MW00985646

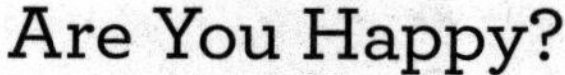

Are You Happy?

ALSO BY LORI OSTLUND

FICTION

The Bigness of the World

After the Parade

Are You Happy?

STORIES AND A NOVELLA

Lori Ostlund

ASTRA HOUSE NEW YORK

Various stories from this collection first appeared in the following publications: "The Bus Driver" in *Story* magazine; "The Gap Year" in *The Southern Review*; "Are You Happy?" in *Colorado Review*; "Clear as Cake" in *ZYZZYVA*; "The Peeping Toms" in *The Kenyon Review*; "Aaron Englund and the Great Great" originally published as "Aaron Englund, July 1970" in *Nashville Review*; "A Little Customer Service" in *ZYZZYVA*, republished in Literary Hub; "Just Another Family" in *New England Review*, reprinted in *The Best American Short Stories 2024* and *The Best Short Stories 2025: The O. Henry Prize Winners.*

Astra House
A Division of Astra Publishing House
astrahouse.com
Printed in the United States of America

Library of Congress Cataloging-in-Publication Data
Names: Ostlund, Lori author
Title: Are you happy? : stories and a novella / Lori Ostlund.
Other titles: Are you happy? (Compilation)
Description: First edition | New York : Astra House, [2025] | Summary: "A collection of stories and a novella from a critically acclaimed writer"-- Provided by publisher.
Identifiers: LCCN 2024037810 (print) | LCCN 2024037811 (ebook) | ISBN 9781662603020 hardcover | ISBN 9781662603037 ebook
Subjects: LCGFT: Short stories | Novellas
Classification: LCC PS3615.S64 A89 2025 (print) | LCC PS3615.S64 (ebook) | DDC 813/.6--dc23/eng/20241127
LC record available at https://lccn.loc.gov/2024037810
LC ebook record available at https://lccn.loc.gov/2024037811

First edition
10 9 8 7 6 5 4 3 2 1

Design by Alissa Theodor
The text is set in AGaramondPro.
The titles are set in Archer-Medium.

In memory of Nancy Zafris, writer, editor, friend
Dearly missed

Wipe your hand across your mouth, and laugh;
The worlds revolve like ancient women
Gathering fuel in vacant lots.

—T. S. Eliot, "Preludes"

Contents

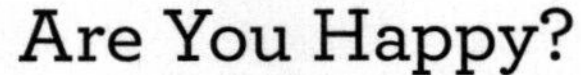

Are You Happy?

The Bus Driver

There were thirty-two of us that first day, standing in a sloppy circle as Miss Lindskoog spoke of cubbyholes and taking turns, none of us doubting that we would soon become friends. We were children, after all. Children like other children. Over the next thirteen years, Jane and I became—and remained—best friends, *unlikely* best friends, our friendship determined less by shared interests than by proximity, which is how it is in small towns. In 1983, we graduated, Jane barely receiving her diploma while I finished at the top of our class, a predilection for academics just one of many traits we did not share. Among the few traits we did share was a love of animals, yet within weeks of graduation, Jane began working full-time at the chicken factory outside of town.

I do not want to overstate the degree to which I—back then—might have been troubled by her job, by what some would call her cruelty or hypocrisy, criticism more reflective of the world I inhabit now, a world in which people have the luxury of dwelling on such things. To be fair, I probably viewed the nature of her job in terms of us—as the first step in our growing apart. The next step came with my departure for college that fall, albeit to a state school just two hours away, where the other students felt familiar because we came from the same farming communities and small towns and because we were the ones who left. The group I found myself drawn to was wild, though I was not. I was the quiet one who sat just outside the chaos, watching the others dance, drunk and high, drawn to them not because I sensed some similar wildness inside myself but because I was curious to know what people looked like when they set inhibitions aside. Until then, I had known only inhibition.

Jane and I did not see each other again until the spring of my senior year, when I spent a long weekend at my parents' house. Something—simple guilt perhaps—had returned me there, to this place that I no longer considered home, dropped off on a Thursday evening by a friend on his way to the Twin Cities. Two nights later, Saturday, I found myself desperate to go out, trapped by a former life that was suddenly too close at hand, present in the way that my mother expected my assistance with dinner while my brothers sat idly on the sofa waiting to eat; in the way that my parents had greeted me, my father asking from the recliner as he lowered his newspaper an inch or two, "Is that Clare?," my mother answering from the kitchen, "It's Clare"—each, from a distance and with a cursory nod of their heads, welcoming me home.

Or maybe I fled that night out of simple boredom, ran from the sight of my family huddled around some detective show, my mother asking constant questions about the most basic plot points, my father predictably absent. He took no pleasure in family time. I later found him in the basement, planting seedling cups. My father kept a large garden that, like the universe, expanded just a bit more each year and provided steady justification for his not spending time with us. When I appeared before him that night, requesting his car keys so that I might drive into town to the municipal liquor store—half package sales, half dive bar—my father looked up from his trays of dirt and shook his head. He disapproved of the liquor store and did not want people to see his car there, but when I promised that I would park in front of his hardware store one street over and walk up the alley to the muni, he reached into his pocket with his muddy fingers and produced the key, for when it came down to it, my father cared most about being left alone. In this way, we were alike.

I had never been inside the liquor store, and when I opened the door that night, I stood for a moment embracing the unknown. The front room—where I entered—consisted of the bar, one pool table, and a jukebox, in front of which, punching in selections, stood Jane. I had received periodic updates on her from my parents, though they reported only on what had gone wrong in her life, a considerable list. I hoped that there were also things that had gone right, but had no way of knowing, for we had not kept in touch those three and a half years. In the beginning, I tried. My first fall away, I sent three letters. All went unanswered. Perhaps the act of penning a letter felt too much like being back in school, like homework, or maybe she had simply recognized the futility of our friendship sooner than I.

"Howdy," she said when I approached her, and I said hello back.

She was dressed oddly—oddly for Minnesota, that is, oddly for our town—in a cowboy hat and boots, a shirt with snap buttons that strained at her stomach. It was the first time I had seen her carry weight. We did not hug. She did not ask about college—what I was studying, whether I liked it, what I planned to do with what I was learning. I did not expect her to.

"I've got kids," she said straight off, her Minnesota accent undercut by something vaguely Texan. "I'm at the chicken factory. Still."

There had always been something childlike about Jane, but that night I could see that she was an adult, someone who snapped necks and paid bills, snapped necks *in order* to pay bills.

"I heard you'd become a mother," I said.

As soon as I said it, it sounded wrong, this talk of *becoming* a mother, as if motherhood were something she had aspired to, when the reality was this: she'd gotten pregnant, twice, and as a result had two girls under the age of three, who, according to my parents, her parents were raising. I wondered, but did not ask, who the fathers were.

Did I feel superior to her as we stood that night regarding each other from our divergent lives? I do recall thinking as I looked at her—twenty-one years old with two children and a mundane job—that only I had a future, for the whole point of the future was that it was unknown, and everything about her life seemed already determined. I recall thinking, too, what a relief my life seemed by contrast. Was I wrong to acknowledge wanting none of *that* for myself?

She went back to punching numbers into the jukebox, and a song began, something country, which was all she'd ever listened to. "I recognize this song," I said. In truth, it sounded to me like every other country song. "Who is it again?"

She snorted. "Conway Twitty," she said, and I nodded solemnly as if to say, "Ah, yes, Conway Twitty."

"So," she said. "I've got quarters on the table."

It took me a moment to understand that she meant the pool table, that she was inviting me to play. "Sure," I said. "Okay."

"I'll gut you like a chicken," she said, still in that strange Texas-Minnesota accent. There was something in her tone, but when I turned to look at her, she laughed.

"I'm not great at pool," I said.

"So you don't want to play?" She sounded neither disappointed nor relieved.

"I'm just warning you," I said, though really, I was filling the silence. The Jane I knew had talked incessantly, but the one before me, this new Jane with two children and a softening waist, did not speak at all, not as she corralled the balls and assessed the cues for warping, nor as she chalked the one that met with her approval, an action that called attention to her hands, which looked strong and capable and like the hands of someone twice our age.

"How's your father?" I asked.

She snorted, presumably at my word choice, "father" instead of "dad."

"He's still got the buses," she said.

"Tell him I said hello. I always liked him."

"Yut," she said, agreeing to tell him or acknowledging my fondness, maybe both. "Break?"

"You go ahead," I said, and she positioned herself at the head of the table, bent low, and, with one brutal jerk, sent the cue ball exploding into the others.

As a kid, I spent a lot of time at Jane's house, in part because her parents were nothing like mine. They drank alcohol, which mine did not, and from a very early age, eleven or twelve, we were allowed to drink with them. There was a part of me that felt I had the best of two worlds: parents who knew that it was inappropriate for a child to drink, friend's parents who let me do so anyway. To this day, I remain drawn to fun and excess in others, wary of it in myself.

On the night of our high school graduation, Jane's parents threw a party just for us, the class of 1983. They lived outside of town, far from streetlights, the nearest neighbors half a mile away, and so there was a shared sense that the night belonged to us, that the rest of the world did not fully exist. Jane's father owned the buses that served our school, which he kept in a large metal barn constructed for that purpose, but that night he had moved two of the buses outside to make room for dancing, and for the keg and the garbage can half-full of punch that left some of the sloppier drinkers with red mustaches. Most of us roamed the property, some playing horseshoes drunkenly in the dark, others sitting in the yard, also drunkenly, wondering aloud how it was possible that we had even reached this point, from which we were now being flung outward.

Miriam, the woman I've been with for nine years, finds it *odd* that Jane's parents hosted such a party, though such parties—keggers—were not uncommon where I grew up. Miriam was raised in New York, having wine at dinner with her parents, who were both from Europe and considered the American attitude toward drinking puritanical, so what shocks her is not that parents allowed us to drink but that they allowed us to get into our cars afterward and drive home, a position with which I agree, now that I have learned how to view my childhood through Miriam's eyes.

Around midnight, I sought refuge in one of the two unberthed buses, settling in the seat halfway back on the left that, until then, Jane and I had considered ours. Soon I heard someone on the steps, Jane's father, whom I liked but did not know well, despite the hours I spent at their house. In fact, I thought of him mainly in terms of this bus—the back of his head and his benign, steady presence as he drove. That night, however, he did not settle into the driver's seat but instead came down the aisle and sat across from me and, eventually, began to talk, and then, to sob. I knew that this was the result of alcohol, but because I was not really an adult, despite the way he spoke to me, I did not yet know that one did not cry because they were drinking but because drinking made them think about the very things they were drinking to forget.

"I should have done something," he said, softly. "I should have killed him."

He did not identify whom he was talking about, nor did I ask, our shared knowledge implicit in the silence that ensued, during which he sniffled and drank some more from a bottle that only then did he offer to me. It tasted awful, but I drank from it again and again because I did not know what to say to a grown man who was weeping.

"I'm glad you're leaving here," he said at last. By then, he had stopped crying. "You can always come back, but the older you get, the harder it is to leave."

I did not say that I planned never to come back. There in the dark, I just nodded. At some point, he added, "You've been a good friend to Jane all these years," and I stood and got off the bus rather than saying what I felt to be true, which was that I had not been a good friend at all.

Jane was athletic. I was not, but for a brief period in my early teens I had wanted desperately to play basketball, not just play it but excel at it. The fall that we entered seventh grade—junior high, as it was still called in the late seventies—we both joined the team. The coach, whom the older girls all claimed to find sexy, was a man in his early thirties who had moved to our small town the year before with his wife and baby son. Coach-wise, he was considered a catch, for in addition to girls' basketball, he oversaw football in the fall and track in the spring, racking up an impressive record of wins his first year. In his spare time, he taught fourth grade.

A couple of weeks into the season—his second, my first—he lined us up at the beginning of practice one day to run sprints, then paused and took the whistle from his mouth. "Ladies, I've been reading some research," he said, "and it seems one of the best ways to strengthen chest muscles is to run without a bra." His voice sounded the way it did when he explained backspin or zone defense, and then he announced that he was giving us another five minutes, in case we needed to return to the locker room. I don't recall whether we all went. I think most of us did. We were serious about basketball, serious about winning—games as well as the coach's praise—and so I imagine that we gladly shed our bras, lined up again, and waited for his whistle. I do recall that later some of the older girls complained, not to the coach or even in front of him, but in the locker room afterward. "My breasts hurt like hell," they said, holding their bare breasts aloft in their hands, like offerings, to relieve the ache.

Jane and I changed directly back into our school clothes and went out into the late afternoon darkness, onto the after-sports bus that was parked at the curb, Jane's father at the wheel. As usual, I greeted him and Jane ignored him, and we made our way back to our seat, where we huddled our sweaty bodies together, shivering.

"Did you see it?" she whispered.

"What?" I said.

"His wiener."

We still used words like "wiener," still found wieners funny. She giggled. I did not, though I had seen it, the polyester of his maroon track pants tented at his crotch as he whistled and we ran, the assistant coach standing to the side, looking elsewhere.

When I told Miriam this story, she said, "And he didn't say anything?" and I said, "Who?" and she said, "The assistant coach. How could he just stand there?"

One of the things that drew me to Miriam was her ability to see justice in very simple terms: when something was wrong, it needed to be called out, remedied, which was why she had become a lawyer. Miriam rarely got tired of arguing a point. It was what made her a good lawyer. It was what made her exhausting to live with.

"The assistant coach was a woman," I said.

"A woman?" she said. "Now I'm even madder."

"Why?" I said. It was not that I didn't understand her anger. "Why are men always let off the hook? She wasn't the one telling us to run braless."

"I'm not letting anyone off the hook. I just don't understand how a woman, in particular, could let something like that happen."

"She was young," I said. "It was her first year at the school, her first job." It had also been her last year, though we did not even know she was leaving until she was gone.

"You're making excuses," Miriam said, "for something that's inexcusable."

I said nothing. It *was* inexcusable. Still, I could not help but wonder whether I might have responded similarly, might also have turned away, that is, and focused—as she, the assistant coach, finally did—on the cart of basketballs in the corner and the straightforward task of picking them up, one by one, and squeezing, as if to assess their firmness.

I did not tell Miriam that I wondered this. I knew what she would say. "What are you talking about? You would have stopped him."

"Human beings like to discuss hypotheticals," I would reply. "We like to sit on barstools and lay claim, with unwavering confidence, to our bravest selves. But really, there's no way to know what I would have done, what I would do." Then, I would say what I always said when we found ourselves engaged in some version of this debate: "I mean, look at how many people talk about how they would have hidden Jews, how few people actually hid Jews."

"That's because most people are weak," Miriam always replied, she who had actually lost family members because this statement was true. "You're not afraid. You would have hidden Jews."

I wanted to tell her that I *was* afraid. I was afraid all the time, of not doing the right thing, of not even recognizing what the right thing was, afraid of how hard it was to be in love with someone who always believed the best of you.

The affair began several months into the basketball season, though, to be clear, I never considered it an affair. "Affair" implies two adults having sex, a victim who is someone else, a spouse—that is, a victim who is not either of them. Of course, Jane did not consider herself a victim. She felt lucky, chosen. At first, I did not even believe her when she said they had had sex. It was not just that I was the sort of child who believed in adults, in their infallibility. It was also that I knew Jane, knew she was not always honest, that she was prone to exaggeration.

Then, one night, our telephone rang. It was Jane's mother. "Oh, you're home?" she said, clearly surprised to find me there.

"I just got home," I said, lying instinctively.

"And Jane?" she said. "I didn't think it would be so late, not on a school night."

"She should be home soon," I said, hanging up before she could reply because how could I elaborate when I did not even know what I was lying about? Almost immediately the phone rang again, and I picked it up, fearing that it would be Jane's mother again.

"My mother might call," a voice whispered. It was Jane.

"She already did," I whispered back. "Where are you?"

"With *him*," she said. "At his friend's cabin. What did you say?"

"I lied," I said. "I told her you'd be home soon, but I didn't even know where you were supposed to be, where *we* were supposed to be."

"We're out having pizza with the team," she said, giggling.

The next day at practice, when the coach blew his whistle and we lined up to run sprints, he said that we were going to handle things a little differently today. "What I'm going to do," he said, "is I'm going to pick the slowest girl on the team and give her a head start, and anyone who doesn't pass her before she finishes, well, that person runs extra sprints."

Whenever he wanted to call someone out—for blowing an easy shot or missing practice—he threw a ball, hard and without warning, enjoying the thump as it hit the girl's chest or back, her startled cry of surprise and pain, and that afternoon, he pivoted and flicked a ball at me, but I caught it, then stepped up to the line, set the ball down, and waited for his whistle.

That day, nobody caught me; nobody even came close. As I stood back at the line, bent over and trying not to vomit, the coach flicked another ball, which ricocheted off my shoulder. "Run like that more often," he yelled, "and you might lose a few pounds."

He blew angrily into his whistle, and the rest of the team lined up and ran ten more.

After practice, as Jane and I sat on the cold, dark bus waiting for the others, I blurted out, "He hates me, and now everyone else does too."

"He doesn't hate you," she said, her voice low. "He knows you're my best friend. He knows you cover for me."

"Wait," I said. "Did you tell him I know about—you know, the two of you?"

"I had to."

"Why?" My voice rose, and Jane's fist came up reflexively, landing a quick blow to my shoulder, that same spot where the coach's ball had hit.

"Shh," she said, nodding her head toward her father. Then, "He heard me on the phone with you last night. He asked if you knew."

Thus began the slippery slope of my own complicity. Over the next year, with me as their occasional accomplice, the two of them continued to meet, mainly at his house on the evenings that his wife attended WeightWatchers. His wife was not fat, at most carried a few pounds left over from the pregnancy as women do, so her participation in this organization perplexed me. I did not yet understand the way that decisions about women's bodies were made, the way that other people, men, tended to chime in, asserting their own wishes. "She's a cow," Jane declared on the bus one day—the regular bus right after school because basketball season had ended—and I knew that she was talking about his wife. When I did not respond, she added, "Who'd want to have sex with someone with such huge, gross tits anyway."

"I hate that word," I said, as though "tits" were the only part of the sentiment I found objectionable, and on the seat beside me, Jane began to cry.

"Well, I hate my body," she said, and she began pummeling her breasts, which had only recently begun to bud. "He's going to leave me." *Leave?* I thought.

"He likes breasts," I said, making my voice consoling because Jane was my best friend after all. "Don't you remember when we ran with our bras off? He got a hard-on."

Jane laughed, a laugh that embraced the change in terminology; we were thirteen by then, no longer giggly girls who used "wiener." No longer girls with girls' bodies.

Jane wanted to win at pool—more precisely, she wanted to beat *me*—whereas I was ambivalent: part of me wanted to let her win, while the other part knew that doing so would be one more betrayal.

I won.

Jane threw her cue onto the table and put on her coat, and I followed her into the cool March night.

"Where are you parked?" I asked, as if we were two old friends ending our evening with easy chatter.

Jane did not answer, instead turned in her cowboy boots toward the grain elevator lot, where people often parked even though parking was never an issue, and I went in the opposite direction, across the street and into the alley that ran down to my parents' hardware store. I imagined Jane getting into the same temperamental pickup that she'd driven in high school and driving home to a tiny room where her two children were not, but there, my imagination stalled, for I had no idea what this room might look like, whether her daughters' absence was a relief or a steady sorrow, whether there was someone there waiting, perhaps the man who was her children's progenitor.

Jane was following me. I sensed it first, then heard the clack of her boots and turned. "Do you have pictures of the girls?" I asked, mainly for something to say.

"They're with my folks."

"The pictures?" I said.

"The girls," she said, an edge to her voice. "They live with my folks. They're better off with them."

"I thought you might have pictures," I said. "That's all."

Throughout much of my childhood, this alley had been home to a stray ginger cat that I courted tirelessly, spending hours talking to it while it regarded me with disinterest. Then, one day it brushed casually against my leg, a small gesture on its part but one for which I had worked so long.

"Remember the orange cat that lived back here?" I said to Jane.

"I hate cats," she replied without much conviction.

"No you don't."

"I've learned to hate them," she clarified. "You're not the only one who's learned things."

"Of course not."

"Of course not," she parroted, and we began walking again.

"How about your brother?" I asked after a moment.

"Works at the bowling alley in Evansville," she said.

We reached the back wall of my parents' hardware store, and with one quick move, she had me up against it. She reached into her jacket, and I saw the flash of a blade. I recognized the knife, the *kind* of knife, that is. My parents sold knives like it, knives meant to gut fish or flay the skin from a deer. I imagined Jane coming in with the money she had earned snapping chicken necks to buy this knife from my parents, one violence begetting the means for the next, for this knife now pressed to my throat.

Her eyes had a slightly unmoored look, a vacant gaze that, back then, I regarded with pity, I suppose—pity in the sense that I felt her incapable of a decisive act.

"It was you," she said. "You reported us."

This was true. I had told someone about their relationship. Mr. Tesky, the guidance counselor, was a new addition to the school, a man who came in twice a week, mainly to help seniors enlist in the army or apply to trade school or college, a man wholly unprepared, that is, for me to sit down in the closet he had been given as an office and tell him that the basketball coach had spent the last year having sex with my friend. I had made the appointment earlier, so by the time I appeared at his closet door that day, he had probably realized that I was only in eighth grade. Had he thought it odd, a thirteen-year-old making an appointment when she was years away from a future?

"Does it feel weird to have no windows?" I asked, stalling.

He looked around, then laughed. "I hadn't thought about it," he said.

The adult me believes that this should have been a red flag—what good could come from confiding in a person so unquestioning of his surroundings—but the me I was then blurted out, "My friend pukes a lot." When he did not respond, I said, "The coach puts his wiener inside her."

I imagine now—not without sympathy—how the encounter must have felt to him, how he had thought that his job was to sit in a windowless room two days a week handing out forms to disinterested teenagers. Was it his fault that he did not know how to make sense of the story that I was trying to tell: about a coach who slept with a girl, a child, for an entire year, dumping her when she began to menstruate, how she began excusing herself from class, returning with glassy eyes and the smell of vomit on her breath, her spine rising from her back in a strange new topography, and how I, her friend, had done nothing?

The guidance counselor stared at the windowless walls. He did not ask, "Who is your friend?" He did not say, "Tell me what happened." What he said was "You'd better get back to class."

Two days later as I sat in science class listening to the teacher explain that gas was made up of particles and giggling with the other students because we were children after all—amused by adults speaking of gas—I received a note summoning me back to Mr. Tesky's closet. His door was open, and I went in and sat down.

"I spoke to the principal about what you—about your visit," he said.

I looked down. I knew that the coach and the principal were friends.

Mr. Tesky coughed and, in a tone that sounded oddly formal, announced, "The principal has informed me that he and the coach went out fishing yesterday and they had a chat, and he has told the coach to keep it in his pants."

It was only years later that I understood that this—Mr. Tesky's parroting of the principal's casual vulgarity—was an admission of anger. There was nothing more to be done. That was what he was telling me. Mr. Tesky looked away, at the spot where he perhaps only then understood a window should be.

So, you see, I had betrayed her. I had done the thing that seemed right and necessary, and, in doing so, I had betrayed her. In college, where I was an English major, I was learning about such things—paradox, irony—grateful to have such words at my disposal, feeling, I suppose, as one does when, after slipping on a pair of glasses for the first time, the world unblurs. But did "paradox" even apply in situations like this, situations far removed from the worlds of the kind of people who invented words and assigned them meanings?

"Why did you do it?" Jane said, the blade a feather at my throat. "You were my friend. You were supposed to help me."

"I was helping you," I said.

"The counselor called our house," she said. "He wanted my parents to come in."

This I had not known. "Is that how they found out?" I said.

"They never found out. I told them Tesky canceled the meeting."

I did not correct her, did not describe her father's sobbing on the bus the night we graduated or the way that he had spoken, as men often do, in simple, violent terms: *I should have killed him.*

"We were going to get back together," she said. "But you wrecked it. You didn't want me to be happy."

As she spoke, her grip on the knife tightened, the blade hard at my throat. Even now, I do not know whether her reaction was one of anger or of muscle memory, that of a hand practiced in daily slaughter. Even now, I do not know which of these—the violence of impulse or of habit—one should fear more. What I do know is that she saw in my eyes that I was afraid, and her stance softened in triumph.

"Of course I wanted you to be happy," I said, my voice softer now, the appeasing whisper that I had used with the orange cat all those years earlier. "You were my best friend."

"You were jealous."

"Jealous?" I said. "I hated him." I did not spell it out, so obvious seemed the logic of my hatred: he had taken a child whose body and innocence and trust were, to him, sexual, destroyed each of those parts, then continued on with his life.

"You hated him because I loved him," she said.

"What?" I said.

She leaned in closer, her breath sour with beer, and for a single heartbeat I thought that she was going to kiss me. Did I want her to? No. The realization came so swiftly that I clung to it—throughout my twenties—as proof that I did not desire women at all when the truth, of course, was that I did not desire her.

She yanked the knife from my throat. "You're a fucking dyke," she announced, and walked away—boots clicking—down the alley.

That was the last time I saw Jane. She was already pregnant that night, with her third child, another girl; this, I would learn from my parents, as well as of the fourth, born years later, just before Jane went to prison for turning her poultry blade on a coworker. Somewhere along the way, I came to terms with desire, *mine*, and was living far away from that town when I learned of her sentence—three years, the coworker had not died—from a newspaper clipping sent by my parents, who considered it their duty to keep me apprised of the ways that my former best friend's life continued to go wrong.

A couple of years passed, then another clipping arrived, this one technically not about Jane, unless you were the kind of people who read between the lines, which my parents were not. They were the kind who took headlines at face value—"Popular Coach Dies Tragically, Run Over by Bus"—never questioning "popular" or even "tragically."

The newspaper article mainly reported Jane's father's version of what happened: that it was dark, nearly nine o'clock, and they'd just returned from an away game, which they'd won. He heard the girls cheering, still, as they ran from the bus into the school to stow their uniforms and call their parents. The coach had gone in with them. Jane's father was sure of that, so when he heard the thud and felt the back wheel rise, he imagined he'd backed into a snowbank. He drove forward then stepped out and saw him there, pinned beneath the wheel of the school bus.

"The man coached my daughter." That was how the article ended, the reporter framing the statement as an expression of remorse.

No charges were pending.

When Miriam got home that evening, I showed her the article, covering up the text beneath the photographs of the two men involved—coach and bus driver—and asked her to guess which was which: who was perpetrator and who, victim.

She waved the paper away. "You need to call the police," she said.

"What police?" I said.

"In your hometown. You need to tell them about your suspicions. That it might not have been an accident. That Jane's father might have murdered that man."

"I don't know that."

"That's why you need to call," Miriam said in her calm lawyer's voice. "You need to tell them what he told you on the bus that night."

When I did not answer, she asked, "Is there a reason you don't want to call?" She was turned away from me, struggling to open a beer, and I could not tell from her voice alone how she meant the question—conversational or probing. Miriam was not a patient person, but she told me once that when you ask a question in court, you need to be prepared to wait as long as it takes for an answer. Of course, we were not in court. We drank our beers—an evening ritual we both looked forward to, a moment when our days came together, collapsed into one—and still I did not answer.

"The coach ruined his life, too," I said finally. By then, we had eaten dinner and were lying in bed.

"So you do think he did it?" she said, as if hours had not passed.

"Well, he did do it," I said. "But you're wondering whether I think it was intentional?"

"Yes," she said. Her voice was sleepy.

"That's not for me to decide," I said.

"But by not reporting it, you are deciding," she said.

Then, she kissed me and turned over and went right to sleep, confident that I would sleep also, that morning would come and I would wake up and do the right thing, that right things existed, that the world spinning beneath us was a world spinning ever closer to justice.

The Gap Year

1.

It was late—well after midnight, Beth supposed—and she was trying to sleep but Matthew was in the kitchen folding origami, the steady whisper of the paper giving itself over to form all she could think about as she lay there in the middle of the night in their empty house—in the middle of their half-over and suddenly empty lives. It was how Beth thought of their lives now, now that Darrin was gone and she could no longer say whether *half-over* was such a bad thing. When Darrin was young, Matthew had stayed up late making origami also, flitting from shape to shape, a turtle followed by a crocodile, a cat, a fish. These he hid inside their son's favorite cereal and in the meat drawer of the refrigerator because Darrin had a fondness for cold cuts, both parents giddy with joy at watching their son discover a swan snuggled with an elephant, there atop his bologna.

Matthew did not mix animals, not anymore, for the whole point was to give himself, his hands, over to repetition. These creatures were not made in anticipation of a son's delight; they had no purpose, no future either. For even as Matthew created them, his hands were already anticipating their destruction, finishing the final fold, then delivering them onto the pile that would become their funeral pyre. This was their morning routine now (and hadn't Beth always liked routine?): Matthew sweeping the pile into a paper bag, taking the bag to the back patio, lighting it. He left the sliding door open, and the smell of burning paper wafted in, becoming their new morning smell, the smell—like coffee or bacon—that told Beth to wake up and face the day.

2.

They met at a gay bar on the west side of Albuquerque, both of them straight, and later Beth wondered whether Matthew came up to her that night simply because, in a gay bar, straight people could pick each other out the way that gay people were said to be able to find one another in every other crowd. In fact, she had never asked him why he approached her that night, perhaps because she never quite got over needing to believe that he saw her there with her friends—the Sapphists, he later called them—and thought, *Now that looks like an interesting person.*

She was wearing glasses with owlish frames that did not flatter her face, for that was her goal back then—to be seen as the sort of woman who conspired against her own beauty. Matthew approached her as she stood at the bar trying to get the bartender's attention. "Excuse me," he said. "Are you near or far?"

He'd meant her eyesight, but she just stared at him, wondering about his scar, a simple white line that emerged from his left eyebrow and continued upward.

"To what? From what?" she said at last, and he pointed at her glasses and said, "Your vision, four-eyes," in a teasing, playground voice. "Are you near- or far*sighted*? I'm twenty-twenty, but that too can be a burden." He sighed, as though struck by the ways that his life had been made more difficult by perfect vision. She was just starting graduate school in linguistics, and she thought about how the Japanese and Chinese looked at a character and arrived at the same meaning yet articulated it with completely different sounds. She recognized all of the sounds this man was making yet had no idea what he was trying to tell her.

"May I buy you a drink?" he asked, and he ordered her some sweet, green concoction involving Midori and pineapple juice. "It's awful, isn't it?" he said gleefully after she'd taken a sip. She nodded because it was. "But very tropical, don't you think?" She nodded again. "When I graduate next year I plan to travel to lots of tropical places, so I'm getting myself in the mood." He paused. "Maybe we'll go together," he said. The pause was what kept her from walking away right then, what assured her that he was not just some smooth talker who went around making preposterous suggestions to straight women in gay bars.

They stood in a corner away from the dance floor and talked. They were the same age, twenty-three, though she was starting a doctoral program while he was still struggling to finish his undergraduate degree in English, struggling because he was tired of having his reading dictated to him by a syllabus.

"I'm tone-deaf," he announced then, as though listing reasons that she should consider getting to know him. "And I was portly as a child."

She asked about his scar. He reached up and stroked it with his finger, and she noticed his hands. She had not known that one could find hands attractive. "It's a rather boring tale," he said, though over time she would learn that this was how he prefaced all of his favorite stories about himself. He went on to describe a pair of glasses that he had invented as a child—two plastic magnifying lenses held together with pipe cleaners and tape—which he'd worn while riding his bicycle one afternoon: down a hill and straight into a tree. But right up until the crash, it was a glorious feeling, everything rushing toward him, so close he should be able to touch it, though he knew better. He understood how magnifying glasses worked.

"Then how did you hit the tree?" she asked.

"Well," he said. "I suppose that even our intellect fails us sometimes."

Around midnight, Lance, Matthew's best friend, approached them, dripping sweat from the dance floor. "This is Lance," Matthew said. "He's a rice queen."

"What's a rice queen?" she asked.

"It means he likes Asian guys," Matthew said. "It's a bit of a problem here in New Mexico."

He and Lance laughed, the two of them collapsing with their arms around each other. Beth did not believe love happened in a flash, love at first sight and all that. Rather, she imagined it working something like a frequent-buyer card, ten punches and you were in love, and as she watched the two of them cackling like a pair of spinster sisters, she looked at Matthew and thought, *This is the first punch.*

3.

Matthew grew up in Los Alamos, New Mexico. When he mentioned this to strangers, they assumed that his father had worked for the national labs, but his father had been a mailman. "Really?" these strangers always said, as though they could not imagine anything as unlikely as scientists receiving mail. Once, halfway through a shift, his father stopped at the post office to drop off several bags of mail and found the entire place shut down, men in white hazmat uniforms combing through the sorting area. "They told him to take the rest of the day off—no explanation—and I told him he should not go back to work until there was an explanation. I was twelve at the time, and he chuckled and said that the mail needs to be delivered, that when I was older I would understand about such things."

Matthew told Beth this story to sum up the sort of man his father was. It was early in their relationship, and she noted how he sounded—at once proud and exasperated—which told her something about the sort of man Matthew was. In the picture he showed her, his parents looked more like grandparents; it was his high school graduation and they stood flanking him, looking pleased but slightly baffled by the occasion. His mother was sixty-two in the photo, his father sixty-eight. They had come to parenthood late.

A few weeks into his first semester of college, his parents' neighbor phoned to tell him that his parents had driven the wrong way down the exit ramp of the interstate and into oncoming traffic. They were both dead. His father took that ramp every day for thirty-six years, so the mistake made no sense, but the doctor said—dismissively,

Matthew felt—that these things happened when one got old. People became disoriented. Perhaps his father had had a stroke.

Matthew dropped out of college for the semester and took a job counting inventory. This was how he met Lance. They both lived in downtown Albuquerque and began driving to work together in the wee hours, which was when inventory was generally counted. Early on, they were sent to Victoria's Secret, where the two of them counted every bit of lingerie in the store. Afterward they went to Milton's diner for breakfast, and Lance looked down at his breakfast burrito and said that he was tired and bored after a night of counting women's underwear. This was his way of revealing that he was gay. They each ordered a second burrito, and Matthew told Lance about his parents. It had been two months since the accident, but Lance was the first person to whom he had spoken of it. Lance had saved him during that first year after his parents died, Matthew told Beth. They were like brothers.

4.

Matthew had learned to fold origami in preparation for their first trip abroad, their first trip together. Traveling would involve lots of waiting, he said, and it was always good to have some trick up your sleeve. He packed stacks of folding paper, from which he produced an endless menagerie, each cat and rooster snatched up by one of the children who pressed in shyly against them to watch him fold.

Once, on a bus in Guatemala, when he was out of paper, he took a dollar bill from his wallet and transformed it into a fish while the little girl across the aisle looked on. He pretended not to notice her interest, but when he was finished he swam the fish across the aisle and dropped it into her hands. Above them on the roof rode two boys no older than twelve, makeshift soldiers with rifles taller than they were. Beth had watched them climb on. They were all she could think about. She was twenty-four, not yet a mother, so she imagined only fleetingly the sorrow that the boys' mothers must feel at seeing their sons already schooled in death. Mainly she considered them from her own perspective, the fear that she felt in this foreign land, knowing that right above her were two guns, their triggers guarded by fingers not yet skilled at shaving. As she watched Matthew fold, she wondered whether he did so to distract himself from the boys and their guns or whether he was like the girl, focused solely on the beauty of the fish taking shape before them.

5.

It was a Saturday afternoon, Darrin's junior year, and they were pestering him about taking the SAT. Finally he came out with it. "I want to travel," he said. "I want to do a gap year." He showed them the website for the program he had in mind: a ten-month trip around the world, working in the rain forest in one country, teaching English in another, while they stayed behind, paying a hefty sum for him to do so, to fly around the world dabbling in local economies. There would be adults, three teachers who would lead seminars, arrange details, and make themselves available by email to anxious parents.

Beth had never even heard of a gap year, but she didn't like the sound of it, the way that it made Darrin's future seem removed from them, made Darrin seem that way also. "I just need a year away from school, a year that doesn't matter so much," he said, and they kept quiet. But later, as she and Matthew lay in bed together, she said, "'A year that doesn't matter.' How is that even possible?" Matthew laughed gently because he understood that she was afraid.

6.

They—not Lance—were the ones who ended up in Asia, the last leg of a one-year trip through a host of hot countries. Matthew had graduated, finally, but Beth quit her program halfway through. Actually, she took a year off, but when she got out in the world and saw what was there, she could not go back. She had grown up in a small town in Wisconsin, and she understood only then that she had been about to exchange one small town for another: academia.

They had been together a year when they started their trip, but their relationship had never really entered the public realm, the realm of parties and shared errand-running, so Beth did not truly know who Matthew was out in the world. She learned on that trip that he talked to everyone. Using Thai or Spanish gleaned from guidebooks and taxi drivers, he conversed tirelessly about the weather and food, about where they were going and where they were from and whether they had children. Beth considered these questions either tedious or nobody's business, often both, but Matthew did not see it that way. He was happy to tell people how much he loved rice, to say, over and over, that they were from New Mexico—"*New* Mexico. It's in the United States."—to explain that they had no children, *yet*. Matthew was at ease, in his body and in the world. Beth was not, but on the trip she learned to mime and gesture and even laugh at herself a bit.

One afternoon in Belize, four elderly Garifuna women lounging on a porch called to them as they passed in the street. Three of the women were large, but the fourth was as thin as a broom, and she sat slightly apart from the others, as though her thinness were something that they did not want to catch. The women were eating homemade fruit Popsicles, and Matthew immediately began flirting with the women, asking which of them might share. He pounded his chest to show he meant business, and the women laughed and told Beth that she had a handsome devil on her hands, waggling their fingers at her in warning.

"You two better come in and eat something," said one of the fat women, and the four rose like a chorus about to sing.

The women gave them rice and the leg of a stringy hen, with watermelon Popsicles for dessert. Later, they asked Beth and Matthew how young people danced these days up in their country, and Matthew pulled Beth up to demonstrate. The women clapped and sang, creating a rhythm that Beth willed her body to follow, and for a moment it seemed to, but the rhythm changed suddenly and her body went in the wrong direction. One of the women leaned forward and slapped Beth's buttocks hard, while the others roared with laughter and shook their hands in front of their faces as though they had chili in their eyes. Matthew laughed also, a laugh that said, *Buck up, four-eyes. This is life. Isn't it great?* It was the laugh of a man who was in love with her, who saw in her stiffness and reticence something exotic.

7.

Mornings had always been their time as a couple, both before Darrin came along and after, for even as a baby, he had no interest in mornings. Sometimes she and Matthew leg wrestled—she got to use both legs—or Matthew brought her coffee in bed and the two of them sat propped against the pillows, talking quietly, wanting this time together, alone. What they had wanted, that is, was not to wake their son, and she wondered now how they could have ever done such a thing, plotted to have even one precious second less with him. But they had. They had reclined together in this same bed, giggling and covering each other's mouths, saying, "Shhh, you'll wake him."

Other days Matthew woke up feeling loud. "I feel loud today," he would say, loudly of course, and he would stand on the bed and sing one of the Bible camp songs from her childhood—"Shadrach, Meshach, Abednego, lived in Judah a long time ago. They had funny names, and they lived far away"—songs that she had taught him in the early days of their relationship when she was first learning to let go and be silly around another human being. Or he would lie on his back with his arms and legs straight up in the air like a dead cockroach and belt out old Carpenters tunes. "I'm on the top of the world," he sang as though he really meant it, for that was the thing about Matthew: he was never sheepish about acknowledging his happiness, did not believe that happiness should be discussed only in terms that were ironic or self-deprecating. Eventually Darrin would come running in, begging to be flown around atop Matthew's extended legs while Beth watched and laughed and tried hard not to picture their son slipping from her husband's feet, tumbling through the air, his head crashing into a bedpost.

Now, she and Matthew got out of bed each morning, still exhausted, and said standard morning things like "How'd you sleep?" They rose and dressed and went into the dining room, where the night's origami awaited them, sometimes a hundred cranes or giraffes, piled up on the table: a heap of wings, a heap of necks.

8.

The first month, Darrin emailed them almost daily, sending pictures of all the things he knew would interest them: his sleeping quarters and meals, his work and the other students, the people and buildings that made up his days. He ended his messages with easy declarations of his love for them because that was the way the world was set up now—easy access to communication, easy declarations of love—and Beth was grateful for both. He rarely wrote more than a few sentences, but she could hear his voice in these quick updates filled with enthusiastic adjectives, for he was like Matthew in this way also, never embarrassed by his ease with superlatives, by the way that he declared her spaghetti "the absolute best" and her "the most wonderful mother in the world" for making it.

It was during the second stop on the itinerary—collecting plants in Belize for medical research—that the girl began appearing in his photos. She was plump with wildly curly hair and a careful smile. Because it was his way, Matthew emailed Darrin, asking about her, and Darrin wrote back days later, saying only that her name was Peru.

"Peru? Were her parents hippies?" Matthew wrote, and Darrin replied, again after what seemed a deliberate delay, "Missionaries."

This, his one-word response without explication, troubled them. Was she religious, they wondered, and if she was, what did that mean for their son? Would he return speaking a language that they did not understand, his conversation laced with earnest euphemisms like "witness" and "abundance"? After years of worrying—with Beth imagining all the ways that they could lose him and Matthew steadfastly refusing to imagine any—was this what it came down to, that their son could simply grow up to be a man they did not recognize?

"Well, please be sure to have safe sex," Matthew wrote next.

"No need to worry" came back their son's reply, an ambiguous response that they also discussed far into the night: Did it mean that he was not having sex, or that he was but the sex was safe? Or was it simply his way of telling them to stop worrying, of declaring his adulthood?

9.

On the plane from Thailand, they each made a list: on the left, cities that seemed appealing, and on the right, cities that did not. They were heading home, but they had not yet determined where home would be. Somewhere over what Beth thought was the Sea of Japan, they decided on Minneapolis. Beth worried that they were making the choice based on the overwhelming memory of heat, a year's worth, but Matthew said so what if they were. Weren't most choices made as reactions to something else? They were in love, but traveling had taught them that they were also well matched:

they knew how the other responded to crisis and boredom; they could live together in a very small space yet not grow distant. The trip had left them broke but had also taught them that they did not need much, and so they rented a tiny apartment in Saint Paul, which was cheaper than Minneapolis.

They were in a new city, both of them working at their first real jobs, Matthew as a high school English teacher and Beth as a newspaper caption writer. It was a job that she both liked and did well, for she had the ability to look at a photograph, feel at once the narrative sweep of it, and sum it up in a few precise words. Each night, they lay in bed talking, just as they had through ten-hour bus rides and bouts of stomach ailments. Matthew dissected his day, celebrating his students' successes one minute and bemoaning their lack of curiosity the next. Mainly Beth listened, preferring to talk about her day when it had gone well, keeping the small frustrations, which were a part of any job, a part of life, to herself. She distrusted how emotions sounded when put into words, the way that words could reduce the experience to something unrecognizable. It was like reading descriptions of wine, she decided, for when she uncorked the bottle and took a sip, she never thought, *Ah, yes, quite right,* nutty *and* corpulent *and* jammy.

10.

Matthew wanted to meet her family now that they were only three hours away. Beth felt that relationships worked best when families were not involved. Early on, she had told him the story of her father and his brother, wanting Matthew to know that she trusted him, but the story had left him keen to meet her father.

He was like many fathers, she said by way of blunting his interest, quiet and largely absent. He worked as an accountant in an office containing a desk and a coffeepot, and what she remembered most from her rare visits to him there were the stacks of cashew canisters along one wall—empties on the left and full on the right, like debit and credit columns—and the way that her father bent over his ledgers, nibbling one nut at a time, brushing salt from the page before turning it.

Each evening he came home at six and the family sat down to dinner, a silent affair because their father wanted them to focus on chewing and swallowing and, especially, on not choking, goals from which talking and frivolity would surely distract. Then he returned to his office, where he stayed until midnight, balancing the books of farmers and beauticians and storekeepers, all of whom trusted her father to keep them safe from financial ruin.

One night when Beth had just turned seventeen, after she had done something stupid and teenager-like—taken the family car out on a muddy road and gotten stuck so that she missed her curfew by four whole hours—her mother came into her room, where Beth was sulking over her father's overreaction, which involved a six-month grounding. Her mother sat on the edge of the bed and took one of Beth's feet in her hands, holding it awkwardly because they were not a demonstrative family.

"Well," said her mother, "it's time you learned about Thomas."

Thomas was her father's younger brother. Until that night, Beth had not even known that her father had a brother. "When your father was a boy, just eight years old," her mother began, "he and Thomas were sent out in the front yard to play one Sunday afternoon. Thomas was four, so it was your father's job to keep him occupied for an hour or two while your grandparents read. At first they made a pile of leaves, planning to jump in it, but it was a windy day and the leaves kept blowing away, so they decided to play hide-and-seek."

Her mother had paused here, but then went on to describe how, as her father crouched behind a shrub while Thomas turned in slow circles in the yard, a brown car pulled up to the curb and a man got out. "He looked kind," Beth's father later told the police, words that had brought his mother to her knees on their kitchen floor.

The man stood for a moment on the sidewalk on the other side of the low fence that enclosed their yard, Beth's hidden father watching. It was this image—the triangulated gaze—that haunted Beth: her father looking at the man, who was looking at Thomas; Thomas, who was looking for her father.

"Say," the man called to Thomas. "Are you the little boy who lives here, the one who likes marshmallows so much?" The man extended his arm and opened his fist: a marshmallow rested in his palm like a tiny pillow.

Thomas turned and stared at the man, then made another half-turn, surveying the yard, torn between hide-and-seek and marshmallows. "Yes," he said to the man, and the man opened the front gate, walked in, and picked him up. Beth's father stood up from behind the shrub; the man stared at him for a moment, the way a magician might stare at a rabbit that he had not meant to conjure. Thomas's pant leg was hiked up to his knee, his calf plump and white, the man's hand wrapped around it like that of a butcher assessing a particularly meaty shank. The man smiled as he took his hand briefly from Thomas's calf to wave goodbye to Beth's father.

In the events that followed—going into the house to alert his parents, describing the man for the police—Beth's father quickly understood that everyone considered him old enough to have been suspicious of the man, so it was not until years later that he told Beth's mother, confessing this for the very first time, that he had stepped forward not to stop the man from taking his brother but to say, "I like marshmallows, too."

In her bedroom that night, Beth had promised her mother that she would never tell anyone about Thomas, especially not her siblings, and she never had, until Matthew. When Matthew finally did meet her parents, he was disappointed to find her father just as she had described, a man whose conversation and demeanor did not reflect a childhood of unspoken guilt. Instead, her father engaged Matthew in "men's talk," offering detailed explanations of the way that gadgets worked, which was precisely the sort of thing that Matthew hated.

"Say, I bet you haven't seen one of these," her father said, showing him the front door lock that he had installed when Beth was young. The lock resembled a rotary telephone, on which she and her siblings had dialed their way into the house. Their friends had all coveted the lock, but Beth and her siblings regarded it as a reproach, proof that their father did not trust them with keys. Their mother had claimed that he installed it because he could not bear the thought of them locked out, waiting in the yard, and only later did Beth understand that her mother was right.

Each time she dialed the lock with her brother and sister standing impatiently behind her, she wanted to tell them about Thomas, but she never did, and she wondered now whether this—maintaining a secret of such magnitude—was what had made her distant from her siblings. Lately, she found herself wanting to call them and confess, but she sensed in this impulse something selfish: she would be offering her father's secret in order to obtain an audience for her own sorrow. In truth, she had no idea what she wanted from anyone now, except to be left alone.

11.

When they had been in Saint Paul a year, Beth learned that she was pregnant, and they began hurtling down the slippery slope of adulthood. The wedding happened quickly, during their lunch breaks, but it took them months to find the right house. They toured a Victorian owned by an elderly couple, the Enquists, who had lived in it for forty-two years but were moving to North Platte, Nebraska, to be near their son, who owned a bar there. The Enquists wrinkled their noses as they spoke, as though something smelled bad—owning a bar, North Platte, being near their son. It was probably everything—the combined facts of leaving their home—but Beth and Matthew did not want to think about the old couple's unhappiness because their own happiness demanded it. They knew that this was the house for them.

That night they were both too excited to sleep, so they lay curled up in bed together, attempting to inventory the house from memory, its closets and windows and electrical outlets. Finally Beth dozed off, awakening with a start when Matthew jumped up and down on the bed beside her, waving a piece of paper—an offer letter filled with embarrassingly intimate expressions of their love for the house and their desire to *make love* in the house. He had used words such as "enamored" and "smitten," had described the appliances as "sexy," the molding as "bewitching." In closing, he had written, "We beseech you to accept our offer."

She remembered even now—especially now—how she had stared at Matthew, who looked strange in the predawn light, unfamiliar, how she had thought, not entirely at ease with the fact, *This man is my husband.*

Though she wanted to say, "These are old people. This is Minnesota. Don't you *want* the house?" she said simply, "It's a lovely letter, Matthew." He smiled and bounced onto his knees on the bed. "I'll take care of it," she said, implying that she would deliver the letter, but at work that morning, in between captions, she rewrote it, stripping it down to the basics of money and time frames and expectations.

The baby that she was carrying inside of her, a boy whom they were planning to name Malcolm, never saw the inside of this house that they purchased for him, never hung his clothes in the closets that they had lain in bed tallying up, never got scolded for forgetting to do so. When Beth was six months pregnant, she stepped on a patch of ice on the sidewalk outside their new house and went down hard, trying to break her fall with her right arm. She was in the emergency room having her arm set when the bleeding began.

A year went by, a year during which they did not talk about children or pregnancies or the treachery of ice, but the following winter they broached the topic of having a child, *another* child, their conversations tentative, circling the subject, until one night Matthew took her hand and said, "Listen, I've been thinking that we should adopt. It's selfish to think we need to re-create ourselves." Beth felt the same way, but there was a part of her—a small part, but a part—that believed what Matthew was really saying was that he did not trust her to deliver a child safely into the world.

About Darrin's origins they knew very little, except that he was Canadian. They went up to Winnipeg on a Tuesday, signed all sorts of forms, and drove home with him that evening, in the course of one day crossing borders and becoming parents. It was winter again, and Beth drove while Matthew sat in the back with Darrin, singing to him and reporting everything, every clenched hand and grimace, every aspect of their son's face, so that by the time they got back to Saint Paul, they both knew him as intimately as if his features were their own.

12.

She left her job because she wanted to have those first years with him, wanted to watch him sleep and to feed him sweet potatoes and pears that she chose from the bins at the produce stand and pureed in the blender, combing through the pap with a fork to find the chunks that he could choke on. She had imagined that she would go back to work when he was two, three at the latest, but by then she had come to realize what a minefield the world was—cords dangling tantalizingly within reach, furniture corners like Sirens wooing the most tender parts of him as he ran drunkenly through the house—and she couldn't leave.

Sometimes, when fear overwhelmed her, she tried to pull back, to take a mental snapshot of the scene unfolding in front of her and produce a pithy line of text for it, and sometimes this even worked and she could see the events for what they were: small, happy moments. *Boy, six, learns to ride bicycle without gouging out eye.*

Birthday boy blows out candles without igniting hair. Tuba player, fourteen, marches in parade without collapsing under the weight of instrument. She understood that an uneventful day was, in fact, the sum of the many moments that could have veered toward tragedy—but did not.

Before she pricked potatoes for the oven, she sent Darrin off to his room. She didn't want him getting ideas about forks. And if he was allowed to watch, she made a point of screaming "Ow!" each time she sank the fork into a potato. "He's going to think you're torturing it," Matthew said as he stood in the kitchen one evening, drinking wine and observing this ritual. "Is that what you want?"

"It's better than him stabbing himself with a fork," she said, as though they had been presented with these two options for their son—sadism or masochism—and made to choose.

Their son spent hours stacking dominoes into neat piles, piles that he toppled explosively but with a giggle, enjoying the fickle sense of power that this stirred in him. Beth liked the dominoes also, not just their ability to enthrall her son but the sound that they made in doing so, the steady clicking like the beating of his heart. On the evening of his third birthday, as she closed the oven door on yet another set of wounded potatoes, she became aware of the house's stillness and walked fast—running would only frighten him—down the hallway to Darrin's room, where she found his dominoes stacked in orderly towers, but no Darrin. Him she found on the bathroom counter, kneeling in front of the open medicine cabinet, an empty bottle of shoe polish in his hands, the white polish that she had used to keep his baby shoes in order.

"Milk," he said, smiling at her sweetly, white parentheses framing his mouth.

In the emergency room, after he had been made to vomit and the doctor assured them that he was fine, Darrin giggled while Matthew rubbed his belly like a magic lamp. Beth could not laugh, not even when Matthew said, "Look, Darrin. Mommy's still wearing her apron." Instead, she drew her coat around her tightly as though it had been pointed out that she was naked.

"Don't you ever get worried?" she asked Matthew later, when the three of them were back home and she and Matthew were in bed, lying on the mattress that remembered the shapes of their bodies so perfectly that she thought maybe she had been silly to be that frightened.

"That's your job," he said, moving against her in the dark.

But later, after they had made love and fallen asleep, Matthew awakened her to say, "We guard him in our different ways, you know. You keep him safe by visualizing every bad thing that could happen to him, as though—I don't know—you think that you can control it somehow, contain it to your mind. But I can't bear that, can't bear living with those images, so my job is to pretend that the thought of them never even enters my mind."

He began to sob, and she held him, thinking about the tenderness with which he had rubbed their son's belly. "I know," she said, for she did know. She understood that fear, like love, took many forms, that it did not have to manifest itself in just one way to be real, and Matthew lay beside her sobbing as though he were confessing an infidelity and not that he, too, loved their son so much that he could hardly bear it.

13.

His emails became less frequent, less effusive, and they did not know whether this was because his girlfriend now commanded his attention or because he did not trust them to understand the details of his new life. In fact, they would never know. One morning when he had been gone six months, as they were drinking coffee and Matthew was singing in his loud, off-key voice, the phone rang.

"This is Peru," whispered the voice on the other end.

"Peru?" said Beth.

"I'm one of your son's teachers. On the trip?"

"His teacher?" Beth said. "I don't understand."

"Oh my God," said the woman, for Beth thought of her that way now—as a woman. "I can't do this." She began to sob.

"Hello?" said Beth, but the sobbing grew distant.

"What is it?" Matthew asked, standing up from the table and coming over to her. Beth shook her head.

A man came on the line then, another teacher, who identified himself as Rob. This man Rob explained to her that their son was dead, electrocuted in the swimming pool of their hotel in Chiang Mai just a few hours earlier. "The students were finished giving English lessons for the day, and Darrin and a few of the other guys were in the pool having a beer." He paused. "An electrical box fell into the water."

Rob waited for her to speak. She wanted to ask, "Why were eighteen-year-olds drinking beer?" and, "Why was there an electrical box above the pool?" and, most of all, "Why was my son sleeping with one of his teachers?" But in the end she said only, "And the other boys?"

"They're okay. Darrin was closest to the box," said this stranger, Rob. "Listen, if it's any comfort, the doctor said that he died instantly."

It was not a comfort. How could there be comfort in the word "instantly," in any word that meant her son had lived even one second less on this earth?

Matthew took the telephone then. She was vaguely aware of him discussing details, two men taking care of business, but then he said, "No, I'm coming for him," and everything about Matthew—his voice, his body, his heart—seemed to break into pieces right in front of her.

He told her that he could go to Thailand alone, but she would not hear of it: they had picked up their son together at the beginning of his life, and she would not consider doing any less at the end. She explained this as she wiped off the counters and washed out their coffee mugs, but when she turned, looking for the dish towel, she saw that Matthew was sitting at the table wearing it over his head like a small tent into which he had disappeared to be alone with his grief.

14.

They did not tell anyone that they were going, except for the cat sitter, to whom they said only that there was an emergency in Thailand. Beth knew that she should call her parents, but she remembered the way that the conversation about Thomas had ended all those years ago. "Did they ever find him?" Beth had asked, meaning did they find a body, for she understood that nobody had ever seen Thomas alive again. "No," her mother had said. "And let me tell you, for a parent, not knowing has got to be the worst thing." Beth knew now that her mother had been wrong, that there was something far worse than not knowing—and that was knowing that her son lay, unequivocally dead, in a hospital somewhere in Thailand.

Later, after they had booked a flight, they went into the bedroom and began to pack, their suitcases lying open at the foot of the bed like two giant clams. They had not spoken of their individual conversations with Rob, had not compared notes in order to create a complete account of their son's death. They had not talked of anything but the logistics of getting to Thailand, of getting their son home.

"Why was he drinking?" she asked Matthew, hurling the question at his back as he filled his own suitcase, and then, "I want this woman arrested. I want her to pay."

Beth lay down on the bed, placing her feet inside her own half-packed suitcase, and began to cry.

Matthew sat beside her, holding his hand to her cheek. "We need to take comfort in knowing that his last days, his last minutes even, were happy ones," he said.

He sounded like a minister or a therapist, someone schooled in the art of discussing other people's pain, and she wanted to tell him so, wanted to say, "You see?" for she had been right all these years and now he was proving it, proving how inadequate words were.

15.

The final punch in Beth's falling-in-love card had come in Thailand, at the end of their hot-countries tour. They flew from

Jakarta to Malaysia, spending an afternoon in Kuala Lumpur before getting on the night train. In Thailand they bought tickets for a ferry that would shuttle them out to an island whose name Beth could no longer recall; the ticket sellers had considered demand but not supply in offering the tickets, and when the ferry began to load, it was clear that there were not enough seats.

"Next ferry tomorrow," called out one of the young ferry workers, blocking the gangplank, but he gestured at the flat, empty roof of the boat to indicate that it was an option.

"Let's do it," Matthew said. Already, disappointed travelers had begun to jump from the dock down onto the ferry's roof.

"Absolutely not," she said. "Have you not heard of something called 'weight capacity'?"

Matthew bent as though to kiss her but instead bit her nose, hard.

"Ow!" she cried out, and he laughed and tossed their backpacks onto the roof of the ferry, leaping down after them and turning to offer his hand. Nearly since they met, Matthew had been declaring his love, to which she always replied, "Good Lord," or "Heavens," intentionally prim responses that made both of them laugh and bought her time, but when she jumped down beside him that day, they both knew that she was nearly there.

The last punch happened two days later on a snorkeling trip with thirteen other tourists. She remembered the other passengers well: a young British woman who vomited uncontrollably and several French boys who laughed at her until Matthew explained to them that they were not helping matters, sounding so reasonable that the boys stopped immediately. There were Germans and a family from Brazil, about whom she had wondered why they would come this far to be in another hot, wet place. Three Thai boys ran the boat, one driving and the other two tending to the passengers' needs, bringing the vomiting woman a pail, picking the Brazilian children up and pretending they were going to toss them overboard. They said nothing to Beth, though they made small talk with Matthew, asking whether he liked to fish and how much his watch had cost. The driver multitasked as he drove, eating and turning to joke with the other two, even pulling his T-shirt off over his head—all without slowing down. He struck her as the sort of young man who would only become more reckless when presented with fear, particularly a woman's, so she said nothing, her face set to suggest calm, though Matthew, who knew better, rested his hand on her knee.

It took them nearly two hours to reach the cove. They were supposed to spend the day there, but around one, the young Thai men began to round everyone up, pointing at the ocean, which had become a roiling gray, and at the dark clouds suspended over it. They departed hastily, a forgotten snorkeling mask bobbing near the shore behind them.

That morning, everyone had conversed happily in English, but the storm made them nationalistic, each group reverting to its own language. The waves grew higher, the passengers quieter, and when they hit a particularly big wave, everyone flew up in the air and came down hard, landing atop one another and making a collective "umph" of surprise and fear. The two Thai stewards pointed into the distance, where an object bobbed on the waves, and as they got nearer Beth could see that it was a boat filled with the same configuration of young Thai men and tourists, except this boat was not moving forward, bucking the waves; it rose and fell listlessly while the people on board screamed and waved their arms.

On Beth's boat the two stewards huddled around the driver, who had been so cocky speeding across the water that morning but now looked tired and very young. They were arguing, she knew, and the driver finally wrenched the wheel, turning their boat toward the stranded one.

"We can't take everyone," called out one of the Germans, a woman who had refused to stop smoking even as her lit cigarettes pocked the arms and legs of those around her each time the boat hit a wave, "or we will all die." She said it in English, the *w*'s becoming dramatic *v*'s, and then she took a long drag on her cigarette and glared.

At first, nobody spoke, and then Matthew said, "Look, there's room." He wiggled closer to Beth, and the others followed his example. The driver maneuvered their boat parallel to the stranded one, and a steward from that boat, a young man—they were all so young!—with an owl tattoo on his left bicep, instructed the men to link hands across the water.

"Why don't we tie the boats?" asked one of the French boys, and the steward explained that they needed to break free quickly when a big wave came or the two boats might be slammed together and destroyed.

Only then did the passengers on the stranded boat seem to realize what was expected of them: that they were to perch on the edge of their boat as it lurched beneath them and then leap across the gap to safety. A few cried, but one by one they jumped, collapsing into the arms of those on the other side. Every few minutes, someone called out "Wait!" or "Quickly!" and the men dropped hands and let the boats surge apart.

On the deck of the other boat sat a woman flanked by two young children, a baby in her lap. She was dressed as though for a job interview, and atop her bosom a large cross bounced. She screamed at her husband in what sounded like Swedish, and though Beth did not know Swedish, she knew what the woman was saying. When the husband grew tired of pleading with her, he picked up the oldest child and carried him over to the side, where he stood for a moment, lips moving, before leaning out over the churning water with his son and letting him go into the hands of the French boys on the other side.

He did the same with the second child, but when he reached for the baby, the mother would not let go. "No, we will die here together," she screamed, in English this time because she wished to include everyone in her terror. After her husband had pried the baby loose, she sat with her head in her hands, refusing to look as her husband leaned out for the third time, offering the baby, their baby, into the outstretched arms of the French boys. As he let go, a giant wave flung the boats apart, the clasped hands slipping from one another like sand.

Later, the father, sobbing, would say that he had heard King Solomon whispering in his ear, "Let go of your son." As he told this story, the baby rested in his arms, mother and siblings on either side, a family reunited. Beth sat beside Matthew, who looked sheepish yet pleased by the rounds of applause in his honor, for in that half second after the baby had been released, Matthew's hand shot into the gap and caught him by his chubby leg. Even as the boat bucked mightily, he held on, held on as though nothing but life were possible.

16.

Lying in their bed listening to Matthew fold origami night after night, Beth does not cry. Crying happens during the day, when every sight and sound reminds her of Darrin: the hole in the wall from an arrow that he had not meant to release; the creak of the refrigerator door; the tubes of toothpaste in a brand that only Darrin liked, sitting in a drawer unused, useless. Today, she goes into his room and vacuums for the first time since he left a year and a half ago. When she is finished, she panics and rips the vacuum bag open on the hallway floor outside his room, sifts through the compressed pile of dirt and dust, looking for something—a hair, a thread from a favorite shirt, a sliver of dead skin, a fingernail chewed off and spit onto the carpet, the lint from between his toes. Some piece of him.

She falls asleep there on the floor, curled up around the vacuum bag as though it were Gertrude, their cat. When she awakens she does not open her eyes right away, but she knows time has passed, can tell that the sun has shifted and is about to disappear. She knows also that someone is sitting beside her. Matthew. She can feel the weight of his hand on her calf. They have not touched like this since before the phone call from Thailand, touched in a way that is not about passion—though there has been none of that either—or practicality, passing the salt and emptying the dishwasher, but that is simply about the intimacy of every day. Then, as though Matthew senses that she is awake, his hand is gone.

"You think I drove him away," she says softly. "That I worried too much." Her eyes are still closed. She hears him breathing and finally the slight intake that means he is about to answer.

"No," he says. He sounds tired, all those nights of sitting up, folding origami. "I don't think that." He pauses, sighs. "The truth is that I don't think at all. I teach, and I grade papers, and I smile at the other teachers to let them know that it's okay when I catch them laughing. I stop and put gas in the car on the way home from school every Friday."

In her pocket are the pieces of Darrin that she picked out of the vacuum cleaner bag—a curly black hair that could only be his and some dried mud he'd dragged in from an all-night graduation party. She knows that if she opens her eyes, she will see Matthew rubbing his scar, as he does when he is thinking, the scar that she had asked him about all those years ago in the gay bar the night they met, when he told her about the bliss of riding his bicycle down the road wearing magnifying-glass spectacles, the world so close, so deceptive. "Have you spoken to Lance?" she asks, because she cannot think of that night without Lance.

"I talked to him last week," he says. She thinks about the last year, how she knows nothing of what her husband's days have entailed—lunches eaten, books read, people talked to.

"How is he?"

"Lance is Lance," he says. "He's still in Albuquerque, still waiting for the perfect Asian man to come along, still counting inventory, if you can believe it. He sends his love."

She never understood Lance—with his degree in political science—counting cans at Albertsons. She recalls all the times that she and Matthew, smug in their own lives, offered commentary on Lance's, saying things like "How's he going to meet someone when he spends his life aspiring to nothing more than counting inventory?"

"Poor Lance," she says, and she means it, but then it occurs to her that she no longer has the right to feel sorry for Lance, Lance who wants more than anything to meet someone, to settle down and just be together.

"He's pretty amazing, though," Matthew says. "He can walk into a 7-Eleven, look around, and predict within two hundred dollars how much merchandise they have on hand."

"I guess that's why he stays," Beth says.

"What do you mean?" Matthew says.

"To have that kind of certainty," she says. Her eyes are still closed.

"Or that kind of fear," Matthew adds and then falls silent.

The day of the funeral, Matthew's hands rested atop their son's coffin, side by side, as though the coffin were a piano that he would soon begin to play. His hands were what had first attracted her all those years ago, the unchewed nails and the veins rising up across the backs. They had seemed at once sexy and capable. She remembers how they came from nowhere that day at sea, grabbing the baby from the gap, and how she had mistaken this as a sign of how their lives would always be.

She begins to sob, quietly at first, but then more loudly, and she waits for Matthew to say something, to try for the right words. "He was the absolute best," she says finally. "The A1 most amazing son in the world."

Matthew laughs, and the sound startles her here in their silent house. She feels his hand on her ankle, tentative but holding on. She does not know whether it is pulling her down or up toward the surface, but she opens her eyes and does not move away.

Are You Happy?

Twenty-four years after the crash, Phil would return to Albuquerque to see his mother and she would ask whether he was happy. She was in the final stages of stomach cancer by then, living—or, more accurately, dying—in his brother's house, and Phil sat there, not sure how to answer her question because they'd never talked about such things. Happiness. She'd always scoffed at people who did, maintaining that happiness was a uniquely American preoccupation, speaking as if she were not American. Even then, at the end of her life, Phil believed she would hold an admission of happiness against him.

He had awakened that morning at home in San Francisco, Kelvin and their whole menagerie huddled around him, his legs stiff from being curled up to accommodate the cats, who stretched across the middle of the bed, rejecting parallelism because they preferred to sleep perpendicular. "Daddy's going away today," Kelvin loud-whispered, phrasing that always struck Phil as vaguely but disturbingly sexual, the "Daddy" part, he supposed. The dogs leapt up and began bouncing between them. It was "away" that got them going—Kelvin had trained them to associate the word with car rides—but Phil liked to pretend that it was his imminent departure to which they were responding.

"Let's all eat breakfast together on the raft," Kelvin said. "The raft" was what he called their bed. It was king-size. "We're a growing family," he'd said when they bought it. They were up to seven now: the two of them, three cats, two dogs. Each night at bedtime, Kelvin called out, "Everyone on the raft," and all seven of them climbed on. There, surrounded by a chorus of snorting and snoring and purring, Kelvin always fell asleep quickly, as if the raft were meandering down a peaceful river, while Phil lay wide awake most nights, gripping the mattress as the current quickened, pulling him toward the rapids.

That morning, the morning that Phil would get on the plane to visit his dying mother, Kelvin got up and brought them all breakfast, arranging the bowls of kibble strategically across the comforter, isolating Ollie, their fat boy, who was fond of sniffing the others' buttocks to distract them and then stealing their food. "Let's have sex," declared Kelvin when they were done eating, because he never felt shy about making his desire known, and he got out of bed again, stacked all seven bowls on the dresser, and herded the animals out of the room. Ollie had to be picked up and dropped just as the door was being shut behind him because even though he was portly, he was quick. "You do know they're sitting out there listening," Kelvin said as he returned to the bed. Banning them was not his idea. "Besides, sex is perfectly natural."

"Sex is natural," Phil agreed, though he did not believe this for a minute. There was nothing natural about the way people's faces contorted in the throes of an orgasm or how they seemed as pleasant and agreeable as door-to-door salesmen beforehand, then cold and occasionally cruel after. Kelvin was the first man he'd met who wanted the same things before and after, in bed and out: intimacy and pleasure and reciprocity.

He reached for Kelvin. "But you want me to enjoy myself, right? And I can assure you that I stop enjoying myself the minute Alfie starts howling along."

Kelvin leapt on top of Phil. "Woof," he said. He burrowed his face in Phil's crotch, and Phil laughed.

The call from work came just as they finished, an emergency that Phil could have asked one of the other vets to attend to, but the family had requested him. Kelvin had taken the day off work—he had a boring but flexible office job—to drive him to the airport, so they rose and dressed and went first to the clinic, where Kelvin waited in the car with Alfie and Madeline while Phil handled the emergency, and from there to the airport. As they stood at the curb saying goodbye, Kelvin began to cry. He looked right at Phil as he sobbed, even stroking his cheek, while the curbside baggage checker stood several feet away, staring and scowling. Phil pretended to focus on his husband, though all he could think about was the baggage checker.

The dogs put their snouts out the half-open car window and began whimpering. "You see?" Kelvin said, his face still wet. "The whole family's miserable."

This—the way Kelvin spoke, without sarcasm or subtext—could have turned Phil off all those years ago when they first met, but instead it had seemed exotic, inviting. When Phil joked with him on one of their first dates, "My God, you're as earnest as a lesbian," Kelvin laughed because it could be both funny and true. Phil discovered that he liked making Kelvin laugh. As a boy, he'd never made people laugh, except at him. This was particularly true of his family, who laughed at him often and considered him overly sensitive for minding.

He met Kelvin at an auction, a fundraiser for an animal shelter at which he'd volunteered when he first moved to Davis, after he'd fled New Mexico and his family and the life he was expected to live there. At the time of the auction, he was in veterinary school, and the listing in the auction program read: *Date with sexy veterinary student!* A group of women with whom he volunteered had come up with the idea, and though the whole thing embarrassed him greatly, he'd gone along with it, which meant that halfway through the evening he found himself up on the stage being told to strike a sexy vet pose. Mainly, the bidders were women his mother's age—*bidding biddies*, he thought, ungenerously. It did not surprise him that bidding biddies were his audience. What did surprise him was the lone man, Bidder 13, who kept lifting his paddle until most of the bidding biddies had dropped away and it became a duel between him and a woman in her sixties wearing cat ears and whiskers. Finally, the man threw down his paddle in defeat. This was Kelvin.

After the auction was over and Phil was standing to the side of the buffet table with Carol, the shelter receptionist, Kelvin approached him, pausing—out of nervousness or hunger—to select a shrimp-and-cucumber canapé. He stood in front of Phil, his face a deep red, which Phil misread as shyness until Carol said, "I think he's choking." She'd spent the last five minutes referring to Phil as the "975-Dollar Man," which is what the cat woman had paid for the date, but her voice turned serious then, the way it got when someone brought in a sick animal they'd found on the street.

"Are you choking?" Phil asked, and Kelvin nodded.

Phil pounded him on the back, and when this did not work, he put his arms around Kelvin from behind, placed a fist above

Kelvin's navel, and administered the Heimlich maneuver, jerking up so hard that Kelvin's feet came off the ground. He did this twice more, and Carol said, "I think you got it."

Kelvin nodded in agreement and spit the shrimp back into his hand. "You're amazing," he said to Phil when he could finally talk, and Phil buttoned his suit coat to hide the fact that he was aroused, turned on by this whole unlikely version of himself.

His brother Tom had someone waiting for him at the airport in Albuquerque, an employee from the family business that Phil had fled all those years ago. The man was in his thirties, nervous and deferential, no doubt assuming that Phil was like his brother. He drove Phil to Tom's house, which was predictably large and nondescript. Tom was there waiting for him—already bundled into his coat—and after the brothers shook hands, Tom left, like they were factory coworkers passing between shifts.

Phil had never been to his brother's house. He went into the living room, where he stood considering the décor, which made sense neither aesthetically nor in terms of what he knew of his brother, who had always valued practicality. There were numerous ceramic reproductions of books, all crudely cast, and above the fake fireplace, framed behind glass, an arrangement of pot holders. Pot holders! He supposed that Sandra, Tom's wife, whom he had met just twice, might be responsible for the décor. He went over to the rocking chair beside the fireplace, but as soon as he sat down, Sandra appeared, and he stood back up. She, too, shook his hand, then explained with some urgency that the chair in which he'd been sitting was "just for show." He did not know what this meant, but remained standing.

After that, neither of them spoke, and when the hospice nurse arrived for her daily visit, Sandra put on her coat and left, so it was the hospice nurse who led him down the hallway to the guest room, in the middle of which stood a hospital bed. There, tucked into the bed, was his mother. She opened her eyes and said, "Oh, it's you," as though she'd seen him just minutes earlier, but he made a point to go over to her and kiss her forehead.

The nurse showed him everything—a list of instructions, broken down by the hour; the packets of nutritional shakes that his mother did not want to drink but needed to; a drawer filled with oral syringes of pain medicine—all while writing on charts and attending to his mother, who alternated between ordering the nurse around and ignoring her. The nurse did not hurry or become impatient, and when she was done with her visit, Phil walked her to the door and thanked her in an apologetic voice.

"She's not so bad," the nurse said. "At least she knows what she wants."

Phil laughed in agreement.

"And she's much calmer, now that you're here. She's been anxious for you to arrive." This, he knew, was one of those things that medical people say, a one-size-fits-all approach that treated the world as a place where families were happiest together.

Some of his friends had told him that the hardest thing about a parent's death was that the argument suddenly ended, but in his case the argument had never really begun. He had withdrawn from the debate, left without telling his family that he was going, eventually contacting them to say that he had settled in California. When he met Kelvin, he let the answering machine announce his relationship—"You have reached the home of Phil and Kelvin"—and his family never asked for details. When Kelvin wanted to accompany him on his infrequent visits back home, he declined, saying, "I'm saving you from them," but the truth was that he was saving himself. As long as Kelvin was not there—sitting at their table asking questions about what Phil had been like as a boy and expecting to sleep in Phil's childhood bed with him at night—they did not have to discuss any of it.

At the airport that morning, the last thing Kelvin said was "Call if you need me to come." He tried to imagine Kelvin here, in his brother's house, wondered how his mother would feel, dying with a stranger beside her. But wasn't he a stranger also?

He waved as the hospice nurse drove off, then went back into the guest room. His mother's eyes were shut, and he sat down in a chair, relieved. It was then, without opening her eyes, that his mother asked whether he was happy. When he didn't answer, she said, "I suppose it was a good thing you ran away like that, even if you just turned your back on everything—your father, the business." She spoke as if they were discussing recent events, not events that had occurred years ago. "I told your father all along you weren't cut out for it—the business. You never liked the direct approach to anything."

Her eyes were still closed, and she sighed deeply.

"Actually, I don't think your father was even disappointed," she went on, either trying to goad him or just talking, which often sounded like the same thing. Kelvin, who was unapologetically influenced by pop psychology texts, said that falling into established family patterns of communication was a self-fulfilling prophecy, that it was within Phil's control to respond differently, a position with which Phil—in theory and from a distance—agreed. In practice, at this particular moment, he said nothing. "The truth is he was probably relieved that you left."

"You know what?" Phil said suddenly. "I *am* happy. Kelvin and I have a wonderful life together. Is that direct enough for you?"

His mother opened her eyes but did not look at him. "You let that crash get the better of you," she said.

After the shuttle dropped them off at the hotel the day of the crash, the three of them—Phil, his mother, and his aunt—went upstairs to the rooms they'd been assigned by the airline and into the smaller of the two, which Phil assumed was his because it had just one bed. None of them had luggage—it was gone with the plane—and Phil felt even more lost without a bag to unpack, toiletries to arrange. He waited, but his mother and aunt did not go into the adjoining room. They just stood there. Finally, his mother drew the curtains closed and climbed into the king-size bed that was supposed to be his, and he and his aunt followed. Except for their shoes, they got in fully dressed, his mother in the middle, mirroring their seating on the plane. It was ironic that they had been sitting that way, for they all three accepted that it was his aunt's job to buffer Phil and his mother from each other, but his aunt needed to be at the window, looking out. She said it was how she kept the plane afloat. Of course, this was ironic also.

The overhead light was on, but no one got up to shut it off. Nobody spoke. What was there to say? None of them wanted to relive the moments just before the crash, or the chaos after. And before that? Before that, they had been on vacation, drinking and laughing under the bright Caribbean sun. Now, they were huddled beneath the blankets, their teeth chattering hard in their mouths. At some point, Phil rose and went into the adjoining room, where he stripped the comforters from both beds, brought them back, and covered his mother and aunt. For the first time in his life, he felt like an adult.

They stayed in bed together for thirty-six hours. Phil did not sleep. Each time he closed his eyes, he felt the plane beneath him, speeding down the runway, the backward tilt as its nose poked upward, the plane hesitating, then falling back, hard. Around him, people had screamed; he had screamed with them.

The morning of the second day, the telephone rang and Phil got out of bed and answered it. It was the airline, checking on them.

"Have you arranged a flight for us?" he asked the woman on the other end.

Directly after the crash, the survivors had been brought to a room at the airport set up with coffee and telephones. Phil and his mother had called his father back home, explaining that there had been an accident. Phil's father was at his office, and even though he was on the phone with his wife and son who were calling because they had almost died, he held the receiver between his ear and shoulder and waved to his secretary to bring him some paperwork that needed signing—or so Phil imagined, given his father's distracted response. For his father, even tragedy could be multitasked.

Phil waited for the airline woman to answer his question, to say that she had booked a flight for the three of them, even though he could not imagine getting back on a plane so soon, maybe ever. Instead, she hiccupped loudly. She did not apologize, but he supposed the ensuing silence had to do with her feeling embarrassed, hiccupping like that into the ear of a crash victim.

"We can't arrange flights quite yet," said the airline representative at last. "We're still identifying bodies." She paused. "That's actually why I'm calling—we need someone from your party to come to the morgue."

"Party?" he said loudly, finding the word strange, almost offensive, in a conversation about morgues and bodies. He was sitting on the edge of the bed, still wearing the clothes he'd had on for the flight—jeans with a button-down shirt and linen jacket, in deference to his mother, who insisted that flying was something you dressed up for. She and his aunt wore skirts, which rode up around their thighs when they slid to safety; now, beneath the layers of blankets, he imagined their skirts had done the same. "I'll come," he said to the airline woman.

"Who was it, Philip?" his mother asked.

"The airline," he said. "I need to, you know, identify their bodies."

When he returned two hours later, his mother and aunt were out of bed, showered, and dressed in clothes that the airline had delivered. Phil had never seen his mother in a T-shirt. Neither woman asked about the morgue, which was fine with him. He did not want to discuss any of it, to hear himself using words like "fungi" to describe how Mr. Milford's left ear had looked, melted to the side of his head.

"Philip," said his mother, "will you take us out for a late lunch, please?"

She had never spoken to him like this, requesting rather than demanding his services. Though his homosexuality was not discussed between them, she treated him like her homosexual son nonetheless, expecting him to escort her to dinner and concerts, on shopping excursions and to the hair salon. Art, the man with whom he was having sex back home in Albuquerque, had told him he needed to learn how to stand up for himself, stop being such a sissy. Art was ashamed of him. Whenever they went out in public, which was rarely, Art walked several feet ahead of him, pretending they were not together.

Art did not walk this way with his wife. Phil had seen them once, strolling along Central with their two children. In bed later that week, when Phil asked Art what his children's names were, Art smashed Phil's head into the headboard. "You think I want their names coming out of your filthy faggot mouth?" Art said.

Phil had wanted to say something clever about what Art wanted from his filthy faggot mouth. "No," he said instead, soothingly. "Of course not."

"Lunch, yes," Phil answered his mother. "Let me just get out of these clothes." He picked up the bag that the airline had left for him and took it into the bathroom. Inside were T-shirts, extra-large though he was a medium at best, imprinted with the airline's logo. He put one on. He looked like a walking advertisement for an airline that had nearly killed him.

The bed was made, neatly, and his mother and aunt sat on it, waiting. "I haven't gone out without a purse since I was a girl," his mother was saying to his aunt. They had obeyed orders to leave everything behind when they evacuated, though in the survivors' room afterward, some women sat clutching their purses, symbols of their betrayal. His mother had surprised him, not because she'd left hers—she was a stickler for rules—but because she'd refrained from commenting on those who had not.

They had only what was in Phil's pockets—some leftover vacation currency and his credit card—but they avoided the hotel restaurant, where the airline was running a tab, and instead took a taxi to a nearby restaurant. They needed to be away from the other survivors, though they did not say this aloud.

As they finished their first course, two businessmen sat down at the table next to them and began to smoke. "How's your soup?" Phil asked his mother to distract her from the smoking.

"Mine is very good," said his aunt, doing the same.

"Excuse me," his mother called to the men. "Please put those out. We're trying to eat." She waved her hand at the cigarettes, and the men laughed.

"Americans, no?" said the younger man.

"Yes," said Phil.

"Americans are always the pure ones in the room," said the older man, sweeping his arm to indicate the other tables, which were occupied by people smoking and drinking and laughing. "But sometimes you just need to live a little instead of thinking every cigarette is going to kill you." He raised his wineglass at them encouragingly.

His mother stood and walked past the men as though she were leaving, but before Phil and his aunt could rise to follow her, she turned back around and went right up to the men's table. "You see me here in front of you?" she said. "I am living."

The Milfords were dead, dead because they smoked. That was the melodramatic way to think of it but also the truth. They had all boarded the plane together, but when Phil, his mother, and his aunt reached the fifth row, they waved goodbye to the Milfords, and the Milfords waved cheerfully back as they continued toward the smoking section at the rear of the plane, the section that would be crushed when the plane dropped back on its tail. As the Milfords moved down the aisle, Phil turned and saw Mr. Milford press his hand lightly to his wife's back. The night before, as the five of them sat in the resort lounge after their final dinner together, Mr. Milford had reached under the table and pressed that same hand to Phil's thigh. Phil's first thought was that Mr. Milford had somehow mixed up right and left, believed that he was caressing his wife's thigh as he stared straight ahead, listening to Phil's mother explain what was wrong with vegetarians, which was that they didn't eat meat. In response, Mr. Milford laughed, but Phil knew his mother was not being clever. She was rarely intentionally funny and never with topics that angered her, like vegetarians.

"I don't trust anyone who doesn't eat meat," said Mr. Milford, his hand climbing higher on Phil's thigh. Belatedly, Phil realized that the comment was intended for him. In those days, Phil was often surprised by people, perplexed by the things they said and did. But had he truly been surprised by Mr. Milford's hand that night? Just hours earlier at the pool, Mr. Milford had chatted with him the way an uncle might, even as he regarded the pouch in Phil's swimming trunks with a steady, almost amused gaze. Phil was used to men being startled by his size, not just the few, generally straight men with whom he'd had furtive sex but all the men he'd ever been obligated to shower beside, in high school and then college. They watched him mince toward the showers, penis swinging like an elephant's trunk, startled but also, he thought, angered at the injustice.

He did not remove Mr. Milford's hand. He didn't know why exactly, except that it was already there, *situated*. Then, Mr. Milford's wife jumped up. "ABBA!" she screamed. "Let's dance, Rob."

Mr. Milford's hand stopped its cajoling and joined his other hand, which was raised in mock protest, but Mrs. Milford—Kate, she'd insisted Phil call her—pulled her husband from his chair anyway. The lounge was dim, but Mr. Milford's crotch, when he stood, was at eye level, so Phil could see the effect the encounter had had on him. Phil's own crotch had registered nothing, which both pleased and baffled him. He supposed it was that his mother was sitting right there across from him, sipping cognac and saying, "I've never cared for legumes."

When Mr. Milford came to his room later that night to finish the furtive fumbling he'd started under the table, Phil invited him in. The sex was fast and not quite as rough as Phil had come to expect from straight men, which was how he regarded Mr. Milford because he had a wife. Afterward, they lay together on the bed and talked. It felt strange and intimate and exhilarating. Mr. Milford lit two cigarettes and passed him one. He showed Phil how to draw the smoke in, hold it, and blow it back out, and Phil followed his instructions, all the while recalling the straightforward dictums from his childhood about the perils of smoking. He'd always trusted straightforward dictums.

Eventually, they had sex again, more slowly this time. When they were finished, Mr. Milford turned toward him, propping his head on his arm. He studied Phil: his body and then his face. "You're such a lovely boy," he said.

"Thank you," Phil said, in a polite voice that made Mr. Milford laugh, and Phil felt compelled to add, "Actually, I'm twenty-two. I just finished college."

Of course, Mr. Milford knew this already. At dinner the first night, when the two families were seated together, his mother had told the Milfords all sorts of things, including how she had presented Phil with the trip as a surprise graduation present, not mentioning that she had done so even though she knew that he hated resorts, hated lying on the beach and sharing the rarefied air of the resort grounds with people who thought themselves experts on a host of third-world countries because they had frequented their resorts. The two families had made plans to meet again the next day, the week taking shape around their new friendship, around some daily configuration of the five of them eating and shopping and going on excursions. When they discovered that they were even booked on the same flight out—a discount shuttle that flew between the resort island and Puerto Rico—they regarded it less as a coincidence than one last outing that they had planned together.

There in bed, he and Mr. Milford did not discuss their departure the next morning or anything having to do with the five of them. "What do you plan to do next?" Mr. Milford asked. "Do you have a job lined up?"

"I'm going to work at my father's business," Phil said. He tried to sound nonchalant.

"Business?" said Mr. Milford. "I don't see you in business." He added, "I don't mean that in a bad way."

"I told you I studied business in college," Phil said. "It's been the plan for both of us, me and my brother, since we were boys."

"I see," said Mr. Milford. He stroked Phil's arm, and Phil wondered where Mrs. Milford—Kate—thought her husband was. "But what would *you* choose? What is it that you want to do?"

"I'm a pragmatist," said Phil. This was not true. He was a romantic, and he did not think one could be both. "Anyway, I'm already enough of a disappointment because of, you know." He gestured at the two of them side by side on the bed, naked. This was the image he would recall as he stood in the makeshift morgue two and a half days later.

What he wanted to be was a veterinarian. He'd dreamed about it since he was six, when Hans came to live with them. Hans was nothing like the dog that Phil had picked out from the lineup of breeds in the encyclopedia—a dachshund. "We're not getting a damn wiener dog," his father had said, and the next day he came home with Hans, but the thing about Hans was that even though he was a big dog—"a man's dog," his father liked to say—Hans loved *him*. He didn't care that Phil had no friends or that he was a boy who thought about other boys. When Phil lay in bed crying, Hans came, and when Phil wrapped his arms around Hans, Hans curled against him and stayed that way, steady and warm, through the night.

He did not tell Mr. Milford any of this that night, but five days later, when he and his mother and aunt finally arrived back in Albuquerque, he got off the plane and went directly to his apartment, packed his car, and drove west to California, then north to Davis, where he found a job working at an animal clinic and volunteered at the shelter. Two years later, he started veterinary school, and then he met Kelvin. He tried not to think about the fact that his own happiness had come about because Mr. Milford died.

The first time Phil went out to dinner with Kelvin's parents, they had on matching T-shirts with the words *We Love Our Gay Son*. Phil asked whether this meant that they did not love Kelvin's brother, who was straight, and they laughed as though he were joking. He supposed he was. The next time, they had new shirts: *We Love Our Gay Son and His Gay Boyfriend.* They sat in the restaurant wearing their public displays of support and eating the calamari appetizer. "Phil," they asked, "how does your family respond to your homosexuality?"

"By not talking about it," he replied, keeping his tone light, but Kelvin's parents drew closer. "These things can't just be brushed under the rug," his mother said. She set down a forkful of tentacles and lifted the corner of her place mat, pretending to sweep breadcrumbs under it with her other hand.

"Would it help if we spoke to them?" Kelvin's father said. "We're happy to give them a call."

"I couldn't ask you to do that," Phil said. "I don't even like talking to them." He laughed, but it ended in a high-pitched squeak that threatened to devolve into tears. His father had always responded to his tears by saying, "I'll give you something to cry about," and then proceeding to do so. Once, when Phil was twelve, his father had yanked down his pants and spanked him right there in the plaza in Old Town as tourists walked by, his buttocks heating up beneath his father's blows and the steady New Mexico sun. The memory was as vivid as the expressions of concern on the faces of Kelvin's parents as they stared at him. He'd looked away, down at their T-shirts. *I love your gay son also,* he thought. He thought about how he would never declare this on a T-shirt. He was crying, and he stood up from the table, pushed back his chair, and left.

Not even a year later, he and Kelvin had moved to San Francisco because he understood by then that he was not cut out to be part of a happy family either. Each month, Kelvin's parents drove into the city to stay with them, and Phil wondered whether they knew that they were the reason for the move. He didn't think so because during these visits, when Kelvin called out, "Everyone on the raft," Kelvin's mother came into their room and lay at the foot of the bed, talking to them as she stroked Ollie's fat stomach, and then she would get up and kiss them both good night.

In her hospital bed, his mother lay turned away from him. He thought she might be crying. He had not seen her cry in the twenty-four years since the crash, not even when his father had died a year earlier. That night, the night his father died, he and Kelvin sat down to eat dinner and Phil said, "Just so you know, the phone's going to ring any minute, but we're not going to answer it."

"Okay," said Kelvin, not asking because he knew by now how this worked, and sure enough, a few minutes later, Phil said, "I did it. You said I needed to, and I did."

"The invitation?" Kelvin said, and Phil said, "Yes," and just like that, the phone rang. They both laughed because there was something funny about saying a thing would happen just before it did. The dogs began to bark, not at the phone but at the laughing. They did not like to be left out.

"We'll let the machine take it," Phil said. He loved answering machines, the sense of control they gave him. "I know it's them. It would have arrived today. I'll call back tomorrow, but for now I just want to feel happy."

He and Kelvin were getting married, finally, after nineteen years, because for the first time they could, legally that is. There would be a brief ceremony at City Hall followed by a party, and the only catch was that Kelvin said Phil needed to invite his family. "Force *them* to make the decision," he said. "Don't make it for them."

"Call me," said his mother's voice from the corner of the room in his tiny house, where his mother had never been. "I need to tell you something."

She sounded strange, a different kind of strange from the strange that had to do with responding to an invitation to the wedding of your homosexual son, and he called immediately. "What's up?" he said, and she said, "It's your father."

"What about him?" He was expecting her to say that his father had told her to call, had made it her job to explain that they had no intention of attending this "wedding"—"wedding," her tone would make clear, in quotation marks.

"He's dead," she said. "The ambulance is here, so I better go. I just thought you'd want to know."

"Dead?" he said. He'd never imagined his father in those terms. "How?"

"He was sitting at the table, eating dinner and looking through the mail. I went into the kitchen to get him another piece of lasagna, and when I came back he was gone."

She paused. "Oh, there was something from you today. Some sort of invitation." Her voice made clear that this was the end of *that* conversation.

As he and Kelvin lay in bed later that night, Phil said, "Do you think it was, you know, because of the invitation?"

"What?" said Kelvin sleepily, and then, "You mean the heart attack?"

That was exactly what he meant.

"Oh, Philip. No. Heart attacks don't work that way." Kelvin took his hand in the dark. "I can't believe your mother, that she had the presence of mind to bring up the invitation as they were carrying your father's body out of the house."

From her hospital bed just one year later, his mother said, "Whatever happened with that invitation, the one that arrived the day your father died?"

He'd always imagined dying as a tunnel that narrowed around you until everything ceased to exist and it was just you, walking alone, no longer caring what those around you said or thought or ate for lunch or even who the next president was going to be, but maybe he'd been wrong. "You're wondering whether Kelvin and I got married?" he asked.

She was still turned away from him, but she was definitely crying, and he pulled back the covers and got into bed beside his mother.

"Philip?" she said. She sounded alarmed.

"Yes," he said. "I'm here." He made his voice soothing, like he was talking to an injured animal.

After a while, his mother said, "Do you remember those men at the restaurant? The ones who wouldn't stop smoking?" She sounded calmer, and he thought that she had forgotten about wanting to know whether he was married. He *was* married, but he wasn't going to insist on telling her.

"Yes," he said. "I remember."

"They made me so mad." She laughed, and he laughed with her.

"I mainly remember how you went over to their table and yelled at them," he said. "I admired you so much at that moment." He realized this was true.

"Really?" she said. "I was sure I'd embarrassed you."

His brother would be home any minute. He would come into the bedroom, take in the sight of Philip in bed with their dying mother, and say, "What are you doing?," his brother who could not differentiate between practical and beautiful.

Phil shifted onto his side toward his mother. Her eyes were closed, but he could see that she was in pain. It was his job to understand pain. "Are you afraid?" he asked.

She did not answer, and he thought maybe she'd dozed off. "No," she said at last. "What would be the use? I just want it to be over."

"Don't say that," he said, a perfunctory response.

"There's nothing more for me here. I'm just waiting to die, and you know I've never liked waiting." She paused. "I'm glad you're here, Philip."

Kelvin had told him that people sometimes softened before death, that they understood—maybe only then—what they'd wished for from life.

"I'm glad, too," he said. He was.

Only now did his mother open her eyes. "Listen. I need you to give me all of it," she said, pointing at the drawer where the pain medicine was kept, several weeks' worth, the oral syringes lined up like the hulls of wingless planes. "No one will wonder," she said. "The hospice people left it, after all," and then, when he didn't answer, "Really, Philip. I thought you'd gotten over all of that. Your timidity."

The emergency he'd been called in to deal with on his way to the airport that morning had involved a dog, just four years old, with a tumor that had proven inoperable. Phil had not known the dog or the family well. They were new to the city, but they had asked for him. The dog reared up just once, when Phil pushed the needle into his back leg. The family gathered around, crying unabashedly, Phil crying with them. "He was a lovely boy," he'd said, Mr. Milford's voice still with him after all these years.

"It's not that," he told his mother. "I'm not worried about getting caught." He thought about all the creatures he'd put down, the relief he'd sensed in their bodies at the very end. "It's just—you're my mother," he said finally, though he knew that this was no reason at all.

Clear as Cake

Marvin Helgarson smoked a pipe. When he listened to us, he nipped at the pipe—*pah, pah, pah*—the way that people who smoke pipes do, and when he told us things about our writing, he jabbed the pipe in the air for emphasis. I liked Marvin Helgarson. He was tall, not just everyday tall but tall even by Minnesota standards, though that's not why I liked him. I'm just trying to give details, what Marvin Helgarson called "salient features."

The class met Tuesday evenings in the Humanities Building library, sixteen of us wedged in around two long wooden tables that came together in a T with Marvin Helgarson at the head. It felt like Thanksgiving the first night, all of us too close together and filled with dread, though later, after Marvin Helgarson explained about perspective, I could see that maybe that was just my perspective.

"Liars and thieves," said Marvin Helgarson to get things going. "That's what you get with a room full of writers." He rose and swept out his arms like Jesus to include us all.

He meant it as an icebreaker, and most of us chuckled, but the woman across from me said, "Oh dear. I didn't know anything about that"—meaning, I guess, that she had a different idea about writers and writing, a different idea about what she had signed up for. Her name was Wanda, and she had large warts on her chin and cheeks, and later these warts would appear on the characters in her stories. We were always nervous about discussing them, worrying, I suppose, that we might read something into the warts that Wanda had not intended and that she would know then what it was that people saw when they looked at her.

"Wanda," said Marvin Helgarson, "I don't mean writers are really thieves." He paused, picked up his pipe, and sucked on it. "It's more like when someone lends you a pen to use, and then you just don't give it back." About lying, he said nothing.

"You're going to be working together intimately," Marvin Helgarson said, "so you need to know who you're dealing with." He asked for a volunteer to begin the introductions, and Fred Erickson, who was wearing a tie with a treble clef on it, jumped right in, describing his family and hobbies and years as the director of a choir in Idaho, a position from which he was now retired. Idaho seemed far away to me, and I wondered how he had ended up in Moorhead, Minnesota, but I didn't ask because I was intimidated by my classmates, most of whom came to campus once a week for this class but were adults with jobs and families the rest of the time.

I took a lot of notes that semester, tips that Marvin Helgarson shared to help us with our writing, like when he told us that sometimes the things that seemed most compelling to write about should not really be written about at all. They were just anecdotes, he said, odd things that had happened to us that were interesting to discuss in a bar but were not literary, by which he meant that they could not "transcend the page." He explained this the first night of class, jabbing the air with his pipe so that we understood it was important, and then he said it again several months later when we discussed the nutty lady's story about a woman who cleaned rest stops along I-94. In the story, the woman and her cleaning partner were finishing the rest area near Fergus Falls when they discovered a body inside one of the trash cans. The story, which was just two pages long, mainly a lot of boring details about cleaning that established authenticity, ended like this: "The woman was dead and she was also naked. We were shocked and scared, and after the police came, we finished the bathrooms and went home."

When Marvin explained to the nutty lady that it wasn't really a short story, that it was more of an anecdote, she stood up. "Anecdote?" she said. "This really happened, you know. It happened to *me*, right after my asswipe husband left and I had to be at that job every morning at six." She snorted. "Anecdote." Then, she walked out. It was late, nearly nine o'clock, and we could hear her footsteps echoing, not only because the building was empty but because she was wearing ski boots.

We didn't see the crazy lady again, but at the beginning of the next class Marvin showed us what she had left in his mailbox: a manila envelope with our stories for the week, chopped into strips with a paper cutter. You see, she really was crazy. But also, she'd had enough of us I think, enough of us telling her stuff about her writing. Three weeks earlier, she'd submitted a story about a woman whose vagina hurt all the time, except when she was having sex. As a result, her husband, who was a farmer, got very tired of having sex all the time and told her that she needed to go to the doctor to have her vagina checked. "I'm putting my foot down" is what he said, which made me laugh, though I didn't say so because I didn't think the story was supposed to be funny.

When the woman and her husband spoke, it seemed like they were from Ireland, but when they drove into town to see the doctor, they drove to Bemidji, which is in Minnesota. I raised my hand and said they sounded Irish, pointing to things like "lassie" and "thar" because Marvin had told us to back up our comments with examples from the text, but the crazy lady looked pleased when I said they sounded Irish. "Yes," she said. "They're from Ireland. They moved to Minnesota when they were young in order to have an adventure and be farmers and also because something tragic happened to them in Ireland and they needed a fresh start."

"I guess I missed that," I said and began shuffling back through the story.

"No," she said. "It doesn't say it. It's just something I know. I was creating a life for my characters off the page, the way that Marvin said we should."

"That's a lot to have off the page," pointed out Thomas in what I thought was a very nice voice. Thomas was also one of the older students in the class. The first salient feature about Thomas was that his parents met at a nudist colony, where they were not nudists because they worked in the kitchen, chopping vegetables and frying meat. The other salient feature about Thomas was that he was a minister. I knew these things because he sometimes wrote his sermons at Ralph's, the bar that I hung out at, and one night we drank a pitcher of beer together and talked, but when we saw each other in class the next week, we both felt awkward.

"But the story isn't about them leaving Ireland," said the crazy lady triumphantly. "It's about"—she paused because I guess even a crazy lady feels strange saying "vagina" to a minister—"the pain in her female parts."

None of us knew what to say, so we looked down at the story, at the scene in which the woman and her husband, who was tired from having sex all the time, visited the doctor. When she was in the doctor's office, lying on the table with her feet in the stirrups, the doctor, who was an elderly man, positioned himself between her legs and called out, "Three fingers going."

This was supposed to be a minor detail I think, but Tabatha, who was a feminist, got mad. "That's ridiculous," she yelled at the crazy lady. "What kind of a doctor would say, 'Three fingers going'?"

"Doctors are just regular people," the crazy lady yelled back. "They get tired of saying the same things over and over, day after day. This doctor is like that. He's old, and he's tired. I am showing that he's a regular person who is exhausted and wants to retire. I am developing his character."

"That's not development," Tabatha said. "Then the story becomes about him, about how he's a misogynist and is going to get sued one of these days for saying things like 'three fingers going' to women when they're in a vulnerable position."

Tabatha was not someone I wanted to be friends with, but I liked having her in class because she never disappointed me. Her first story, called "Cardboard Jesus," was about this guy Bart who spends all day watching television, and then one day a cardboard man jumps out of the TV and starts going on and on about how Bart needs to change his life, so Bart names the little man Cardboard Jesus. Finally, Bart gets tired of Cardboard Jesus making him feel bad about his life, so he puts Cardboard Jesus in the garbage disposal. The story ends with Cardboard Jesus getting chewed up, and the last line is him calling out from inside the disposal, "Why hast thou forsaken me?"

Most of us did not really care for "Cardboard Jesus." I pointed out that it seemed unlikely, and Marvin said, "Are we talking character believability?" and I said that I couldn't really put my finger on it but that there wasn't a character worth *rooting for* in the whole piece. Tabatha snorted and said, "It's not a football game," even though we weren't supposed to talk when our story was being discussed.

"Maybe it's the dialogue," I said finally.

Just the week before, Marvin had explained about dialogue, how it's supposed to sound like a normal conversation except less boring. Our dialogues, it turned out, had too much verisimilitude. "Look," Marvin had said. "Imagine a guy goes into McDonald's and says, 'I'd like a Big Mac and fries,' and then the cashier says, 'Okay, that'll be four dollars and five cents,' and the guy pays and walks out with his burger and fries." He paused. "Typical conversation, right?" And we nodded. "So what's wrong with putting that conversation in a story?" he asked.

Tabatha's hand went up. "Why is everything always about McDonald's?" she said. "I would never have that conversation because I would never go to McDonald's." She looked around the table. "Or Burger King," she added, preempting the possibility of a setting change.

Marvin Helgarson sighed. "Fine," he said. "But my point is that this conversation is only interesting if one of them says something we don't expect, if the cashier says, 'No, sir, you may *not* have a Big Mac and fries.' Then you have a story."

Tabatha had started to speak, probably planning to point out that the cashier was doing the man a favor, but Marvin held up his hand at her. "Dialogue," he explained, "is all about power shifting back and forth." His pipe had volleyed illustratively through the air.

"What's wrong with my dialogue?" Tabatha asked, looking at me and making her eyes small.

"I don't know," I said. Her dialogue was the opposite of what Marvin had cautioned us about. It didn't have any verisimilitude. "I guess it just feels sort of biblical."

The crazy lady raised her hand and said that there was nothing biblical about the story. She said the story was libelous, and Marvin said, "I think you mean blasphemous," and she said that she knew what she meant and so did God. Thomas said nothing, even though he was a minister, and then Tabatha announced that everyone had missed the point, which was that "Cardboard Jesus" was a "modern-day crucifixion story."

Each Sunday after church, my parents called my dorm room, my mother dialing because the telephone made my father nervous. Though only a week had passed since the last conversation, my mother always had plenty to say because my mother was the sort of person who conversed in details. She began with who had been in church that morning, and who had not and why, and moved on to what types of bars and cookies were served during the coffee hour afterward, and from there, to what she planned to serve with the ham that was baking in the oven at that very minute. Then, she broadened out to cover the specifics of the preceding week: what they had eaten for supper each night, what illnesses had beset the town. During these conversations, I often became abrupt with my mother, though she seemed not to notice, for I do not think that it occurred to her, ever, that I was not interested in these details, all of them adding up to a life I did not want.

Of course, there was more to it than that. I had stopped believing in God. I didn't even know when it had happened, just that one day I understood that I did not, the way that you look out the window and realize the leaves are gone yet you can't remember seeing a single one fall. I had told no one about this, certainly not my parents, who would have said, "Well, what do you expect?" and then prayed for me, which I did not want.

"There are no saints or sinners," Marvin Helgarson had taken to saying when he criticized a character for being what he had, at the start of the semester, called "cardboard" but switched to calling "two-dimensional" after Cardboard Jesus. "None of us is all bad—or all good."

Unlike Marvin Helgarson, my parents did believe that people could be all good; in fact, they believed not only that people could be all good but that they should be. My parents did not think that people's weaknesses were interesting or literary. They just thought that weakness led to sin.

Eventually, my father would demand the receiver. "Not much to report," he would say, and I would reply, "Me neither," and then he would ask something general about my classes and something specific about my bank balance, and as he prepared to hand the phone back to my mother, he would add, "Remember, Renee, communism is Satan at work," the way that other parents, I imagined, might admonish their children to study hard.

These were the Reagan years, so many people in the town where I grew up referred to communism in daily conversation, right alongside talk of droughts and price ceilings and all the other evils of the world over which they had no control. Still, even within the narrow parameters of our small town, my parents' fears felt different.

They saw communism lurking everywhere, behind everything that was new to them or unfamiliar, behind everything that I had gone off to college and found myself drawn to: philosophy, feminism, poetry, my professors, even the Peace Corps, as I had discovered when I mentioned that I was thinking about applying, a revelation that made my mother cry. In the sixth grade, when four of my classmates showed up at our door on Halloween with UNICEF boxes, requesting contributions to help poor children, my mother told them, "You can have candy or nothing," explaining, "We don't support communists in this house." She held out a Baby Ruth bar, gauging whether they were beyond salvation. They were.

That year, we had been presented with a new teacher, Mrs. Keller, who was not from our town, which meant that she was an outsider, and this meant that I paid a good deal of attention to everything she said and did. Early in the year, on a rainy afternoon when we were all feeling restless, Mrs. Keller had tried to teach us levitation, which we enjoyed so much that some of us went home and reported about our fun to our parents. I did not, for though I was just eleven, I sensed that levitation was one more thing that would be regarded with suspicion by my parents. Nonetheless, word came quickly back to the principal that we had been practicing levitation, which—it was acknowledged by nearly all of the parents—was a form of witchcraft and thus satanic. We knew that Mrs. Keller had been spoken to, and for days we sat quietly in our seats, too ashamed to lift our eyes, but gently she wooed us back. Then, several weeks later, she played a scratchy recording of Poe's "The Tell-Tale Heart," which terrified us, and which we loved and begged to hear again, but which, it turned out, was also satanic, and again she was reprimanded. We watched as the joy that she took in teaching us diminished, her spontaneity replaced with uncertainty, which spread to us so that we began to believe that we must say nothing of the excitement we felt in her classroom, as though excitement itself were suspect.

The day after Halloween, I sat at my desk and watched the four girls who had come to our door turn in their UNICEF boxes to Mrs. Keller and report, shyly, what my mother had said, how she had begged them to accept candy bars and called them communists. Mrs. Keller started to say something but caught herself, her initial response giving way to a few bland comments about the good deed that the girls had done. Then, at the end of the school year, Mrs. Keller packed up her carefully decorated room—the maps of the world, the recordings of jazz and poetry, the picture of her daughter, of whom we were all just a little jealous—and moved on.

When Marvin Helgarson asked us to introduce ourselves that first night, I said only that I was a humanities major, one semester away from graduation. The humanities department had recently declared a slogan—*Confronting the Ultimate Reality*—to explain what it was that we did in the humanities, for apparently there was some confusion. I had found that we spent a lot of time reading and talking about concepts that required capitalization—Beauty and Love, Suffering and Death, Guilt and Art. We also wrote papers about them, and often my professors wrote "interesting" or "hmm" next to my points, but they never wrote "correct." This was starting to feel stressful. It was like playing Find the Button, with people calling out, "You're getting warm!" every once in a while, but no matter how long you played, you never actually found the button.

Because there wasn't really a button. I got that. I understood that the Ultimate Reality was nebulous. Still, I was one semester away from graduation, and I knew that the Ultimate Reality was not something that you talked about at job interviews, to employers who wanted to know what relevant skills you had acquired over the last four years. Moreover, when I looked around at other students, they were learning how to generate spreadsheets and teach children to read, concrete, practical knowledge of the sort that you imagined people going to work and using, while I was becoming less equipped for the world with each passing day.

To make matters worse, when I visited my parents, which I did infrequently even though they lived just an hour and fifteen minutes away, they always asked about my job prospects, sometimes while I was still getting out of the car. "What you want is to look for a company that'll keep you until you're ready to retire," my father said the last time I visited, and I said, "Why not just kill me now?"

This was the sort of comment that made no sense to my parents, that made them think I had gone off to college and gotten myself hooked up with communists. Most nights, I lay in bed awake, imagining myself jobless and forced to move back into my parents' house, where we would sit at the dinner table eating overcooked pork chops and potatoes from my father's garden while they pointed out again and again that they were not surprised by my inability to find a job because nobody they knew had ever heard of such a thing as humanities.

Tabatha and the crazy lady argued about "three fingers going" until Marvin said that it was a good time for a break. Usually, I stayed in the room during breaks, reviewing the next story up for discussion, but that night I went into the hallway and stood around with the others. I had trouble getting my structure straight before I started writing, and Marvin said that the problem might be that I did not figure out the *emotional thrust* of my stories early enough, which was probably true because, overall, I found *emotional thrust* an elusive concept, but I can see now that before I explain why I went out in the hallway, I need to explain about Clem.

The easiest way to begin is to say that Clem and I were friends, though, in retrospect, this seems dishonest because Clem annoyed me much more than he amused me, which is not to say that he couldn't be funny, but this story will mainly deal with annoyance because annoyance was the salient feature of our friendship. Our friendship began because Clem was crippled—"crippled" was his word, the one he insisted on—though not actually *because* he was crippled but because he blamed everything, including the fact that he had no friends, on being crippled. I befriended him primarily to prove him wrong about people, though it's clear now that Clem knew all along that that's what I was doing, which just proves that he was a very lonely person. I've always been intrigued by people like that, people who are mean and hate everyone and do everything they can to repel others—and then feel lonely about it.

Clem was mainly crippled on the left side; when he walked, he held his right arm aloft like the Statue of Liberty and pulled the rest of his body toward it. He told me that before the accident he was athletic but shy, that he gravitated toward solitary sports like golf and running. He was jogging when the accident happened, the morning after his high school graduation, and he lay on the side of the road for over twenty minutes until a truck driver spotted him because the car that hit him had just kept going. He found out months later, after he came out of his coma, that the car had contained four of his classmates, all of whom had been too drunk to even realize what had happened.

The accident turned Clem into a completely different person. He told me this one night as we looked through his senior yearbook, and I wondered—though did not ask—whether he remembered being that other person. I assumed that he did not, for it seemed to me that if he did remember, he would still *be* him.

"Do you think I'm good-looking?" he would ask after a few beers, a question that I refused to answer because I knew that it was a trap, knew that either answer would confirm what he already felt about people, which was that we were cruel, insincere, and stupid. The accident had left him disfigured, though—except for some scarring on his face, which he partially concealed with a black beard and sideburns—disfigured in a way that was not so much ugly as startling. His tongue appeared too big for his mouth and often lolled outside. The truth was that he looked like someone parents would instinctively move their children away from.

His brain had been damaged in a way that caused him to perceive everything as upside-down and backward, so that what he saw as a *6* was really a *9*. Over the years he adjusted by learning to write so that the words appeared upside-down and backward to *him*, a process that was slow and messy. The college provided some assistance in the form of students who typed for him, but most tired of him quickly because he mainly dictated things that were pornographic, like the first story he wrote for class, about a cow named Bessie who had large udders but also a penis. He called the story "Bessie the Hermaphrodite Cow, No Bull," and nothing really happened in the story except that Bessie had sex nonstop with both bulls and cows. When it came time to critique the story, nobody said anything, not even the crazy lady, and finally Marvin did a line-by-line critique of the punctuation, which he said was "creative but at odds with the story."

In the year that Clem and I hung out together, I took him to doctor appointments, shopped for his groceries, and listened to him rage. I drew the line at doing his homework, which he never did himself and which meant that he failed all of his classes and had been doing so, to the best of my knowledge, since he enrolled in college three years earlier. His parents called me when they wanted to know how much money he had left or whether he was "keeping his spirits up" because they were afraid of him. I met them only once, on his birthday, when the four of us went to Mexican Village and he made his mother cry by announcing that she smelled like "crotch rot."

Clem never missed an opportunity to suggest that he and I have sex, posing the question—always—in the most vulgar of terms. Thus, while Tabatha and the crazy lady argued that night about the gynecologist, he was hard at work on a picture of the two of us as naked stick figures, which he labeled "Three Fingers Going." He slid it across the table toward me, and it took me a moment to understand the drawing, not only because it was poorly sketched but because it made no sense to me—there in a library, surrounded by books and people talking about words. As I ripped it up, Clem said, "Just so you know, before the accident, I wasn't into fat, ugly chicks." For the record, I wasn't really fat or ugly, but I wasn't exactly out of the woods when it came to fat and ugly either. Still, I knew that the sudden anger I felt had less to do with the words themselves than with the realization that I was sick and tired of Clem.

Out in the hallway, several of my classmates were standing around smoking and eating chocolate Easter eggs. Marvin once told us that we should use specific nouns, that instead of writing "candy," we should say exactly what kind of candy—chocolate Easter eggs, for example—but he also told us to use details to establish time and setting, so I realize now that people are going to think that this happened at Easter, but it was actually several weeks after Easter and Melinda brought the eggs because she was tired of seeing them in her freezer.

Nobody acted surprised that I was joining them in the hallway that night. Melinda offered me an egg, just as she did everyone else, and I stood next to her, unwrapping it and thinking about what to say. "I liked your story about the drummer whose drum set falls out of the back of her truck," I told her.

She narrowed her eyes, not because of what I had said but because she was taking a drag from her cigarette. "Thanks," she said, blowing out smoke.

Sometimes Melinda wore leather to class, so I asked her whether she had actually been in a band.

"Sure," she said, as though I should have known the story was about her.

"Why'd you stop?" I asked.

"You read the story," she said.

"Couldn't you have bought new drums?"

"Well, yeah," she said. "But that's not really the point."

I nodded, though I didn't really know what the point was. Finally, I said, "I'm sorry, but what is the point?"

She smoked for a moment, and I felt better because it seemed then that maybe she was not sure of the point either. This was one of the advantages of smoking. It gave you the chance to think about what to say next without making it obvious that that's what you were doing. "I guess the point is that sometimes you reach a place in your life where you just want things to add up at the end of the day." She took another drag. "Do you know what I do now?" she asked.

"No," I said, worried that she had mentioned this during introductions the first night.

"I keep the books for the beet plant. Every night before I go home, I close out the books for the day, and I make sure that everything adds up. If something doesn't add up, I stay until it does. It's very gratifying—to go home each day knowing that everything has added up."

I nodded because I could see how this would be gratifying. In high school, I had been enamored of math, and it shocked everyone—friends and teachers and family—when I declared my intention to major in something else entirely, something that involved "reading and the world," an inexact phrasing that reflected how little I understood of what I was after. Math came easily to me, too easily, and in my romanticized view of the world, this had struck me as a problem.

Around this time, the results of a battery of aptitude tests to which I had submitted began rolling in, all bearing the same news: that I was destined to become an engineer or a statistician or an accountant, careers in which things were meant to add up. I soon stopped showing these results to my parents, who were already bewildered by my earlier announcement and could not imagine reading as an end in itself or what sort of living this would provide, but eventually, the results, each new one mirroring the others, had begun to worry me also, for I thought highly of tests, believing them almost infallible. Finally, one of them dealt a wild card, concluding that I was uniquely suited to be a forest ranger, no doubt because I had responded agreeably to questions about solitude and working alone. Still, this came as a great relief because there were few things that interested me less than nature, which meant that the tests had no more insight into me—or my future—than I did.

Of course, I did not say any of this to Melinda that night outside the Humanities Building library as she spoke of things adding up. I simply nodded, she finished her cigarette, and we went back to class. But the truth was that I had found myself missing math terribly: the logic and asymmetrical beauty of the equations, the straightforwardness of the signs and symbols, unequivocally urging me to add or subtract or divide.

In fact, I missed it so much that I had enrolled in a calculus class. Nobody knew, not my parents, who would have felt vindicated, or my humanities friends, who would have seen it as a betrayal. The professor, Dr. Dillard, was a thin man in his forties with a habit of thrusting the chalk into his ear and twirling it nervously, only to become flustered when it no longer worked on the board. He regarded students as his natural enemies, and when we asked questions, which we did often since his explanations lacked clarity, he prefaced his equally hazy clarifications with the words: "Am I teaching complete and utter imbeciles?" We dealt with this the way that students generally deal with such things. We hated him.

Thus, when he arrived one morning several weeks into the term with his zipper open, nobody said a thing. We let him stand up there at the board, writing out equations and delivering his incomprehensible explanations with his fly not just undone but gaping like a hungry mouth. We did not laugh, but probably most of us took some pleasure in the situation, until finally an older man from Togo raised his hand and said in a kind, almost apologetic voice, "Excuse me, Doctor, but your zipper is not closed." He had a French accent and a low, buttery voice, which made even the word "zipper" sound appealing. Dr. Dillard asked the man to repeat what he had said because he had trouble understanding the man's accent. Actually, what he said was "I can't understand a damn word you're saying," and the man from Togo repeated it, enunciating and speaking more slowly but sounding just as kind and sensuous as the first time.

It was clear that Dr. Dillard did understand then, for he turned quickly around and stared at the equation that he had been working out for us on the board, stared at it while we stared at him. He did not speak or reach down to fix his fly or attempt in any way to move the situation along, and finally, after ten minutes of terrible silence, we understood that class was over, and though we all hated him, I believe that in that moment we felt sorry for him, sorry for how small and hunched he seemed, for the way that he stood with his back to us, staring at an equation that had lost its meaning.

Dr. Dillard arrived for the next class with his zipper up. He stood at the front of the room and announced that we would begin with a quiz, which we all failed because the quiz was over material that we were supposed to have covered during the last class. When he handed the quizzes back to us after the break, he did so in a frenetic, almost jaunty way, running up and down the aisles and announcing our grades—"Zero, zero, zero"—loudly before tossing the quizzes down in front of us, and I realized then that even in math, things didn't always add up. Sometimes, there was just one side trying to be greater than the other.

After class that night, Clem acted as though I were going to drive him home as usual and then sit around watching him get drunk while listening to him explain that the world was made up of assholes, but when he started lurching after me, I turned and yelled, "Find your own way home," and then I walked away fast while he shouted after me that I hated cripples. He knew that I hated that kind of thing: screaming and public arguments and having strangers look at me, look at me and think that it must be true that I hated cripples because there I was, running away from one. Instead of going home, I went to Ralph's, which I had been avoiding because of something that had happened there a couple of weeks earlier, and though it was probably just an anecdote, it was an anecdote that nearly broke my heart. It had to do with this old man who spent every night at Ralph's, doing the splits for anyone who would buy him a drink, which, it turned out, was a lot of people. After I watched him do the splits seven times in two hours—and drink seven drinks in those same two hours—I'd gone over and asked him how old he was.

"I'm seventy-six," he said, holding his hand up and wiggling the thumb and index finger, as though seventy-six were an age that could still be conveyed with fingers.

"Wow," I said unconvincingly. "You must be in very good health." I did not really know how to talk to old people.

"Yes," he said proudly. "I'm in perfect health." He proceeded to tell me a long story about how he had been diagnosed with a bad liver just six months earlier. He imitated his doctor telling him, "You've got to give up the booze," and then he told me, with a wheezy chuckle that made his nose squirt, that he had not given up *the booze* because he liked *the booze.* Instead, he had prayed about his liver before he went to bed one night, and during the night God came and performed surgery on him, actually fixed his liver while he was asleep.

"But how did you know that God operated on you?" I asked because how would you know such a thing?

"I'll tell you," he said triumphantly. "I knew it clear as cake cause when I woke up there was blood in my long johns, and I'll tell you what else—I got right out of bed and did ten push-ups. I had the energy of a horse." He neighed, which made his nose squirt some more.

Honestly, I did not want to hear about the blood in his long johns because hearing about it made me picture it and picturing it made me queasy, especially on top of his squirting nose, but I thought about how lonely he must be to tell such a thing to a stranger. I bought two pickled eggs because that was the only food available at Ralph's at that time of night, and we sat at the bar to eat them, his teeth clacking as he chewed. I wanted to ask him about the expression he had used, "clear as cake," which I had never heard before, but I didn't ask because I suspected that "clear as cake" was something left over from an earlier life.

Two boys came over then with a shot of vodka, and he nearly fell off his stool following them. I did not want to watch him do the splits again, especially now when all I would be thinking about was the blood in his long johns, so I left, but from outside, I could still hear the laughter and clapping that meant he had made it down to the floor again.

When I got to Ralph's, I sat at the bar and the bartender who had dished up the pickled eggs that night came down to where I was sitting. I ordered a beer and tried not to feel bad about running away from Clem, and when the bartender set my beer in front of me, he said, "Did you hear about Elmer? Died last night in his sleep."

"Who's Elmer?" I asked.

"Old guy that does the splits," he said. "Elmer."

"Oh," I said. "I know Elmer."

Some humanities friends waved from a booth for me to join them. "Elmer died," I said as I sat down, and they said, "Who's Elmer?" just the way I had a few minutes earlier. "He's that old man who always did the splits," I said just the way the bartender had because when it came down to it, that's how everyone knew Elmer. For most people, doing the splits was Elmer's salient feature.

"Well, he was old," said one of my friends and the others nodded.

I don't know why this made me angry. It wasn't that I didn't think Elmer was old. He *was* old. I guess I just felt that what they were saying was that dying didn't mean anything when you were old. I wanted to tell them about how Elmer believed that God had operated on him in his sleep, about the blood in his long johns and how he said "clear as cake" because he'd once had a family, people who all sat around saying "clear as cake" without ever having to explain themselves because "clear as cake" meant something to them. I wanted them to understand that he wasn't just some old guy who did the splits for college students.

Instead, I went home and wrote my final story for Marvin Helgarson's class. In the story, an old man named Elmer does the splits—which I tried, unsuccessfully, to change to chin-ups and then cartwheels—in an unnamed bar popular with college students who buy him drinks. Agatha, the main character, is majoring in math, and she saves Elmer by realizing that he has amnesia. She finds his family, who, it turns out, has been looking for him for three years, and when she calls them, she knows she has the right family because when Elmer's son describes the day that his father disappeared, he says, "I remember that day as clear as cake." In the final scene, Agatha drives Elmer to his family's house, even though he doesn't really want to go. This takes most of the day, and when she gets back to campus for her math class, the professor gives a pop quiz, which she aces even though she did not have time to study because of driving Elmer home. The story ended like this: "Agatha felt the knowledge taking shape inside of her, becoming a part of her, and then spilling onto the page, everything adding up."

When we discussed the story on the last night of class, Tabatha immediately raised her hand. "First of all," she said, "amnesia's such a cop-out." She looked at me as though I had offended her in some very personal way.

"Okay," Marvin said. "Can you explain what you mean by 'cop-out'?"

I did not really want her to explain, but she said, "It's such a cliché. Plus, Elmer's just some old guy who's going to be dead any day, so it really has to be Agatha's story."

"And you don't think it's her story now?" Marvin asked.

"It is, I guess. I just don't like her." She turned to me and said, "Maybe your life is like this, but nobody wants to read a story about some Goody Two-shoes who always knows what to do. I think the story would be better if Agatha drinks too much because *she* doesn't know how to help Elmer, and the next morning *she* wakes up, and *she* doesn't remember anything."

"So she should just sit there having a good time while Elmer does the splits until he dies?" I said, even though we were not supposed to talk while our story was being discussed.

"Okay," Marvin said. "What else?"

"I like the sex stuff," said Clem. We had not spoken since I ran away from him the week before.

"What sex stuff?" I said.

"When she's thinking about the blood in his long johns," Clem said.

Marvin jumped in then, asking what the story was about, and someone said, "It's about aging, I guess," and Marvin said, "Is it?," the way that teachers do to keep the discussion going. Someone else said that it was about age versus youth, or maybe hope, or knowledge, and when Marvin asked me what I thought it was about, I said, "I don't know. Compassion, I guess," and Tabatha looked at me as though I'd said it was about chewing gum.

"There's no compassion," she said. "She just pities him. They're not the same thing."

"Go on," said Marvin, but she shrugged as though there was nothing more to say.

"She just wants to feel good about herself," Clem said, surprising everyone, I think, because he generally restricted himself to making lewd comments. I knew that by "she" he meant me and that Marvin Helgarson maybe knew this also because he did not ask Clem to explain. Instead, Marvin said that class was over.

That was the last time I saw Clem, though I think about him from time to time. I picture him sitting in Marvin's class semester after semester, another student, always a woman, shuttling him home afterward, watching him drink and failing him in the same way that I did because I understand now that the kindest thing I could have done was to tell Clem what he already knew: that I would not have sex with him because he repulsed me, that I didn't even like him.

I got a B- in Marvin Helgarson's class, which didn't surprise me because I knew by then that I had no business being a writer. In his final comments, Marvin Helgarson said that my main problem was that I was actually *too good* a student, that I had followed every one of the rules and, in the process, I had "suffocated" my story, which was the way it worked in writing. I ended my stories as though it were the reader's birthday and I had tied everything up in a bow and handed it to the reader like a present. Readers, he said, liked to figure things out for themselves, but it seemed to me that if someone had read the whole story, they would want to know how things turned out: that I did not move in with my parents or join the Peace Corps, that I moved instead to New Mexico, where my plan was to forget about the Ultimate Reality and go back to studying math, that I somehow imagined this would be easy and everything would start adding up. But it was like Marvin Helgarson said: sometimes, you thought you knew what your character wanted and then you got to the end of your story and realized that you didn't understand this character you had created at all.

The Peeping Toms

It's Tuesday night, and Clarice and Miriam are already in bed, lying side by side on their backs, books held aloft in their right hands. Most nights, they are exhausted by ten. They own a business, an Asian furniture store called Two Serious Ladies, and all day long they deal with people. Sometimes, these people actually come in to buy furniture, though more often they come in to kill time or make jokes along the lines of "I just wanted to see what serious ladies looked like." There are also those who come in looking for friendship, strangers looking to be less lonely. They tell the women oddly personal stories, and sometimes, especially if they have just had wine with lunch, they cry and solicit hugs. Clarice and Miriam had not been expecting any of this when they started the business six years ago. It's not that they didn't know the world was filled with lonely people or that they are unsympathetic, but they spend their days writing ads and balancing the books and oiling furniture because everything is their job, yet these strangers think nothing of interrupting all of that to share the most intimate details of their lives. So, it's no surprise that bedtime has become the best part of the day, the two of them reading together in pleasant anticipation of sleep.

On this particular Tuesday night, Clarice glances up in a thoughtful or maybe idle way, as one does while reading, and sees a man's face at their bedroom window. The man is gripping the security bars, his face framed between them, and her first thought is that he looks like he's in prison, like he is on the inside, except that would put them outside, even though they are lying comfortably in bed, and in this way, the whole thing resembles a dream, nonsensical yet so real.

It's dark, so Clarice does not really make out his features. Everything just happens so fast. "A man!" she says. He lets go of the bars and his face disappears, but his hands hang in the air, fingers wiggling. It is as though he is waving goodbye.

She and Miriam lay their open books across their stomachs like saddles and stare at the window. "It was probably just some kid from the neighborhood, some boy whose friends dared him to find out what lesbians do in bed," Clarice says finally. "And here we are, two lesbians in bed! Reading!" She begins to laugh. Miriam takes longer. "Reading!" Clarice says again, encouragingly, and they imagine his shock and disappointment and laugh some more.

They named their store after a novel called *Two Serious Ladies*. This novel was the reason that they met. Clarice was sitting outside a café that is closed now, a café that everyone in Albuquerque seems to miss, this nostalgia expressed through shared memories of the café's exceedingly poor service. She was reading (*rereading*, actually) *Two Serious Ladies*, which, it turned out, was Miriam's second-favorite novel. Miriam had just moved to New Mexico from New York and was not expecting to come across someone reading *Two Serious Ladies*. She had come to New Mexico because she wanted to be away from New York, but she carried certain notions with her, notions about what people in New Mexico read. For the record, she had never once come across anyone reading *Two Serious Ladies* in New York, but that was less important than the fact that she expected to. She had not said any of this to Clarice right then.

Instead, they discussed the author, Jane Bowles, about whom both women seemed to know a lot: that she married Paul Bowles, whose writing they both liked, and moved with him to Morocco, where she fell in love with an illiterate peasant woman named Cherifa and, eventually, fell apart. When Jane died, some people claimed that Cherifa had killed her, that she had been slipping strychnine into Jane's food. Neither Clarice nor Miriam knew what to make of this theory, though they both admitted to being perplexed by the relationship. They supposed that there was something romantic about it, about the way the two met at the market in Tangier, where Cherifa was selling grain, but what it came down to was that neither Clarice nor Miriam could imagine falling in love with someone who could not read.

For hours they discussed Jane Bowles—her marriage, her lover, her death—with the casual confidence that had to do with being young and having never, either one of them, sustained a relationship. Specifically, Clarice, at twenty-five, was bookish with a fear of intimacy that was reflected in her approach to food: she had never cooked for another person, not even scrambled eggs, and she shopped for groceries in the middle of the night because she could not bear people looking into her cart. Miriam, on the other hand, in the years before it occurred to her that she might prefer women, had dated two men, the first a primarily sexual endeavor, a means of dispensing with her virginity, which she had considered superfluous at twenty-one. The second was a man in his forties named Alvin. Alvin was not interested in sex so much as in intellectual debate. They had stayed together for six months even though Alvin was crazy because they shared a love of arguing a point right into the ground. One night they argued so heatedly that Miriam picked up her typewriter and heaved it out her second-story window. Nobody was hit on the sidewalk below, but she had had a realization akin to what a person must feel upon waking up hungover to the recollection of having driven home drunk the night before. That is, she saw how quickly one's own desperation could affect other people, even strangers. The thought had terrified and sickened her, and that was the end of things with Alvin, the end of attempting love—until she moved to New Mexico two years later and met Clarice, with whom she would discover that what one needed in a mate was to temper, not mirror, oneself.

Clarice had moved to New Mexico to attend graduate school, but once she finished her master's degree, she stopped. She came from a small town, which she had escaped, and she could see that academia would be another small town. She began teaching history at the community college and spent her afternoons at the café, being attended to by a host of ever-changing though equally incompetent servers as she graded papers and read and waited for something to change. She understood that waiting for something to change was an ineffectual approach, even if many people did subscribe to it. She was rereading *Two Serious Ladies* because it was about women who wanted to go out in the world, but when they did, the world was just too much for them, which was what she was thinking about when Miriam approached her table.

Just four months later, at this same café, Miriam and Clarice made the decision to move abroad. They had a vague notion that living together in a foreign country would either destroy or cement their nascent relationship, and they were willing to accept the possibility of the former in order to more quickly achieve the latter. They both felt ready for intimacy, the sort that came from seeing how another person dealt with distress and boredom.

Though they had planned to stay two years in Indonesia, where they had both found jobs teaching English, they lasted not even a year. This had to do with the heat, which they both disliked (though Clarice more so) and with the way that time seemed frozen in the tropics, but mainly it had to do with being watched everywhere they went, with having people look at them and talk about them, even reach out and pluck the hairs that grew on their arms. It was because they were foreigners, they knew, but knowing this only got them so far. They began making up silly songs—"We are interesting people, we do interesting things"—which they belted out, jauntily, as they walked along the streets of Jakarta, but the songs did not help. Eventually, on their nonteaching days, they stayed inside, not even going to the market, because they lacked the energy to be approached, over and over, by people wishing to know where they were going and where they were from, why they were so tall and what they planned to do with the vegetables they had purchased.

The thing about *being* watched, they learned, is that it leads to *feeling* watched, which sounds like an exercise in semantics, unless you've been there. By the end, they had stopped touching and kissing, stopped cooking together and grading papers side by side, stopped cuddling together at night and then in the morning. In short, they stopped doing everything that was intimate because feeling watched had become the norm.

Miriam and Clarice do not get up to pull the blinds, nor do they move closer together or hold hands. They just lie there with the books that they have been caught reading still open across their stomachs, discussing practical things, such as how the Peeping Tom came to be hanging from their bedroom window. Like all of their back windows, it is seven feet off the ground because the house is built into a hill. When they had the security bars installed, they wanted to do only the front windows, but the installer gave them a package deal; now it feels as though they spent good money making some Peeping Tom's work easier. Moreover, there is a fence around the yard that is taller than they are, each board rising to a point, and a gate that opens onto the alley. The gate is secured with a very large padlock, the key for which they are almost sure is in the cutlery drawer. They never go into the alley anymore.

Their neighborhood is considered one of the safest in Albuquerque, which means that the police are rarely around, though over the last year, this—the absence of police—has made their alley increasingly attractive to people with something to get rid of. Finally, just a few months ago, the city closed the alley to vehicles because everyone, the residents and the police, had gotten tired of finding stuff dumped there, mainly old mattresses and broken appliances but also a sacrificed goat and a U-Haul stolen out of a motel parking lot all the way up in Denver, and then the last straw: the body of a drag queen from over on Central.

Their store is located on Central. They never saw the body, but they could not help but wonder whether it was *their* drag queen, the one who used to come in each week to admire their Indonesian batik caftans. Her name was Peggy, but when they spoke of Peggy to each other, they sometimes slipped up and said "he." They were ashamed of this—of the slipups, which had maybe to do with Peggy's hands, large, workman's hands with dirt embedded in the knuckles, though the nails were painted a glossy red—and later, ashamed of the fact that they'd called her a drag queen to begin with, even if that was the way that Peggy had referred to herself. "I'm just another drag queen working the drag," she'd say.

Peggy had a nondescript way of dressing—black stretch pants, clogs, and a blouse—but she loved the caftans and listened raptly as they explained how batik was made, how one had to apply the wax to the areas one did *not* want dyed. "Isn't that something," she would say, her voice sweetly Southern, and then she would add, "Come payday, ladies, I'll be back for one of these marvelous creations."

One day, Miriam asked which caftan was her favorite, and Peggy touched a pink-and-black floral on silk, stroking it as though it were a cat.

"Take it," they both said.

"You ladies are too kind, but I couldn't possibly," she replied, and she held her big hands up demurely, as though refusing a second slice of cake. But they insisted, and finally, she reached out with her grubby, red-tipped hands and accepted the bag into which they had folded the caftan. She thanked them profusely and left. They never saw Peggy again. Aloud, they worried that something had happened, that she had been hurt or arrested, or had moved back to Georgia. They did not want to admit the truth, that in forcing the caftan on Peggy, they had taken something from her: the illusion that they regarded her as a customer. They hardly knew Peggy, yet they had taken so many things from her.

"What did he look like?" Miriam asks. They are still in bed.

Clarice does not know. It was a man. He had hair.

"You mean he wasn't bald?" Miriam clarifies.

"I don't know," Clarice says. It was so fast. "He might have been."

"Maybe you imagined it," Miriam says finally.

The book that Clarice is reading, the one that straddles her stomach still, is *Pride and Prejudice.* She tells Miriam huffily that *Pride and Prejudice* is not a book that would conjure up Peeping Toms. She wants to go into the backyard right then to look for proof, but Miriam will not let her. "That's the sort of thing they only do in horror movies," Miriam says, "and everyone in the theater gets annoyed because they know that no one would ever do that in real life."

Clarice agrees to wait until morning, and then when it is morning, it's so bright and sunny that she thinks she might have imagined him after all. She goes out onto the deck still wearing the T-shirt and boxers she slept in and looks at the mountains. When she and Miriam bought the house, the assessor described the view as "average," and they had laughed smugly the first time they sat on this deck together and watched the sun set, feeling that they had gotten away with something: they had paid for an average view but gotten this.

Clarice takes a sip of coffee, looks away from the mountains, down into the yard, and there it is: the watering bucket that they always keep beneath the deck, tipped onto its side beneath their bedroom window. "Miriam," she calls as she trots down the deck steps. She's excited, not about the bucket but about being right.

Miriam comes out dressed in her running gear, and Clarice points at the bucket. "Looks as though our Peeping Tom kicked the bucket," she says, chuckling. Clarice is from Minnesota, so she laughs about things that others might not, things that frighten her, for example, like a bucket beneath her bedroom window or a face pressed against it.

There's something else: the rosebush near the window has been trampled. Neither of them likes roses, but the former owner had been so proud of the bush that they'd felt obliged to keep it. Now, it will probably die, which is a relief.

"We better call the police," Miriam says.

The thing about living in a safe neighborhood is that the police accept that the neighborhood is safe; that is, they accept its unwillingness to become unsafe. Miriam and Clarice understand the unfairness of this—after all, most people want their neighborhoods to be safe—but in the moment they just want the police to do something. The police tell them that they will send a squad car to circle the block every night for a week, and they do. After a week, the squad car disappears, but the Peeping Tom does not reappear, which is the important thing because Vera will be arriving soon, and they do not want to deal with a Peeping Tom on top of Vera. Vera is Miriam's grandmother. She is ninety-five and a lot to handle. They will need their sleep.

Four years earlier when they bought this house, Vera began making yearly visits, staying for a month in the guest room, which they had painted a cheerful yellow. “It is the color of crazy houses in Russia,” Vera, who is from Russia, never gets tired of noting. Still, she calls their house her “Albuquerque spa,” which just means that they do all the cooking and cleaning, and that their place is not a fifth-floor walk-up like her apartment in New York.

“You girls are perfect hosts,” Vera tells them at the beginning and end of each visit, and Miriam, the linguist in the family, says, “‘Host’: from the Latin ‘hostis,’ meaning ‘enemy’”—but only at the beginning of the visit, when it still feels like a joke.

Because she does not have to cook and clean and climb up and down five flights of stairs, Vera has lots of free time when she is with them, which she uses to conduct research, empirical studies of topics that interest her. One day, for example, she walks to a nearby McDonald’s, and as the workers take their breaks, she interviews them, recording the answers in a notebook: *How often do they eat the food they serve? Do they bring it home to their children? How much do they weigh?* Miriam thinks the questions are “too personal,” but Vera says that Miriam is being silly. She is just trying to understand why Americans are so fat. “With science,” she explains, “there is no room for feelings.” This, she says, is what she likes about science.

Vera was a scientist, *is* a scientist. To this day, she refers to drinking glasses as “beakers”; she calls cutlery “implements.” She is a terrible cook, largely because she follows recipes with a scientist’s precision, not bending to the inexactitudes of cooking times or salt requirements. When she came to this country—from Russia via Germany and then France and finally Portugal—she worked as a biochemist, sleeping on the laboratory floor most nights to be near her experiments. She mainly did research on arteriosclerosis, and when people who know nothing about arteriosclerosis, their friends for example, ask her to explain her research, she gives answers that are like listening to a textbook being read aloud. Eventually, Miriam or Clarice will interrupt to say, "Arteriosclerosis is a hardening of the arteries," which was all the person usually wanted to know. Vera does not notice when people are perplexed or bored or just don't care. She will be the first to admit that she does not understand human nature.

Still, Vera is the only member of either of their families who truly accepts their relationship. She calls them Miriam-Clarice, writing it with a hyphen, as though they are one person. Early on, she coined the term "unisex ménage" to describe their relationship, gay relationships in general. "Unisex ménage is more egalitarian than other relationships," she tells people as a conversation starter, strangers who have no idea what she is talking about. She tells Miriam-Clarice that they should write a book, a handbook for those who could use some pointers on unisex ménage.

"With unisex ménage, there is no need to argue about cooking and cleaning," she informs Miriam and Clarice at dinner one night, even though they argue about these things all the time. They do not correct her because they know what she means, that there is no need to argue about whether the woman is doing more than the man. "It is very convenient," Vera concludes, assessing unisex ménage as though it were a bus stop.

Once Vera starts thinking about something, she cannot stop. It was why she was so good at her research. It is why she is so tiring to live with. "How do lesbians have sex?" she asks Clarice a few mornings later, when Miriam is out running. Clarice cannot imagine explaining such things to a ninety-five-year-old woman, certainly not at breakfast. Also, Vera has her notebook open, her research notebook. She is holding a pen.

"Use your imagination," Clarice tells her.

"I am too old to use my imagination," Vera says dismissively.

Over dessert that night, Vera says that her friend in New York told her that lesbians have a machine that they strap themselves into. Miriam and Clarice cannot stop laughing. They picture something like a rocket. Vera leaves the table. She does not like to be laughed at.

Miriam and her grandmother fight constantly, over silly things: whether Miriam's parents use mothballs, whether it's possible to predict where a roulette wheel will stop, whether their cat Gertrude is a vegetarian. Sometimes, these arguments end with Miriam having what her grandmother calls "blowouts," the word malapropistically accurate, for when Miriam explodes, it is like a tire blowing out: a sudden, loud burst that leaves her deflated.

Clarice does not like to argue, though she will if the topic merits it. She does not think that mothballs or roulette are such topics. "Set the table," Clarice will tell Vera in the midst of these arguments. "Miriam, go out to the deck and pick some thyme." Clarice's job is to be the peacemaker.

"Truly, you are a blessing for her," Vera tells Clarice. She uses words like "blessing," though Vera is not religious. She says that she has seen too much to be religious. Sometimes she tells them stories about what she has seen, stories in which she goes bravely out to secure food or visas, but the stories end abruptly with things like her on a train, surrounded by drunken soldiers. "The rest is not interesting for us to think about," she will say.

One morning, when Vera has been with them for two weeks, Clarice goes into the backyard to remove laundry from the clothesline and notices a gap of empty line between a towel and a T-shirt. Something was hanging there, she knows, but she cannot recall what. She hopes that it was nothing intimate. That evening, after Vera has gone to bed and they are cleaning up from dinner, Clarice says, "Someone took something from the clothesline." It's an annoyingly vague sentence. She can hear that.

"What do you mean?" Miriam asks. "When?"

"I don't know," Clarice says because she doesn't know *when* it happened, but she also knows that's not what Miriam means. Normally she would have told Miriam immediately, but there's something about having Vera around that makes them interact differently with each other, something about the way that Vera accepts their relationship on one hand, yet makes it clear that she considers relationships, in general, superfluous.

Vera has been alone since Miriam's grandfather died, shortly after the family arrived in New York. Vera was not yet forty. When she tells Miriam and Clarice this story, which she does often, always matter-of-factly, she says that she had liked her husband, had loved him also, but that she prefers solitude. "I've been alone fifty-five years," she says, sounding less resentful than proud. They cannot imagine it: fifty-five years without touching another person, without holding hands or sleeping close together.

"I noticed it this morning," Clarice says. "When I brought the laundry in just before we left for work."

Miriam is reaching up to put the olive oil back in the cupboard, but it slips from her hand. She *lets* it slip, Clarice thinks.

The oil is everywhere—splashed across the cupboards and refrigerator, pooled on the Saltillo tiles, darkening the cuffs of Miriam's jeans—and Clarice bends and begins picking up glass. "I'll get it," Miriam says. She sounds angry, so Clarice stands aside, watching Miriam pick up shards and sop up oil with paper towels. She uses the mop to swab the floor until the film of oil is completely gone, and then she sets the mop out on the deck to dry.

The next morning the mop is gone. "Who steals a mop?" Miriam says. She sounds angry—angry again or angry still, Clarice isn't sure—though they both feel better now about the missing laundry, for they assume that someone who steals a mop probably does not have an underwear fetish.

They walk along the fence searching for breaches, for something that would explain how the mop thief is getting into their yard. "Look," says Clarice. Near the back fence are six cigarette butts, scattered in the dirt.

"We should save them," Miriam says. She is thinking about evidence.

While Miriam is in the house getting a baggie, Clarice does her own bit of detective work. She stands with her back to the fence in the same spot that she imagines the smoker standing, and sure enough, when she looks up, she has a perfect view into their bedroom. She can see the headboard of their bed and Gertrude lying asleep on top of the bureau, which they used to call the "dresser." They started saying "bureau" because they realized that they liked the sound of it, especially liked referring to Gertrude, who spends her days stretched out atop it, as a "bureau-cat." They chuckle each time they say "bureau-cat" because that is how their relationship is. They make up words and say them again and again. They like the feeling that they are the only two people in the world saying these words, but now Clarice imagines someone standing here in the dark, smoking and listening to them say "bureau-cat" to each other, and she wants to cry because she knows that they will never say "bureau-cat" again.

In the next window over, she sees Vera, awake and standing beside her bed, struggling to get dressed. She is shirtless, her breasts exposed, and Clarice cannot stop herself from thinking that they look like dead squid, the gutted sacs that they buy sometimes at the Vietnamese market. Vera looks up then and sees Clarice, and she covers herself with an angry flapping of her arms, as though she knows that Clarice is thinking about squid.

Clarice and Miriam circle their block, knocking on doors. They explain to their neighbors about the Peeping Tom and the missing mop. "Have you seen anything?" they ask. "Anyone hanging around who looks like he doesn't belong?"

The woman next door tells them that she doesn't mind being watched. She is used to it, she says, smiling serenely, and after an awkward silence, they realize that she means God. Everyone else has a theory. "A sleepwalker," says one. "That kid that delivers pizzas," says another, as though there is just one kid in all of Albuquerque who delivers pizza. The woman who lives behind them suspects the boyfriend of the girl who lives next to her. The boyfriend visits at night, after the parents are asleep. "Plus, he's Korean or something," she says.

"Are Koreans known for mop-stealing?" Miriam asks. Clarice is annoyed, too, but she knows that this is what happens when you ask people to speculate about who does not belong.

On the other side of them lives a man in his forties who used to have a wife, two children, and a job but now has only a dog that barks more often than they would like. Actually, they would like if the dog never barked, or if it barked at useful times, like when someone was stealing a mop from their deck. When Clarice and Miriam first moved in, this neighbor, Tom, mowed their lawn along with his own and rolled their garbage cans down to the curb on Tuesdays. When Gertrude disappeared once, he helped them put up flyers, which he took down, without being asked, after she came home. He told them that he loved cats, but his daughter was allergic to dander, so he hoped that they would not mind if he enjoyed Gertrude from afar. One time, they came into their living room and found Tom standing on the other side of their picture window, his face pressed to the glass. Gertrude lay stretched indifferently across the back of the sofa while Tom tapped on the glass and cooed to get her attention, but when he saw Clarice and Miriam, he looked startled and ducked away, and they said nothing to him about it, ever, because they did not want him to feel bad about being neighborly.

Now, Tom's family is gone, and so is his job. He does not do neighborly things anymore because he is depressed. They would like to know which came first, the losses or the depression, but that is not a question one asks one's neighbors. Instead, they respond the way that neighbors do, with gestures that make a nod toward the elephant in the room without ever saying, "Listen, about the elephant." Specifically, they bring him halves of things: halves of banana breads and

Moroccan chickens, halves of lasagnas and cakes. They say, "We thought that you could help us with this," but then they hand these halves over at the door and leave so that he is "helping" them all alone, sitting in his house by himself eating half of their rhubarb pie in front of the television.

"Maybe we shouldn't bother Tom," they say, but he lives right next door and is always home, now that his life has collapsed, so how can they not ask whether he has noticed anything? They knock, and he finally opens, blinking against the sun. He reeks of stale smoke.

Clarice says, "We just wanted to give you a heads-up. We have a Peeping Tom."

They both feel awkward then because his name is Tom. "That's awful," says Tom. He looks truly upset by the news. "I'm home a lot these days. I'll keep an eye on your place."

This is actually Clarice's second Peeping Tom. The first was back in college in a cold town on the border between Minnesota and North Dakota, where she lived in a house with four other students. One day, one of the roommates was writing an essay on the toilet, and when she stood up, her pen fell in. She flushed anyway. When Clarice asked her why she had not fished the pen out first, she said, "I was too embarrassed," which made no sense because the fishing would have been a private act while embarrassment, by definition, required an audience. Also, it was far more embarrassing to have to explain about the pen to the landlord and the plumber, except explaining such things, along with collecting the rent and paying bills, had somehow become Clarice's job.

The landlord arrived wearing a tie that stopped two inches above his navel. He was in his fifties, her father's age, and he made his tone avuncular when he asked about her classes and then about her love life, all while standing too close to her there in the bathroom beside the backed-up toilet. "Oh, by the way," said the landlord, "I found a tenant for the studio upstairs. Young guy. Single." He lowered his voice. "He's got a peg leg."

"A peg?" she said.

"Well, one of them fake legs," he explained. He fiddled with his tie, yanking it down toward his navel, and the plumber finally arrived.

The next week the tenant moved in. Clarice imagined that they would hear his leg tapping above them as he walked, but mainly they heard his television. Twice, packages were left for him on their porch, and Clarice carried them upstairs. His place looked like an old lady's: there were doilies and a cuckoo clock, an afghan in lurid pinks and gold. The second time, he asked her to stay for pizza, and when she said that she had a paper to write, he said, "Oh, I remember those days." As she made her way down the steps, he called after her, "Hey, by the way. I work at a bank." She felt sorry for him that he had no idea how to make himself seem appealing, but she kept on walking down the stairs.

Two weeks later, it snowed hard throughout the night. Clarice woke early the next morning to the sound of a shovel scraping on the sidewalk. It was the tenant. She stood at her bedroom window and watched him fling snow from the sidewalk to the yard, wondering how he could do this—scoop, pivot, fling—on ice with a wooden leg. She had no romantic interest in him, though not because of the leg. She was a lesbian, and though she was several years from knowing it, the outcome was the same. Of course, women sometimes try to convince themselves otherwise, but Clarice was not tempted, for reasons having to do with the fact that his leg was the most interesting thing about him.

Eventually, he sensed her watching. She could tell because he glanced at the window a few times and began to shovel more energetically, lifting bigger and bigger scoops of snow, flinging them farther over his shoulder. Finally, he flung so much snow so hard that he lost his balance and fell backward into the very pile that he was creating. Clarice ducked and moved quickly away from the window, but then she worried that he might be hurt, so she went into the kitchen and peered out that window, watching him struggle to his feet. She saw him glance at her bedroom window, looking relieved that she was gone.

Later that week, when she was in the shower rinsing shampoo from her hair, she opened her eyes and found the tenant staring at her through the bathroom window. Actually, he was in the garage, which was four feet from the house, which meant that he was peeping at her through not one but two windows. She dried off, got dressed, and ran outside, but his truck was gone. He had watched her shower and then gone off to his job at the bank.

She went back inside and called the landlord, but when he asked in his business-y voice what was wrong, she became shy and said only that there had been an "incident" with the tenant. "What kind of incident?" he asked.

"He was in the garage," she said, and the landlord said, "Well, remember the garage is shared space." He seemed about to hang up, so she took a breath and gave an overly precise account of what had happened, and the landlord said, "I see."

For a moment, they both were quiet, and then he used his avuncular voice to explain that it had probably been a misunderstanding. The same thing had happened to him once, he said, but when he told her the story, she found that the same thing had not happened to him at all. It had happened to *his* neighbor, whom the landlord had seen getting ready for bed. "She's in her, you know, brassiere," he said, "and then she looked up and saw me, and we both had to laugh." He laughed loudly into the phone to let Clarice know that it was okay to laugh about these things.

"This wasn't an accident," she said. "That garage is a mess. It takes a lot of work to get back to that window, especially if you've got, you know, a peg leg."

"Okay," he said. "I'll have a word with him."

That night, Clarice saw the tenant pull up in his truck, get out, and walk quickly back to the stairs that led up to his apartment. His telephone rang, and she tried to hear what he was saying, but she could not hear anything, and then her own phone rang, startling her. It was the landlord. "I just spoke to your neighbor," he said.

"Yes?" she said.

"This is awkward for me"—he laughed as though he were maybe enjoying himself—"but, well, he says that you were watching him first."

"I wasn't watching him take a shower," she said.

"But you were watching him?"

"Shovel snow," Clarice said.

"Well," said the landlord. "You made him fall. That's what he says." He sighed. "Listen, I don't know what's going on between the two of you, but leave me out of it."

On the Friday before Vera is supposed to leave, she falls and breaks her hip on their deck. She will not let them call an ambulance because she considers hospitals a one-way trip at her age, and Miriam says that she cannot force her. She is afraid that Vera will become agitated, that she'll have a heart attack. Clarice assures her that the paramedics are trained for these situations, but she knows that it is not just a heart attack that Miriam fears. She is thinking that calling the ambulance behind Vera's back would be a betrayal. She is thinking that Vera will not forgive her because Vera does not forgive betrayal. Clarice understands, but still, they have a ninety-five-year-old woman with a broken hip stretched out on the floor in their guest room.

Vera, on the other hand, is mainly worried about needing to use the bathroom. For the rest of the day, she does not eat. She drinks precisely a tablespoon of water an hour because she has some theory, some theory about a tablespoon of water and survival. The floor is her idea also. She lies on it doing breathing exercises as though she is in labor, breathing in, blowing out the pain. All through the night, they hear her panting. They do not sleep either, not really, though around three Miriam gets the vodka from the freezer and brings it back to bed, where they sit drinking shots in the dark. They doze off around four, awakening nauseated and hungover two hours later, and sit in the kitchen, wondering what to do.

Clarice was the one who found Vera, when she came home to throw in a load of laundry. Through the laundry room window, she saw Vera standing on the deck, fiddling with her hearing aid.

The deck rails were lined with her bedding, which she aerated every other day, and paper towels, which she dried and reused until they fell apart. When Clarice finished loading the washer and turned back around, Vera was gone. She went upstairs and out onto the deck, where she found Vera lying crumpled in on herself like a bat.

Vera looked up at her and asked how business was. She asked what they had eaten for lunch. She made no mention of her situation, of the fact that she was lying on their deck in pain. "I need to pack," she said. "Please take down my valise from the shelf."

"Okay," Clarice said, and she went into the house as though she were going to attend to the valise right then.

Instead, she called Miriam. Miriam said that she would ask some customers to drive her home. The customers were people they knew, not friends exactly but a husband and wife who came in often and made a point of buying things from them. Clarice went back out and covered Vera with one of the aerating blankets and then sat beside her to wait, but Vera said that there was no reason they both should waste their time.

"Go inside and read," she said. Clarice laughed, imagining herself in the living room with a book while Vera lay in a heap outside.

The customers did drive Miriam home, and the husband even came in and carried Vera to the guest room. He was a sculptor, a large man who came across as calm, almost serene, but his cuticles had been chewed off in bloody strips down to his knuckles. They did not look like hands that created art. Clarice felt queasy when she looked at them, but she understood about the need to appear calm, how it sometimes felt that appearing calm would make you calm. He laid Vera on the floor, and she clutched his bloody hand and asked him questions about his art, the sorts of questions that people want to be asked. Vera was like that, especially with people she did not know.

"She needs to go to the hospital," he whispered as Clarice walked him to the door. He did not want Vera to hear him because even strangers did not want to disappoint Vera.

Around seven, Vera calls to them. They are still sitting in the kitchen drinking coffee and feeling sick from everything—the vodka, the lack of sleep, not knowing what to do. Vera needs to go to the bathroom, so Clarice carries her. She is strong, a robust Minnesotan made stronger by moving furniture every day. She picks Vera up under the arms and carries her tipped back against her chest, waddling toward the bathroom with Vera's feet dangling inches from the floor. She stops each time Vera cries out, which is often.

Vera stays on the toilet for three hours. Each time one of them opens the bathroom door to see whether she is finished, she yells, "Go away," and finally they have no choice: they go over to Tom's house and ask to use his toilet. They say that their toilet is backed up, not wanting to admit that they have a ninety-five-year-old woman with a broken hip sitting on it, that her hip has been broken for eighteen hours now. They have not been beyond Tom's front steps in months, so they are surprised when they enter his house to find the refrigerator and stove gone, their absence like the gap of two missing front teeth. Where the sofa and coffee table and console once congregated, forming a living room, only the television remains, propped up on a cardboard box. They suspect that Tom, needing the money, has sold everything, but they stand there saying nothing, pretending not to notice all that is missing from Tom's house: the furniture and appliances, his children and wife.

Saturday is their busiest day at the store. It's not a day that they can afford to miss, so they go back home and Miriam strips down and takes a sponge bath in the kitchen sink, dresses, and goes off to work because she is not strong enough to carry Vera back to her room, and besides, she needs a break from Vera and from not knowing what to do. Around one, she calls to check in, and Clarice reports that Vera is off the toilet and back on the floor. She does not report that when she brought Vera her last hourly tablespoon of water, Vera had waved it away, saying, "I'm not thirsty," and that Clarice had laughed. She doesn't know why she laughed, except that there was something funny about thinking that a tablespoon of water had anything to do with thirst, or about thinking that you could lie on the floor forever, waiting for a hip to mend. Now, Vera has stopped speaking to her. She lies turned onto the good hip, staring at the yellow walls that signify a crazy house back home in Russia.

When Miriam returns at six, she goes directly into Vera's room. She is feeling bad about abandoning Vera for the whole day. Clarice hears them talking as she cooks, a low hum of words. She cuts the ends from a pile of string beans, enough for three people though she knows that Vera will not eat. She hears Miriam say, "Can't you just be gracious, Omama?," her voice rising, and Clarice puts down her knife and tiptoes into the hallway.

"Gratitude," she hears Vera say. "That's all people think about."

"I didn't say 'gratitude,' Omama. I said 'gracious.' They're completely different things."

"I know what they mean," Vera says, "and I also know what you mean."

This is normally where Clarice would step in, but she just stays out in the hallway listening. They are quiet for a moment; then Miriam says, "We just want to help you, Omama," and Vera says, "Do you think that I have lived this long by requiring help?"

Later that night, they are lying in bed and Clarice says, "What if it's Tom?" She knows that they have both been thinking it.

Miriam does not answer right away. "Why would he do that?" she says at last, and Clarice isn't sure whether she means this in a general way—why would he peep on people?—or a personal way: why would he peep on *them*? "We brought him food. We're his neighbors." She means the personal.

"Maybe he's lonely," Clarice says. She is thinking about his family leaving and him sitting inside all day alone, smoking and watching television and waiting for his life to change. "Besides," she says, "how different is watching television from watching us?"

"How different?" Miriam says. "What kind of a question is that? We're not people on some television show. We didn't give him permission to stand in our backyard watching us."

"That's not what I meant," Clarice says. She does not know exactly what she did mean, but she was not talking about this, the right-and-wrong of it all.

"Well," Miriam says. "What else could you have meant?"

"I guess I meant from his perspective. You know, what's the difference to him if he's watching people on television or through a window?" She pauses. "We haven't been very good neighbors." She is thinking about all of the halves they've brought him. She can see now that halves are not enough.

"Clarice," Miriam says. She is mad. Clarice knows this because Miriam only uses her real name when she is mad. Otherwise, she uses one of her nicknames. They have lots of nicknames for each other. "What is wrong with you? He's a Peeping Tom."

"Well, yes, but we don't know that for sure." After a moment, she says, "Remember that neighbor I had in college, the one who watched me take a shower?"

"With the wooden leg," Miriam says.

"Yes," she says. "Him. Here's what I've been wondering: How was it any different, him watching me shower, me watching him shovel?"

"Well, first of all, he had his clothes on when he was shoveling," Miriam says.

"I know," Clarice says, and she does know. She understands that this is important, that it changes everything. "I just feel like maybe I didn't think about him, his feelings, that day that I watched him shovel." She does not know what she is trying to say, and neither does Miriam apparently, for she doesn't reply. Instead, they lie there, listening to Vera pant in the next room.

"We have to do something," Clarice says. She means Vera now. "We have to think about what's best for her, not about what she wants or says she wants."

"I know," says Miriam.

Vera's hip has been broken for thirty-two hours, but when the 9-1-1 operator asks whether they have an emergency, they say *yes*, they do have an emergency. Then they go into Vera's room, turn on her light, and Miriam says, "Omama, the ambulance is on its way."

Vera says nothing. Her eyes are glossy. She looks like Gertrude when they take her to the vet, like a wild creature, a creature that does not recognize them as the people who feed and stroke her, a creature that knows only that she is up against the world.

"Do you smell that?" Clarice whispers. Miriam does. It's a cigarette.

Soon enough, there will be the sound of sirens and the flash of lights waking the residents of their safe neighborhood, but for now there is only the quiet and the darkness outside, the two of them holding hands in the yellow room. Miriam looks down at her grandmother, who is looking away, and Clarice stares out into the dark, listening for the sound of a lighter, the creak of the fence, the quiet breathing of someone waiting to be seen.

The Stalker

In the mid-nineties, during a stretch of years that offered little to differentiate themselves as I slid ever further down the hole of adjunct teaching, Raymond appeared in my class. Already, Esther and I had begun referring to this period as my indentured servitude, though it was really Esther who came up with the description, Esther who shouldered the burden of hating my job for me. *Jobs.* I had three of them—three different schools and commutes and ways that colleagues could be petty with one another. Esther had recently returned to teaching high school, so we saw little of each other during the week, spending time together only as we slept. Saturdays, we drove around Albuquerque, stocking up on groceries and Gertrude's cat food, and always there would come a moment, maybe after I'd sighed heavily one too many times, when Esther would look over and say, "You need to burn your bridges," by which she meant that I should do something so egregious at one of these jobs—even all three—that I could never go back. Esther was a New Yorker. The notion of burning bridges seemed to come more easily to her, but I was from Minnesota; we were not bridge burners.

Student-wise, it was a good semester, the spring that Raymond appeared, even if I was teaching six classes—all of them expository writing—and growing increasingly weary of the overly confessional tone that expository writing seemed to lend itself to, which is not to say that I didn't like knowing things about my students. I did. Just weeks in, I already knew that Felicia was in the midst of a nasty divorce and that Enrique spent weekends volunteering as a youth minister in one of those ubiquitous strip mall churches. Then there was Jorge, who wanted to be a fireman and had voted for Ross Perot, two disparate pieces of information that he was skilled enough to weave together in his diagnostic essay, the essay that they had written in class the first night.

The students in that particular class—Raymond's class—had developed a camaraderie in which I felt included; only Raymond sat on the periphery, in a state of self-imposed exile that the others picked up on and did nothing to countermand. He had shown up a year earlier in the small farming community where the campus was located, had arrived with seemingly no connection to the place: neither familial roots nor the promise of a job. After class one night, he mentioned that he had spent the last eighteen years in the navy, but when I asked him—jokingly—whether that was what had drawn him to the desert, he looked at me as if I intended something more by the question, a criticism perhaps.

"What do you mean?" he asked.

That was the first time I saw it: a flash of anger in his eyes. Gone just like that, replaced with something docile, almost bovine.

"I just mean that after being surrounded by water all those years in the navy, I bet it's nice to be here where everything is dry and brown," I said.

The school was a branch campus of the main university, a forty-five-minute drive from Albuquerque, and lay along a gravel road with nothing to indicate that a university was nearby. The students had grown up around here and did not require signs, but in those pre-GPS days, I did. I had developed a system of landmarks: left at the barn painted with *Jesus Saves* in large, black letters, past the farm with the neon-blue house, too far if I came upon the goats.

Some days, though, I left for work early just to see the goats. I would drive past my turnoff, then pull over to the side of the road and sit there, watching them frolic. I'd read that goats were social animals, and I could see that this was true. Of course, after everything started with Raymond, I felt strange sitting out there enjoying the goats. I worried that the people who owned the goats might wonder whether they were being watched, and once this notion took root, I could not rid myself of it, and I stopped visiting the goats.

Raymond's diagnostic essay, composed in class that first night, read like a family tree in paragraph format, a series of one-line descriptions rippling both outward—to embrace second and even third cousins—and backward. It made for tedious reading, which is the case with most family trees, certainly one's own, and in my feedback I complimented his memory for details before suggesting that he choose one idea to drill down on, questionable advice I knew, for the paper did not really contain *ideas*. The revised result was a thorough examination of the many ways in which his sister was clean, which he had given a title that was apt, if not a bit on the nose: "My Sister Is Clean." At the beginning of class that third week, I handed the revisions back, and Raymond looked down at his grade, a D, then lifted the paper to his mouth. Over the next seventy-five minutes, he sat in the back—outside the half circle of desks created by the other students—and ate the essay with its offending grade.

When he was finished, he rested his head on his desk, left cheek down, seemingly engaged in a postprandial nap, but when I moved around the room, talking with the students about their returned essays, I could see that his eyes were open, focused blankly on the wall.

"Raymond," I said, "do you have questions about your essay?" He was my last stop.

"I ate it," he said loudly, sitting up in his chair. He opened his mouth wide, and a burp emerged, delicate given the burp one might expect from a man his size but potent enough that the other students turned and looked at him, then quickly at me. I understood their curiosity, the fascination with which such a student is regarded by his peers, the collective interest in observing how the professor will respond.

I was not yet thirty, younger than Raymond by at least a decade, half his size, and while I was technically in a position of authority, the hierarchy seemed tenuous. "Tell me," I said of his recently consumed essay. "Now that you've had time to digest my comments, how are you planning to approach the next essay?"

He burped again, which I ignored, instead pointing to the board, on which I had earlier written the next assignment, an essay meant to introduce the rhetorical modes of classification and division:

Consider the various parts of your identity, and choose three to write about in an essay of approximately 1,000 words.

I picked up the chalk and drew a pie, which I then sliced into pieces.

"I'm asking you to pick three pieces of your personal pie," I said. I pointed at Enrique, one of the shyer students. "The Pie of Enrique, for example."

Everyone but Raymond laughed. Teaching is like that. If the students are well disposed to you, they laugh. "Maybe this slice is religion," I said, pointing again to the pie, to one of its more generous slices. They all were religious, but for Enrique it was more than a matter of how he'd been raised. It meant something. "And this one is that you're Hispanic."

Enrique nodded, and Gil joked, "Can I be a pizza pie with pepperoni?" and the class laughed at this also. You see what I mean. They were a good-natured lot, and I did not want Raymond to ruin that; teachers know that a class is only as good as its most problematic member.

"You can be any kind of pie you want," I said. "Just don't forget to include the most important slices."

Only I understood the irony of my issuing such an injunction, for back then, in the mid-nineties, I routinely skirted student questions—innocuous, well-intentioned questions—about whether I was married and what I had done with my weekend. That was what living in the closet required: a whittling away at the everyday details of one's life. Thus, I stood before them demanding that they write honestly, fully, about who they were, about their whole pie, even as I had missing pieces.

Later that week, the chair of the department called me into his office to ask whether everything was okay. I hedged, unsure whether his question referred to something specific, something that I should know about but somehow did not—had a student complained?—or was strictly routine. Dr. Dant was an attentive boss, the sort who trusted us to oversee our own classrooms but—as he reminded me frequently—was there to help. I did not want help. In those days, I feared that needing help would be perceived as a weakness, a function of my youth and gender, and would, on some unspoken level, make him regret hiring me. There was no reason that I should feel so dispensable, beyond the fact that I desperately needed the job. Esther and I had purchased a house, and it felt as though our very relationship rested on our ability to keep that house afloat.

Not long before Dr. Dant called me into his office, I had woken up in a funk. That was how it usually started, with something settling inside me during the night, already there, in full bloom, when I woke up. This particular funk was marked by a sense of desperation, a feeling that my life would be always only *this*, an unceasing stream of compositions to be graded, a certainty reified by the awful math that I performed in my head throughout the day—as I sat down to grade, and commuted from class to class, and lay in bed at night trying to still my thoughts: the number of students per class (usually 28), times the number of classes (6), times the number of essays written per student (12), a semesterly total of over 2,000 essays.

The previous fall, the community college—with campuses on opposite sides of town that I ping-ponged between—had hired a consulting firm that managed to conclude that adjunct salaries were actually too high, research that my colleagues responded to in ways ranging from angry to resigned. One colleague had purchased a two-minute hourglass, two minutes being the amount of time he was being paid—albeit still poorly—to grade each paper; when the last grain of sand slipped through the neck, he stopped reading and put a grade in the margin. I responded by taking my calculations into dangerous territory, dividing my earnings by my hours—which I had begun tracking—to arrive at an hourly wage: twenty-two cents. Twenty-two cents per hour.

"Any problems with either of your classes?" Dr. Dant asked more specifically when I did not respond to his first softball of a question.

"It's really too soon to know," I said. It was too soon.

"How about this guy?" Dr. Dant asked, and he read me Raymond's full name.

I did not use this opportunity to tell my boss that Raymond had written six hundred words about his sister's cleanliness or that he had eaten that essay over the course of the previous class period. "He's quiet," I said, because I could see that he was expecting more than just another version of wait and see.

"You know that this is his third time taking the class," he said.

I did know, though that was the case with numerous students. I taught nights because I was the newest instructor, but I had actually come to prefer the night students, many of them single working mothers who kept numerous balls in the air—work, school, children—though sometimes a ball fell, a child became sick or their work hours changed, and when this happened, they disappeared completely or started arriving late and missing deadlines, and sometimes, they brought a child to class, which we were not supposed to allow, though I knew that the alternative was the family car out in the parking lot. In fact, several times a semester, a security guard appeared at my door, having discovered a child, sometimes children, sitting patiently with their homework open on their laps, flashlight in hand, a picnic of snacks beside them. I did not consider the mothers negligent. On the contrary, the parking lot seemed safer than leaving the children at home alone, safer because their mothers were nearby.

Dr. Dant looked up. "It's just that—"

He stopped, and I did not know whether I was meant to coax him into completing the sentence. "Is that all?" I said instead. I had four essays left to grade. Still, I regretted my tone—which sounded abrupt, even confrontational—so I paused in the doorway and said, "I just don't like to be ill-disposed toward a student from the outset." This was true and even, I felt, ethically defensible. It was also, I would decide in the days to come, a form of hubris.

The following week, when the class appeared with drafts in hand, I paired them up to work on peer critiques. "I want to work with you," Raymond said to me, after I announced that he would be working with Jorge. Jorge had become one of my favorite students—despite our incompatible political views—my age with two young daughters whose schoolwork he often brought in for my perusal. What I mean is that the pairing was not punitive. Somebody needed to work with Raymond, and Jorge seemed temperamentally equipped. When Raymond refused to work with him, Jorge smiled, perhaps in relief, and formed a trio with the women next to him.

"I'm not a peer," I told Raymond, adding, "but I'm happy to meet with you during office hours." My office hours were before the first of the two classes that I taught each evening.

"I can't come then," he said. "I need to do it after class."

He knew, of course, that I often stayed late, working with students or chatting as we walked to the parking lot, extending classroom discussions in this way because they were hungry to talk about ideas.

"Have a safe drive," they would call out as we got into our cars, knowing that I was heading back to Albuquerque, though not that I had someone waiting for me. Of course, Esther was not technically waiting. She was always fast asleep, and the only thing waiting was a pot of cold spaghetti tossed with butter and steamed broccoli. In those days, I put a lot of energy into resenting broccoli, the cellar-like smell that permeated the house—our new house—and Esther's disinterest in cooking anything else.

"Okay, fifteen minutes," I told Raymond.

That night, class ended but the pairs went right on critiquing while Raymond sat in unpaired silence, refusing even to take his essay out until the others were gone; when they finally were and he finally did, I sat in a desk across from him and began to read.

He was missing a thesis statement, and without looking up, I noted this, saying, "Remember, you need to establish the three pieces of your identity pie up front." He had launched right into the body of his essay: "I am a former soldier, but once a soldier, always a soldier. The military taught me skills and discipline. It taught me how to use a gun. I love guns."

I pointed to the last sentence and said that here he had begun to veer off topic, and he said, "You said to write about my identity, and my identity is that I love guns."

"Yes," I said, "but this paragraph is about your identity as a soldier, not a gun lover."

His right hand, which sat atop his left, twitched and flopped, and for a second, it seemed like a thing alive, separate from the rest of him, his cuticles bloody like the gills of a dying fish. He sighed loudly. "You really don't want to know who I am," he said, his voice neutral as he spoke, so I wasn't sure which way he meant this: as a statement of displeasure at feeling misunderstood, or as a threat, *Just keep pushing and you'll see who I really am, but I can assure you that you really don't want to know.*

I moved on to the second paragraph, which began, "Dogs are the best creatures God invented."

"You need a topic sentence," I said, "something to connect dogs to you and your identity. After all, you're not a dog, are you?" I joked.

"Woof," he said, attempting levity back, or so I assumed, except he kept on barking in an uninspired monotone.

Finally, I looked up at him. "I can't focus if you're barking," I said, but I was suddenly too tired to read more. "That's fifteen minutes," I said. "I need to head home."

"Home to your girlfriend?" he said, and barked again.

I tried to control my expression, not wanting him to sense my unease, but from the way he smiled and crossed his arms, I knew he had.

"Yes," I said, and I handed him his essay, adding, "Work on your controlling sentences." He smirked. "I mean that you need a thesis statement and topic sentences."

I stood and made my way through the desks, making a point not to rush, then gathered my papers into my briefcase and erased the blackboard. Raymond was still at his desk.

"Turn off the lights when you leave, please," I called, and he barked.

I left the building and walked across the courtyard to the English department office, where the secretary, a work-study student, sat tapping her stapler like a telegraph operator.

"Hi, Bernadette," I said. "Working on your Morse code?"

"I don't know Morse code," she said agreeably. "I'm just waiting to close up for the night." She had been in my class the year before, and I knew her as a placid student who composed essays around platitudes, a solid C student who aspired to Cs, so the class had at once met her expectations and taught her nothing.

"Of course," I said. "I just need to make a phone call."

I went back to the faculty room and closed the door behind me and sat down by the telephone, but once I was there in that familiar room with the fluorescent lights overhead, the walls adorned with posters of cartoon characters shaped like punctuation marks, I thought of Esther already asleep, how the ringing would startle her, and I picked up my briefcase and went out.

"Good night, Bernadette," I called, and she said, "Have a good night, Professor," and I walked out into the courtyard again. A trio of students burst out of the library, chattering noisily as they left behind its constraints, but the campus was otherwise still, the trees on the far side of the parking lot dark and looming in the distance. I thought about how this campus had maybe been all trees once, but the thought of nothing but trees did not make me feel better.

I hurried to my car, keys laced between my fingers, the tips peeking out between my knuckles like some sort of medieval weapon. I fumbled to unlock the door, and when the interior light came on, I checked the backseat.

The previous semester, a man in one of my classes had raised his hand at the beginning of a group discussion one night to announce that he did not accept that the world was experienced differently by men and women. He was responding to an essay that we had read, an essay that made this observation in passing. "The world is the world," he continued, his voice rising, "no matter who you are. That's just fact."

"How many of you agree with Thomas?" I had asked. The men immediately raised their hands, and soon a few women joined them. One of the things I liked most about teaching was the challenge of the classroom—moments like this, when the air felt charged—but that night, I had struggled to respond. Should I note the ease with which Thomas had laid claim to fact and suggest that the ease had to do with gender? Or take aim at the claim itself?

Some of the women—not the ones who had raised their hands—looked at me expectantly. Thomas sat back with the easy confidence of one who had truth on his side.

"When you leave class each night," I asked finally, "and go out to the parking lot to your cars, how many of you check the backseat before you get inside?"

To be clear: I did not ask this with the dramatic flair of a TV courtroom lawyer, sure of the outcome. But this time the women did not survey the room. They raised their hands, as one, and the men—their hands lowered as one—had looked at the women, startled, and then quickly down at the floor, as if the very ground were shifting beneath them.

On this night, the night that I stayed late with Raymond, my backseat was empty, but the fact that one night it might not be, that women know this? Well, that is the specter of violence that women live with. I got into the front seat, locked the door, started the car, and headed down a narrow drive that wound around a stand of trees and away from the school before meeting up with the main road. At the end of the narrow road stood a stop sign, at which I always stopped because I was, at heart, obedient, even of a stop sign that was little more than a formality on a desolate road at night. As I approached the sign, a shape appeared beside it, bear-like. Raymond.

I took my foot from the brake and rolled past, not stopping. He waved and said something, something I could not hear but understood nonetheless. "Woof."

Then, his waving hand became a make-believe gun, which he pointed at me as I passed.

Bang. Woof.

Esther had forgotten to turn on the outside light, again. Still, as I pulled into our driveway, I could make out the shapes of the two large rocks that sat, tipped together, in the middle of the yard, a housewarming gift from friends who christened them "the kissing rocks." Esther and I liked to joke that they resembled headstones holding each other up. In the street behind me a car passed, moving slowly I thought, and I sat unmoving in my dark car, waiting for it to disappear up the street. The two stones stayed pressed together, evoking love or death.

The whole drive home, I had imagined walking into the house and immediately waking Esther, but once I was inside, the door locked behind me, I went instead into the kitchen, where I found a plate of tofu and rice with string beans. String beans! I put the plate into the microwave and watched it turn as it warmed. Only then did I begin to cry, at the unexpected pleasure of something besides broccoli and of the plate turning in predictable circles. When the microwave beeped, I dried my face on a dish towel and took the plate into the bedroom, where Esther had fallen asleep with the lamp on, Gertrude curled up beside her.

I got into bed with my plate of tofu and string beans and whispered "Esther?" over and over. "The string beans are really good," I said once she was finally awake.

"You woke me up to say that you like the string beans?" she said.

Gertrude had risen and stood sniffing the plate. "There's nothing for you here," I said, elbowing her away. "No," I said to Esther. "I did not wake you up to discuss string beans." I paused. "So, how was your day?"

Esther had given up on bartending and writing poetry and gone back to teaching, this time at a private Catholic school where she kept having run-ins with the principal, who wanted her to be more of a religious role model for the students. She told me a sleepy, disjointed story about how he had actually pressed her that morning to take Communion, even though she was not Catholic and had never pretended to be. "I'm Jewish," she'd told him, yet again. "A bad Jew to boot. I told you that at the interview. Is that what you'd like me to model?"

I laughed. This was what I needed, to be at home in bed with Esther, Gertrude purring between us.

"Something happened with that Raymond guy," I said at last, and began narrating the evening's events while Esther listened in silence, but when I got to the part about how he'd stood like a sentry at the exit, Esther said, "You have to report him. He's crazy."

"I know," I said. I did know. "But what if he's just, you know, trying to scare me?"

"He *is* trying to scare you, and he's succeeding, so it doesn't matter whether he's truly capable of something or only wants you to think he is. Really, Ella, it's an irrelevant distinction."

"I know," I said, a little impatiently this time. At that moment, I wanted nothing more than for the conversation to leave the realm of reason.

Esther picked up a piece of tofu and held it to my lips. "It'll be okay," she said. "You'll talk to Dr. Dant tomorrow. He'll know what to do."

I opened my mouth and Esther placed the tofu inside, like she was delivering the Eucharist. On our quiet street another car crept by.

When he answered his office phone the next morning, Dr. Dant sounded distracted, but when I asked whether there was a better time to call, he said no, in a voice suggesting that this moment was certainly inopportune but he could not imagine his day offering a better one. "What's up?"

"Remember when you asked me about Raymond Richardson?" I said, and just like that I felt his attention galvanize.

"Yes," he said, and I could hear him stand up and close the door of his office. "Did something happen?"

"Maybe it's nothing," I said, "but, well, he wrote an essay, and it left me feeling"—I debated between "scared" and "uncomfortable" but went with the latter. It was my nature to choose the middle ground, but also, the middle ground was what made men listen.

"Uncomfortable how?" he asked, and so I repeated the story, feeling oddly removed from it, there in our sunny kitchen nook in our new house on our quiet street in the light of day.

When I got to the part about how Raymond had become angry at my feedback, Dr. Dant asked how I knew this. "Knew what?" I asked, and he said how I knew that Raymond was angry. I said, "Well, because he barked," and there was a long pause on the other end of the line.

"Okay, and then what?" he said, so I told him, a little more haltingly now, that Raymond had been standing at the end of the long road that led down from the campus, waiting for me.

"You're sure he was waiting for you?" Dr. Dant asked, and this time, I was the one who paused, and Dr. Dant said, "I don't mean to suggest that I don't believe you. It's just that I need the full story in order to proceed properly. You understand?"

I did understand, I said. Of course I did.

"Is there anything else?" he asked, and I did not say, "He told me to go home to my girlfriend," because I would have had to preface it, like a poorly told joke where just before the punch line, you say the thing that you forgot to say early on, the thing that the punch line rests on—the runway to this punch line being something along the lines of my being a lesbian.

"Nothing else," I said.

"Listen," he said, "your safety is the most important thing. You're not the first, you know." Two other instructors—one male, one female—had had similar experiences. "Paul failed him two semesters ago for an essay about his favorite hobby." He hesitated. "He wrote about his pornography collection."

"He failed him because he didn't agree with his hobby?" I asked, the part of me that believed people should be allowed to write about pretty much anything in conflict with the part that was secretly happy that Paul had failed him for bragging about porn. I knew that men listened to other men, which did not mean I wasn't tired of my words meaning less.

"He didn't fail him for the topic, per se," said Dr. Dant. "The paper lacked any sort of thesis statement or real development." He paused as though not sure how to say what came next. "One of his supporting points was that he was drawn to this 'hobby' because he was fascinated by rape."

"And then what?" I said. I meant what had happened afterward, after the failed paper, the failed class, because about his supporting argument, I had no idea what to say.

"It was the end of the semester, so there wasn't much Paul could do. He suggested that Raymond choose a different topic, and Raymond said he'd need time to first cultivate a new hobby. His interest in other hobbies was 'flaccid,' he explained, and Paul told him that the word didn't work that way, that, in fact, a misuse of words had contributed to his having failed the class."

I, too, had noted Raymond's attraction to words that were similarly malapropian, similarly sexual, among them his description of his sister "spread-eagled" as she scrubbed the floor, though I had done little more than circle them. I did not mention this to Dr. Dant. I simply asked how Raymond had responded.

"He told Paul that he was wrong about the word, that this was just one more attempt to censor him. And that was the end of things. Well, until the next semester—last semester, that is. The first day of class, Paul went out to the parking lot, and two of his tires were flat."

"And he thinks it was Raymond?" I said.

"Nobody saw him do it, of course, but since there were two flats, Paul wondered. Then, while he was waiting for the garage to send someone with a second spare, Raymond appeared and just stood there, staring at the tires. Finally, Paul asked him how his semester was going, what classes he was taking, and Raymond smiled and said, 'What happened to your tires, Professor? Looks like they're flaccid.'"

The bodyguard was not my idea—it was the university's—nor was he technically a bodyguard. "Pick a student," Dr. Dant had said when he called me back later that day, presumably after he discussed the situation with administration, with people, that is, whose job it was to know how to handle such things. "A male student, of course."

I chose Jorge, despite his predilection for Ross Perot, because I knew that he could be counted on for almost everything that the situation required: regular attendance, discretion, equanimity. What he lacked was size. He was a good foot shorter than Raymond.

"What about his grade?" I asked Dr. Dant.

"Raymond's?" he said, and I said, "No, Jorge's. My bodyguard. Do I need to give him an A?"

"Why would you have to give him an A?" he said.

"I don't know," I said, because I didn't know. Nothing about the situation seemed obvious. "It's just that he signed up to learn how to write, and now he has to guard his professor also?"

"Do you think he'll have a problem with that?" asked Dr. Dant. "I mean, I hope he understands the gravity of the situation."

Dr. Dant said this like someone who did understand the gravity—that is, like someone who believed that assigning one student to protect a professor from another student was proof of this urgency. When I called Jorge into my office the next day and explained the situation, he said, by way of agreeing, “The guy who ate his essay, right?”

As soon as he left, Dr. Dant poked his head into my office to let me know that the evening security guards had also been alerted. There were two that semester, both of them work-study hires who could as easily have been given jobs shelving books or monitoring chalk supplies, meaning that there was nothing about them—on their résumés or in their demeanors—that made them particularly suited for the job of providing security, but neither did the campus seem to require much security. At least that was what I had always believed.

“But Raymond is friends with one of the guards,” I said. In fact, I had seen the two of them smoking together as I walked from my car just minutes earlier. I said this in an anxious voice because I felt anxious, so Dr. Dant responded in what he thought was a soothing voice, which just sounded patronizing.

“That’s why he’s so perfect for the job,” Dr. Dant said. “He can keep an eye on Raymond without Raymond getting suspicious.”

“Unless he tells Raymond I’m nervous,” I said.

He chuckled as though there were some way to interpret what I said as humorous.

“Who was Raymond’s professor last semester?” I asked. We had not discussed the other professor on the phone the day before, just Paul with his flaccid tires, but when I’d related the conversation to Esther, the first thing she asked me was about the female instructor. Well, the second thing. The first was why Raymond couldn’t just be kicked out of class, even banned from campus, and I said that this had not come up in any of my conversations with Dr. Dant, and she said maybe it was time to bring it up. “I don’t think things are at that point yet," I said, because if they were at that point, then wouldn't it have come up? And she said, "You can't always wait for other people, Ella," and I said, "I feel like now we're back to burning bridges."

"It was Linda," Dr. Dant said.

"Linda?" I repeated, a question.

"She's not here anymore, so you might not have met her. She only taught here one semester."

"Why did she quit?" I asked.

"Oh, I think that 'quit' is too strong for the situation," he said, which meant that she had definitely quit. "She just felt the school wasn't the place for her. You know, she had a baby, and babies require attention, and—"

"Listen," I cut in. "I just need to know what happened. I think I deserve to have all of the information."

Dr. Dant looked away for a moment, then back. "Raymond wrote something about her."

"About her?" I said.

"Well, about her baby. They were reading 'A Modest Proposal,' you know, the Swift satire? Poor people selling their babies to be eaten by rich people?" I nodded. "Well, Raymond wrote that Linda's baby would make a perfect Sunday roast."

"Had he seen her baby?" I asked. This felt like the wrong question, a question that seemed to suggest that Raymond's comment was somehow more troubling if the baby did, in fact, resemble a suckling pig, but neither did I know what the right question was.

"That remains unclear," said Dr. Dant. "He seemed to know something about the child."

"In what sense?" I said.

"Well, that he existed, for one thing. Linda claims she never mentioned the baby in class."

"Claims?" I said, and he gave an agreeable nod.

"And Peter?" I said, my voice louder now. "Did he *claim* to have flat tires?"

Only then did he seem to understand my point, for his face took on the look of one unaccustomed to being challenged.

He turned to leave, and I said, "Do you know that I make just twenty-two cents an hour?" I imagined him reporting this to the dean later, saying, "And then, out of the blue really, she *claims* to make just twenty-two cents an hour."

When he did not reply, I continued. "I keep track. I spend fifteen hours in the classroom each week, another six in office hours, and the rest of the time I grade. I wake up at five every morning, and I grade for eleven hours most days."

"Are you asking for a raise?" he said finally.

"A raise?" I said. Now I was the one who laughed.

The next morning, Gertrude was there in the kitchen as usual, waiting. Only when I had settled myself in the breakfast nook did she begin to eat, crouched at her bowl, tags clinking merrily against it. She had always needed one of us to bear witness to her pleasure. She was predictable, as cats tend to be—right up until suddenly they're not—which meant that she would eat her fill and then go out into the predawn darkness to hunt, into our backyard, fenced and private and safe. That was how we had described the yard to each other, Esther and I, the very first time we entered the house, this place that we occupied together but had no time to think of as home. I cannot put into words, even now, the profound loneliness I felt at that particular hour—five A.M.—staring down a day that would be unflinchingly like the last: the sky would lighten and then darken again, one essay would give way to the next as I made careful comments on each that research suggested would never be read.

The previous night—my first with a bodyguard—class had felt strangely normal. Jorge had been a little on edge, it was true. He had maneuvered his desk to have a better view of the whole room, and when class ended, he waited patiently for me to answer questions and erase the board. Raymond sat in the back throughout all of this. He was still there when we left. In the hallway, peering in through our classroom window, was his friend, the security guard. Jorge seemed unclear about the extent of his duties, so he walked me to the parking lot, and when we arrived, I waved him off. "Go home to your girls," I said.

There were only a handful of cars left, and when I got to mine, I went through the usual protocol—unlocking it, checking the backseat—but this time, I also opened the trunk. I don't know why. It was empty, of course, but I placed my briefcase inside it because I needed to do something to justify having opened it.

Then, I got in the car and started it, locked the doors, fumbled with my seatbelt. When I looked up, he was there, Raymond, crouched outside my car window.

Earlier, as Dr. Dant and I parted ways, I'd joked, "Off to teach my stalker," but Dr. Dant had looked alarmed.

"Stalker?" he'd said. "Let's not get ahead of ourselves."

"I forgot to turn in my essay," Raymond said, the night so quiet that I could hear him clearly through the closed window, and he pressed his essay to the glass.

"It was due at the beginning of class," I said, but he remained crouched there, his essay inches from my face. I could either open my window and accept it, or drive away. In the end, I did both. I lowered the window an inch, and he rose and fed the pages through it like bills into a vending machine, and I drove off with them scattered across my lap. In my rearview mirror, Raymond waved.

His essay—those pages that had fluttered into my lap the night before—was on top of the stack, so I started there. Why not? I had to start somewhere.

"Dogs are the best creatures God invented," it began, with that line that had gotten him barking just one week earlier. By way of developing the point, which was what I had advised after all, the paragraph continued: "Gertrude would be a good name for a cat, if I didn't hate cats and wish them all dead."

As if on cue, the cat door flapped, predictable Gertrude heading out to begin her hunt.

Soon, at a reasonable hour, I would call Dr. Dant and tell him I quit, but until then—until a reasonable hour arrived—there was nothing more to be done. Inside, the essays sat in their stacks. Outside, Gertrude growled. I rose and stood at the nook window staring out into the darkness, but all I could see was what anyone looking in would see: a woman gazing into her backyard, unable to see what was out there, what was waiting or not, or was all just maybe in her head.

Aaron Englund and the Great Great

They visited August on a Sunday. Aaron remembers the way that his father sat in August's tidy living room and read the Sunday paper, looking bored and only occasionally pretending to listen to the conversation. Aaron's father had been opposed to the visit because he found August peculiar, particularly the fact that he was a bachelor yet maintained such a spotless home, but Aaron's mother said that she was tired of the way that his father always managed to find something objectionable about her relatives, the way that he referred to them as "imbeciles, kooks, and semi-crooks." August lived alone in Park Rapids, the town where Aaron's mother had grown up. There, he occupied what—Aaron had to agree—was an exceptionally neat house, though Aaron, unlike his father, did not find tidiness cause for concern. On the contrary, he appreciated August's house, especially the dustless shelves that August had built to hold not books but the clocks that he had been unable to repair, yet had not had the heart to discard.

August had extremely large fingers, his mother had explained beforehand, a trait that was normally considered a hindrance in his line of work. "But people bring their timepieces to him from miles and miles away," she added proudly. His father snorted. As they got out of the car and stood picking at the clothing stuck damply to the backs of their legs, August came out of his house and looked at them from his enclosed porch. He was nearly seven feet tall with stooped shoulders, and at first Aaron was frightened of him because he was so tall and unhappy-looking, but once August was sitting, Aaron did not feel his height so profoundly, and he saw then that August looked unhappy largely because of his eyebrows and mustache, both of which drooped, giving him a defeated expression. His mother introduced August as her "great-uncle," and at the time, Aaron had believed that she was using "great" to convey her opinion of her uncle, but later she explained to Aaron that August was her grandmother's brother, which made August her great-uncle and Aaron's great-great-uncle. The "greats," she said, were just a way of moving back in time. Aaron was fortunate to have a great-great-uncle because most people did not have great-great-*anythings* since "greats" generally got old and died long before they could acquire the second "great."

His mother prepared coffee in August's kitchen while August hovered nearby, showing her where things were kept and putting them away again as soon as she was finished with them. August's coffee was not like his parents' coffee, which was coarse, like sand, and came in a metal container. August's coffee was shaped like beans, which he ground using a wooden machine with an iron handle that Aaron was allowed to help turn. August told Aaron that he had made the machine himself, many years ago when he was a young man, and that his favorite part of the day was when he woke up each morning and ground the coffee. "The smell of the beans bursting open," he told Aaron, "is better even than the coffee itself." He waved his hand over the grinder, fanning the smell toward Aaron.

"Do you know what anticipation is, Aaron?" he asked. Aaron said that he did not.

"It means that you're looking forward to something. Sometimes in life, you'll find that it's not so much the event itself that's important, Aaron. It's having it to look forward to that means something."

"What about the other way?" Aaron asked. "When you're waiting for something to happen, but it's something you don't want to do?"

"Ah," said August as he worked with a small brush to remove the leftover coffee dust from the machine. "I believe it's dread you're speaking of." He paused. "How old are you, Aaron?"

"Five," Aaron said.

"What does a five-year-old have to dread?" asked August, not unkindly, reaching down from his great height and resting his hand with its extremely large fingers on Aaron's shoulder. Aaron expected the hand to be heavy, but it was not.

"I'm going to kindergarten," Aaron explained.

"I see," said August, nodding his head thoughtfully.

During this discussion, Aaron's mother had arranged powdered doughnuts on a plate and removed cups and saucers from the wooden hutch that sat in the corner of the dining room. She assembled everything on a large tray, including a glass of juice for Aaron that August had made out of something called chokecherries. The three of them went into the living room, and Aaron's father set the newspaper aside reluctantly so that they could begin *visiting*, as this whole process of sitting and drinking coffee and talking was called. The chokecherry juice was terrible, though Aaron thought that perhaps he was not able to assess it fairly given its name, which implied something about the berry that he found impossible to disregard.

Aaron and his parents were in the midst of a vacation, their first—and what would turn out to be only—family vacation, a two-week affair involving long stretches in the car. Some days they drove for six or seven hours at a time, his father stopping only for gas or to drink water from the thermoses that he kept in the trunk. It was hot that summer, unbearably so, and the three of them spoke rarely as they drove, though, in truth, this had less to do with the heat than with the sort of family that they were.

"How long?" Aaron asked from time to time, and his mother gave cryptic responses involving hours and minutes, which meant nothing to him, while his father threatened to pull over and give him "a good spanking" if he did not shut up, which did mean something.

Aaron had no idea where they were going, knew only that the road seemed endless, the heat unbearable, his father's head always in front of him. He began to think that this was how his life was going to be, the days toppling like dominoes. He had no affinity for time, a condition that would persist into adulthood, when he would come to think of time almost as a religious inclination that had passed him by, something that others felt instinctively, that gave structure and meaning to their lives.

As Aaron sat holding his glass of chokecherry juice, his mother described for August what they had done on their vacation, and then she asked, "Now, what have you been doing with yourself these days, August?" and August explained that he was spending his evenings recording the story of their family history. "I'm writing it out longhand," he said, an expression that Aaron had never heard and which he understood to refer to the length of August's hands.

August left the room briefly and came back with what he called his book, which was not a book at all but a stack of paper sandwiched between cardboard and held together with two large rubber bands. He removed the rubber bands and slipped them around his wrist, where they hung like bracelets, and then he opened the stack across Aaron's mother's lap, revealing page after page of spidery script, the handwriting so severely slanted that it looked as though the words were asleep on the lines.

"What is the book about?" asked Aaron.

"Well, Aaron, right there on your mother's lap is the whole story of how we came to be in this country," August said, looking around the room as though by "we" he meant the four of them.

His mother flipped through the pages of the book, far too quickly to actually be reading. "I can't believe how much you've written," she said to August, turning several pages at once while Aaron's father snuck glances at the sports page on the table next to him.

August cleared his throat. "I have something in my bedroom that I believe will be of great interest to you," he announced, clasping and then unclasping his hands nervously, and they all stood, except for Aaron's father, who had no interest in seeing other people's bedrooms. Aaron and his mother followed August down a narrow hallway to his room, which was small and smelled of maple syrup. Tucked against one wall was August's bed. It was neatly made but looked far too short to accommodate August, who had to duck his head each time he passed beneath a doorway. Aaron tried to picture August lying in the bed, his legs pulled up against his chest, but he couldn't imagine that adults slept like that, the way that he slept when he was cold or scared or very tired.

As he pictured August's droopy eyebrows sticking out the top and his feet and calves hanging out the bottom, it brought to mind a lunch that Aaron and his parents had eaten together just before the family vacation. Normally, his father left for work in the morning and came home just in time for supper, but that day he appeared unexpectedly as Aaron and his mother were sitting down to eat their soup. It was barley and beef, which his mother made without celery, and she quickly stood and ladled up another bowl, but his father wanted hot dogs, claiming that he had driven home specifically to have them, and Aaron's mother was forced to admit that she had not thought to buy hot dog buns when she did the grocery shopping that morning.

Aaron watched his father, the way that he gathered anger inside himself, pulled it in like a man desperate for air. Then, letting it out, his father screamed, "You never think," slapping his spoon into the soup that Aaron's mother had put before him.

The absent buns had only intensified his father's longing, and so, while Aaron sat with his soup growing cold before him, his mother boiled three hot dogs for his father, who pressed each one into a hamburger bun and lined them up on a plate in front of Aaron's mother, who looked steadfastly at her soup. Aaron, however, had not been able to take his eyes off the hot dogs, struck by how unnatural they looked, their long, pink tips protruding by an inch on either side of the buns. At the end of the meal, before he stood up and went back out to his squad car, Aaron's father made a point of drinking every bit of the water in which the hot dogs had been cooked.

Directly above August's bed hung the room's only decoration, if "decoration" could be understood not as an aesthetic term but as a reference to anything beyond the strictly necessary. This particular decoration was a photograph, a very large, ornately framed, sepia-tinted photograph of a woman who did not smile or in any way acknowledge the camera, though she was obviously posing. She sat erectly on a chair, sidewise, the chair's back almost completely obscured by her hair, which was thick and black and reached for the floor with the severity of a storm funnel. Once it hit the floor, however, the tension disappeared from it, and it puddled around her like the steadily expanding oil stain on their garage floor at home. Aaron could not imagine why August would want to sleep with this photograph directly above him, to awaken to the fleeting feel of her hair like a rope at his neck.

The photograph seemed like something out of *The Guinness Book of World Records*, a book that terrified Aaron, even as he could not get enough of it. His favorite photograph in the book featured a man whose fingernails had grown so long that they flared out from his hand like five fleeing snakes. After Aaron closed the book, he recalled nothing of the man but his fingernails, and so he made a point to focus on the man's other features, to study the turban that the man wore around his head, for example, and to learn the precise shape of his eyes.

The book had become Aaron's preferred source of bedtime stories, his mother sitting beside him, explaining who was featured in the photographs and how they had come to be included in the book. "This is Charles Osborne from Iowa," his mother told him, adding,

"Iowa's right below us, you know," making it seem as though Iowa were located in the dark, terrifying space beneath his bed. His mother skimmed the text and then announced that Charles Osborne had been hiccupping since 1922. "That's longer than your father and I have been alive," she said. "He was weighing a hog one day, and the hiccups just started."

That night, he dreamt that he was Charles Osborne, his sleep punctuated by a series of jolts from which he had awakened screaming. When his mother came into his room and turned on the light, he told her about the dream. "I was in Iowa," he said because he did not know how else to explain it to her. He gasped for air, hiccupping as he had in the dream. His mother brought him a glass of water, into which she threw a lit match just as he was about to drink. His hiccups disappeared immediately, but a terrible taste remained.

"It tastes like eggs," he told his mother.

"Yes," she said, "that's from the match. It'll go away, and anyway, it's better than a lifetime of hiccups."

"This woman," August announced with a slight nod toward the photograph, "is my grandmother Ragnilde, who is responsible for our family's presence in this country. I would be happy to give you the brief version of the story, but even for the brief version, we must be comfortable." They studied the photograph for a moment longer, and then August led them back to the living room, where Aaron's father still sat with his newspaper.

"Ragnilde, my grandmother, and her husband, my grandfather Jacob," August began eagerly once they had reseated themselves, "lived for the first nineteen years of their married life just above the

Arctic Circle, in a valley that had been logged to extinction by a British lumber company that shipped the lumber home to England. When the trees were all but gone, the company abandoned the valley, following the last load of lumber back home to England, and the Norwegian government announced that the land was available for settling. Five families, Ragnilde and Jacob's among them, arrived there to begin farming. At first, they had just one child, a boy, but over the years, six more were born. As you can imagine, it was not a climate suited to farming, so they were often hungry, and lonely as well. Besides the four other families, their only neighbors were Lapps, who moved around, chasing after their reindeer."

Aaron heard this as "laps," of the sort that his hands were resting in at that very moment, and he began to laugh because the idea of laps, which were by definition sedentary, chasing after reindeer, which could not only run but—as far as he knew—fly also, seemed extremely funny to him.

"Don't be an ass, Aaron," snapped his father, and Aaron stopped laughing immediately, though his father stared at him a bit longer for good measure. "Well, go on," his father said to August, as though he had done him a favor.

August had distributed napkins with the coffee but failed to use his own, not in the habit of doing so after years of living alone, so his mustache was dusted with powdered sugar from the doughnuts he had eaten, which gave him a bewildered look. In that moment, Aaron saw that even though August was very old, he did not know what to say to Aaron's father either. Finally, August said, "The Lapps didn't like them much at first, but later they all got on well enough," and something seemed to occur to him then, for he paused and turned toward Aaron, explaining that Lapps were a group of people who raised reindeer. They were nomads, he said, which meant that they moved around, following the reindeer, which liked to wander.

"Can the Lapps fly?" asked Aaron, who knew what reindeer were.

"Don't be an idiot," said his father. "Of course they can't fly—they're people."

"Aaron," said August quickly, "do you know that my grandmother told me this story many, many times when I was young, when I was right around your age, but I never once thought to ask her *why* they moved to the Arctic Circle in the first place, why they wanted to go to a place where the ground was always frozen and the only thing they could really grow was potatoes, and even those not so well? You see, Aaron, when you're young, the story is just the way it is."

He paused then and looked at Aaron as though he meant this final point not to be dismissive of youth but simply hopeful.

"Well," he went on, "as you can imagine, life was hard for Ragnilde and Jacob. There was frost, even into the summer, and they mainly planted on the south sides of slopes so that the midnight sun would warm the leaves." Aaron stored "midnight sun" in his memory so that later he might ask his mother what it meant. "So, there they were, potatoes growing only on the south sides of hills and them with nine mouths to feed, and one day, Ragnilde up and announced that the entire family was going to America, where she'd heard there was plenty of farmland and they wouldn't need to be constantly fighting the frost. Ragnilde was the boss, you see." August said this proudly, and Aaron's father snorted, but August did not look at him.

"By that time, two of the other families had already left for America, and within a month, Ragnilde and Jacob had packed up and said goodbye to the two remaining families. They went first by boat across the ocean, and it was on this crossing that the youngest child, Ingrid, who was just three, climbed into another family's trunk and suffocated.

"Ingrid would have been my aunt had she lived," August told Aaron sadly, his face growing red. This was one of the many features of time that confused Aaron, the way that it required him to imagine this little girl, younger even than he, crawling into a trunk and dying, and, in the next instant, to resurrect her as a full-blown adult, as a woman old enough to be the aunt of a very old man.

August blew his nose noisily into a handkerchief, dislodging most of the powdered sugar from his mustache in the process, and then folded the handkerchief into a tidy square, which he tucked into his shirt pocket.

"Well, two more of Ragnilde's children died along the way, and then just after they landed in Canada, Jacob went also. They spent nearly a year trying to gather the money to make the long trip down into Minnesota, but eventually they arrived. This was just before winter, so they dug a big hole and lived in it until spring. I think of them down there, how endless the winter must have seemed, but they were used to being cold, my grandmother told me. She said that she'd always been of the belief that if you couldn't change something, there was little use dwelling on it. When spring came, they built a sod house and started farming. By then, it was just Ragnilde and her four remaining kids, all of them boys.

"The youngest, Carl, was born deaf"—August pronounced this "deef"—"and Ragnilde had some notion that being out in the fields all day wouldn't be good for him. But I think that he was just her favorite, and she wanted him with her around the house.

He helped with the animals and the cooking and the garden, and every couple of months, she sent him by foot into the nearest town to do errands.

"Now, in those days, Aaron, there weren't roads to take you anywhere you could possibly want to go, so he'd walk until he came to the railroad tracks, and then he followed the tracks into town. Of course, he couldn't hear the trains coming, but he could feel the rail vibrating when they got close, and he'd hop off and walk alongside until the train had passed. My grandmother said that Carl was crazy about trains. The conductors waved at him, and he loved being close to something moving so fast. He felt about trains the way that most boys feel about them, I suppose."

Aaron's father looked over at Aaron, and Aaron did not look up to meet his gaze because he knew that his father was smirking. Aaron hated trains, cried at the sounds that they made, sounds that the books his mother read to him tried to present as funny and harmless—chugging sounds and *whoo whoo*s. Most of all, he hated the sudden panic that rose up inside him when a train passed, for even from the safety of their car as they sat waiting at the railroad crossing in Moorhead, he felt the train's power.

"One day," August continued, his voice growing solemn, "Carl was walking along the tracks, and, well, nobody knows what happened exactly, why he didn't get out of the way." August passed his napkin over his face again. "The conductor reported the accident as soon as they got to the next stop. They found his body a good forty feet from the tracks. One of the men said that he was doubled over a tree branch like a rug hung out for a beating."

"What a terrible thing to say," Aaron's mother said, though she had been quiet until then.

"I suppose it is, Dolores," said August. "Do you think I should leave it out of my book?"

Aaron's mother looked flustered at being asked. "No," she said at last. "We shouldn't go changing how things happened, even when we don't like the sound of something."

August fiddled with one side of his mustache. "I suppose not," he said, and then, "Well, after Carl went, Ragnilde was down to three children. One of them was my father."

He sat back in his chair, letting them know that the story was over, and Aaron wondered whether they should clap. They were saved from responding by a tentative knock—two raps instead of three—at the front door. August hoisted himself up from his chair and swung the door open. On the porch stood a stooped man with a large wooden radio clutched to his chest like a baby. He wore a gray felt hat with a small yellow feather tucked into the band, and when he saw them sitting there holding coffee cups, he flushed a purplish red.

"Oh," he said. "You've got folks in. I'll just stop again, August."

"Nonsense, Earl," said August, and he took the radio from the man and set it on the sofa next to Aaron. "It's acting up again, is it?"

"Yut," said the man. "I hope that's not the end of her."

He left, ducking his head at them as he backed out the door.

"I'm just going to get this settled in my workroom," said August, as though the radio were a guest who had come to spend the night. He tucked it beneath his arm, started to leave, and then turned and said, "Aaron, would you care to see where I perform my surgery?," laughing in such a pleasant way that Aaron wanted nothing more than to follow. They passed through the kitchen and into the breezeway, on the other side of which lay a small, dark room filled with radios and clocks and the insides of radios and clocks, everything arranged neatly like goods in a store.

"Will you fix them all?" asked Aaron.

"I'll try," said August, laughing again in his awkward, pleasant way. He took an old pocket watch from one of the bins atop his desk and handed it to Aaron, who was shocked and impressed by the weight of it. "I worked on this one for days," August told him regretfully, "but I couldn't revive it. There's nothing to be done for it I'm afraid." He spoke as though the watch had been drowning and he had pulled it from the water too late.

Aaron studied the watch. Its two hands stood perfectly still, not racing along as the hands on his father's watch did. "It's better this way," he said.

"Would you like to keep it, Aaron?" August asked shyly.

Aaron looked up at him and nodded just as shyly.

"Well, let's make it official, then." He took the watch from Aaron, switched on several overhead lamps, sat down at his desk, and carefully bent to his task, holding the turned-over watch in his left hand while he pressed a small tool to the back of it with his right, moving his hand as though writing. The steady, calm way that August worked filled Aaron with a pleasure that was like an ache. The tiny metal shavings curled up along the edges of the carefully formed script, and though Aaron could not yet read, he knew that the words referred to him. When August was finished, he read aloud what he had written: *Aaron Englund, July 1970.*

The watch was in the pocket of Aaron's shorts when they returned to the living room, and neither of them mentioned it to Aaron's parents. August seemed to understand the need for secrecy, and Aaron was impressed by this and grateful. He could not bear the thought of his father asking to see the watch, inspecting it and laughing at its frozen hands, waiting until later to remark, "Well, it looks like the old fart really pulled one over on you"—for that was how his father referred to August when they got back in the car. "The old fart," he said over and over as they drove away. Aaron did not understand how his father could think of August that way, August, who had two "greats" in front of his name and had built a machine that ground beans into dust, who sat in his tidy home night after night writing down the story of their family, who knew how to fix clocks and keep time moving but did not find it odd that Aaron preferred time stopped.

A Little Customer Service

That fall and well into winter, Tara lived with a woman seventeen years her senior, though most days she felt like the older one; she attributed this to the fact that the woman—her name was Gretchen—was rich and always had been, a state of affairs that had resulted in a certain type of arrested development. Tara had lived long enough without money—thirty-two years, which was her whole life—to know that money separated people from both misery and common sense. She was not overly familiar with lesbians, so she did not realize that Gretchen's arrested development might also be caused by that, not by being a lesbian per se but by having spent the first forty years of her life ignoring desire, channeling it into gestures and activities better suited for a schoolgirl. Take, for example, the way that Gretchen wooed her into having sex the night they met: by inviting her to leg wrestle. They lay on the rug in front of the fireplace—hips touching, heads in opposite directions—on the floor of Gretchen's adobe house on Canyon Road in Santa Fe, New Mexico, and all Tara had seen was the luxury around her and not the strange and almost heartbreaking fact of a forty-nine-year-old woman coaxing intimacy out of leg wrestling.

They'd met earlier that night at a tourist restaurant, all coyotes and turquoise, where Tara was waiting tables and Gretchen was eating a Cobb salad, seemingly without enjoyment, as though eating were more of a job than waitressing. When Gretchen was done sighing over her salad, done lifting her fork and knife up and down as though they were a set of barbells, she began waving frantically for the bill, even though she could see that Tara was covering too many tables, or should have been able to see this if she knew anything about waiting tables—or seeing the world through someone else's eyes. When Tara handed her the bill, Gretchen handed it back with her credit card, making a point to not even glance at the total. Tara did not know whether she was demonstrating her faith in Tara's math skills and overall character or reflecting her casual disregard for money, but either way, Tara was not impressed. Then, after Tara had swiped the card and delivered it back to the table with a mint, a pen, and the receipt, after Gretchen had signed the receipt, pocketed the pen that was not hers, popped the mint in her mouth, and was free to leave, a need that her wild gesticulating minutes earlier had seemed in service of, she stayed at her table another forty minutes, watching Tara take orders and fetch condiments and be polite to a group of six men whom Gretchen would later declare undeserving of politeness.

The men were dressed in matching sky blue T-shirts that said *First in Customer Service*, though the phrase "Customer Service" was in quotation marks, so the T-shirts actually said *First in "Customer Service."* Tara laughed when she saw the shirts. She wished that she could laugh with someone, but she did not work with people who thought about things like irony and punctuation. In fact, just the week before, the manager had pulled her aside to say that the kitchen staff had complained about the way that she recorded her orders.

"It's all the extra codes," he said. "You're confusing people."

"Codes?" she repeated, truly perplexed, and the manager pulled out her last order—"Burger on whole wheat; hold the mayo and cheese"—and tapped his pen on the semicolon.

"This," he said.

"That's not a code," Tara said. "That's a semicolon." She took classes at the community college and hoped to cobble together a career someday from the things that she was good at, among them punctuation and multitasking. "A code is"—she paused, hearing her tone become instructive—"you know, for when you don't want other people to understand."

"Well," said the manager, "congratulations. Nobody understands!" and then, "You need to knock it off."

As she waited for the bartender to fill another pitcher, she studied the six men. She knew their story, knew, that is, that the shirts had been presented to them—probably along with this trip to Santa Fe—to reward them for a job well done, just as she knew the sort of men they were, men proud to be good at their jobs, to be the recipients of shirts that proclaimed as much, or claimed to proclaim as much. She wondered whether even one of them understood that the shirts were actually mocking them. "Nice shirts," she said, setting down their third pitcher. All six men smiled proudly. Most people did not want a waitress who corrected their grammar. It was like going to a dentist and having him try to save your soul, which had recently happened to her. Tuition was due, and she needed her tips, so she smiled back and moved on.

Twenty minutes later as she steered a fourth pitcher onto their table, one of the six leaned forward and touched her wrist, asking, "Can I interest *you* in a little customer service?" and the others howled as though this were as clever as life got. It probably was. The men led the kind of lives that they wanted to lead, lives filled with routine and family and the pleasure of paying bills—not joyless lives, but lives that relied, nonetheless, on tired saws about "the old ball and chain" or jokes like this that made them feel like men. But she also knew that on a different night, each of these men might come in alone and sit, docile as a lamb, showing her pictures of his family. He would stare mournfully at the menu, settle on the meat loaf, and leave a carefully calculated fifteen-percent tip, as though anything more were taking food from his kids' mouths.

Gretchen, who had been watching her interactions with the men, held up her signed credit card slip with an exaggerated casualness that suggested she expected Tara to rush over and look at it immediately, so Tara retrieved the slip but waited until she was back at the register to take a peek. *Forty dollars.* Forty on a thirty-eight-dollar check. Next to the tip were a phone number and the words *Call Me.*

Tara had never been hit on by a woman, not that she knew of, and she tried to imagine (not entirely out of insecurity, though there was always that to consider) what had caught Gretchen's interest. Her hair was her best feature, but she was required to wear it back at work, so she knew Gretchen had not been able to take in the healthy swing of it. She decided on her shoulders, which none of the dozen men she had slept with had ever mentioned but which saleswomen noted admiringly all the time. Nice shoulders seemed like the kind of thing that only women would care about.

Earlier, Gretchen had asked whether the restaurant monitored its carbon footprint. It was the sort of question that Tara was used to after two years in Santa Fe, but she knew nothing of the restaurant's carbon footprint, for though she considered the environment important, the details of it bored her. She had invoked her polite Minnesota voice to say, "I'm afraid I don't know the answer to that, ma'am," making herself sound overly obsequious because she sensed that this would bother Gretchen. She had *wanted* to bother her. But was that flirting? She did not think so. First, she was not the flirting type. Yes, she had wanted to provoke Gretchen, but that was because she did not like the way that Gretchen sighed as she ate or her tone as she asked about the restaurant's footprint. It was the same tone that Tara's neighbors used in advising her to keep Toots, her cat, indoors. It was true that Toots was a hunter. One recent Sunday morning he brought down a rabbit, which he dragged through the open sliding door that led from the backyard into her bedroom, where he proceeded to pluck it merrily while she sat in bed reading. When she finally noticed, she leapt up and scolded him as she nudged the rabbit onto a dustpan, but her scolding was half-hearted: the rabbit was bigger than Toots, so she saw in his choice of prey an ambitiousness that she admired. When he nuzzled her chin later, she nonetheless pulled away, for though she loved Toots more than anything, bits of rabbit fluff still clung to his mouth, and she found herself unable to forget his ruthlessness with the rabbit.

Here was the thing: the neighbors, who were also her landlords, did not know anything about Toots's predilection for rabbits when they suggested that she keep him indoors. They were just asserting their opinion, unsolicited, in the way of people who owned a very big house and rented out the tiny caretaker's cottage behind it, not for the income but because they liked knowing that someone was there when they went off to spend time in their other homes: a house in Los Angeles, an apartment in New York, and what they called a "bungalow" somewhere exotic, Bali maybe. In short, they wanted

Toots confined forever to the same six hundred square feet while they could not stay in the same very big house (or apartment or bungalow) for more than a month before flying off to the next.

When Tara got home, she fed Toots and counted her tips. She kept a running tally in her head throughout the evening, but she took pleasure in the ritual nonetheless. At closing, the six customer service reps had handed her forty dollars, smiling because they believed it to be an impressive amount, even though their bill had come to three hundred. She thanked them, not profusely but sincerely, because there was no reason to make people feel bad that they did not understand what a good tip was or have the means to leave one, even if they did have the means to order six pitchers of beer. Men were said to be better tippers, and Tara supposed that they were, but men also convinced themselves that a waitress paid attention to them because they deserved it and not because the woman was trying to earn a living.

Anyway, the important thing was that she was on track to making her fall tuition. She existed in a perpetual state of studenthood, perpetual because something was always getting in the way—money or work. It was hard to find the right balance. It was summer, so she was taking just one course, memoir writing, for which at this very moment she was supposed to be writing an essay. The topic was her first sexual experience, an assignment that Tara found both overly prescriptive and voyeuristic on the part of the professor. His name was Bill, which was what everyone called him, except Tara, who called him Dr. Vance. Dr. Vance was forty with severely crossed eyes about which he made frequent jokes that were meant to put the class at ease: when he returned homework he said they had crossed from grading too many papers, and when he assigned the sex essay, he said it was time to come clean—they had crossed because he thought too much about sex as a boy.

By way of illustrating the assignment, Dr. Vance had told them about finding his father's stash of "horse porn." This, he said, had shaped his notions of sexuality. Tara thought that by "horse porn" he meant horses having sex with each other. She had grown up on a farm, but she could imagine an audience, primarily urban, for whom such images might be a novelty. When Tara said this in class, linking it to an earlier discussion about knowing your audience, everyone laughed, and Carol said, "I think the professor means bestiality." The first night of class, Carol had introduced herself as "seventy-three years young." She favored pantsuits the colors of Easter eggs and lipstick that made her look crazy. Her first essay was about gardening, her second about canning. Yet somehow even Carol had understood that horse porn meant bestiality.

"Carol is correct," said Professor Vance. "I believe that horse-on-horse is what we call the *Nature Channel*."

Everyone laughed, not necessarily at Tara but at the professor's joke, which felt like the same thing. She had heard some of them talking about her in the parking lot one night, saying, "What's she so competitive about? It's a memoir class."

Dr. Vance's goal was to make them comfortable with themselves as writers, and the first step, he explained, was to make them comfortable with themselves as sexual beings. The other students seemed to accept that this was the only way to become a writer. Tara did not, but when she stayed after class to tell Dr. Vance that she did not think she could write about her first time, he laughed and said, "It's that good?" She blushed because she had not meant this at all.

"I knew you'd call," Gretchen said when she called. "Come over for a drink?"

"Now?" said Tara. It was nearly midnight. Still, she showered away the smell of the restaurant and got into her car, but when she was finally standing on Gretchen's doorstep, she decided that she had misread the situation, that Gretchen had invited her over simply so they could drink wine and chat like a couple of girlfriends—*girlfriends* in the sense that deeply heterosexual women used the word.

When Gretchen opened the door, she was no longer wearing the pressed linen outfit she had had on at the restaurant. Instead she wore a tank top and shorts cut so high that her buttocks tumbled out with each step as she led Tara inside. Tara looked away. Summer clothing made her uncomfortable.

"This is the living room," Gretchen said, as though she did not think Tara capable of determining this on her own. It was true that the coffee table looked like an old piece of farm equipment, but Gretchen explained that it was actually a weaving platform from Java. On it sat two glasses and a bottle of wine still bearing the price tag. When Gretchen was sure that Tara had seen the price, $95, she swooped in and said, "Oh God, I can't believe I forgot this," working a manicured nail under the sticker. The walls were hung with the sort of art that Tara saw when she strolled through many of the galleries in town, art that did not make her feel anything except shock at the combination of price and mediocrity.

Gretchen poured them both a good helping of wine and then stretched out on a Navajo rug, drawing her bare right leg up over the knee of the left. She rested her wineglass—containing roughly $25 of wine—atop her stomach. Tara sat on the sofa above her, stiffly, as though occupying a pew in church. The wine was red, so each time she took a sip, she wiped the corners of her mouth.

"I noticed your accent at the restaurant," Gretchen said. "It's very *Fargo*."

"I'm from Minnesota," Tara replied, though she knew Gretchen was referring to the movie and not the town itself.

"I'm from the East Coast," Gretchen said. She mentioned her surname with the casualness of someone used to people recognizing it, of knowing who she was. Tara took a sip of wine, and Gretchen said, "You've never heard of us, have you?" She giggled and announced cryptically, "Paper." Only later did Tara understand that paper was the source of Gretchen's family's wealth.

"You know you gave those men far more attention than they deserved," Gretchen said.

"How much did they deserve?" Tara asked, not combatively.

Gretchen stared up at her, flexing her calf. "Let's leg wrestle," she said. She sat up with the fluid grace of one who worked out daily and set her wineglass on the coffee table. Tara lay down on the floor beside her, head to feet as instructed. As Gretchen counted, they swung their legs up and down, up and down, and on three, Tara felt herself being turned upside down.

In the memoir class, before they were assigned to write about sex, Tara had wanted to write about the time she saw her father throw a litter of kittens against the barn wall. She was fourteen. When confronted, her father had defended himself by saying that that was how his own father had dealt with kittens, and moreover, he had not known she was watching. Tara said what mattered was what he had done, not who had seen it. "Even if I hadn't seen you, God did," she added. About this, she had doubts, but she knew her father believed it, and that was what counted.

Later at supper, her father threw down his knife and asked what she thought would happen if he did not control the cat population.

"We'd stop having mice," she said calmly.

Her father snorted. "Look at that young couple up the road," he said, meaning the couple from the Cities who had bought the Halsruds' farm. "They started out with six pigs, and now they've got sixty-two last I heard, but they're still getting their meat in town because they can't bring themselves to kill anything." Tara's mother laughed as she often did when something was not funny but she thought it might be, and then the meal continued in silence.

The next morning Tara had gotten on her bicycle and pedaled up the road. She wanted to see the pigs for herself, but she got only as far as the Andersons' place, which still sat empty though it had been a year. In their yard was a *For Sale* sign, which she couldn't imagine did any good on a dead-end road that only the locals used. The Andersons had moved away after what happened with Sheila, their daughter, and Tara had not heard anything from them since, even though she and Sheila had been friends. They were the same age, but the friendship had been a recent thing. One night, Sheila's parents phoned Tara's to ask whether the girls might spend some time together. They did not say that they were at their wits' end, but Tara's parents knew they were. Everyone in town knew it.

Sheila was adopted, and people said that the Andersons had not known what they were getting themselves into.

"This is your chance to be a good influence," Tara's parents told her.

Tara agreed to the request because she had no friends. While adults generally knew how to see past her know-it-all demeanor, her peers wanted nothing to do with her. As a result, she was deeply lonely but had the know-it-all's singular ability to say precisely the sort of thing that intensified her peers' animosity. She wore her loneliness haughtily, as a preference. Sheila was a tall, hulking girl with poor posture. The Andersons were both short, especially by Minnesota standards, and one of the first things that Sheila told Tara after they became friends was that whenever she stood near her parents, she looked down at them and thought, *These are not my parents*. She had been held back in the first grade and nearly held back again in the fifth, after she explained to her teacher that she had not completed her homework because voices had urged her not to. The Andersons asked the teacher, as well as the school nurse, librarian, principal, and bus driver—in short, anyone who had contact with their daughter—whether they should have her checked by specialists, but everyone said the same thing. Sheila was just lazy. She was laughing at them all. Only the bus driver said that they should have her checked, but he could not really explain why. "She's just off," he said finally.

Their first afternoon together, Sheila read to Tara from a magazine called *Penthouse*, a story about a woman who liked to have sex when she was menstruating. Tara had been shocked by the story, which was titled "Red," and even more shocked by the casualness with which Sheila read, as though the story were an assignment for school. "Your parents let you read stuff like this?" she asked, a question that later embarrassed her greatly.

"I've never met my parents," Sheila said without looking up from the magazine. "And the Andersons don't know. They're not allowed in my room. Anyway, it's none of their business."

Tara tried to imagine telling her parents that her room and what she did in it was none of their business. She pictured the way that Sheila walked down the aisle of the school bus, ignoring the kids who called her names but then occasionally punching one of them hard. She thought Sheila was wonderful.

Gretchen had mice. When Tara woke up the morning after the leg wrestling—in Gretchen's bed—she went downstairs, and there they were. It was no wonder. The kitchen was set up like a smorgasbord for mice: open cracker boxes, chunks of cheese on the counter, a fifty-pound bag of organic brown rice seeping onto the floor. Of course, they made a show of running away when they saw her, disappearing into holes and cabinets, but as soon as she set the espresso pot on the stove, one poked its nose up from the burner ring. She'd leapt back, just as two boys appeared in the kitchen doorway. "Do you live here?" she asked. It was a silly thing to say to two children standing in their pajamas when she was so clearly the intruder, but Gretchen had made no mention of children, not before the leg wrestling, when they sat making small talk, and not after, when she coaxed Tara into spending the night.

"Oh, no thank you," Tara had said in polite horror when Gretchen first suggested she stay. Tara considered sleeping together, namely waking up together, more intimate than sex.

Gretchen propped herself up on one elbow. “What do lesbians do on their second date?” she whispered.

It was the lead-in to a joke, an attempt to ease the mood, but Tara understood this only belatedly. She shook her head, and Gretchen announced, “Rent a U-Haul!”

Tara did not laugh, and Gretchen said, “What’s wrong?” They were still lying on the Navajo rug in front of the fireplace, surrounded by the innocuous art that did not look any less innocuous to Tara in her post-sex-with-a-woman state.

“Nothing,” said Tara, and then she confessed, “I just don’t really get the joke.”

“You mean you don’t think it’s funny,” said Gretchen.

“I mean I don’t get *why* it’s funny. I don’t understand what U-Hauls have to do with anything.”

Gretchen laughed. “It’s funny because lesbians rush into things. They go on a date and then they move in together. The U-Haul symbolizes that.”

Tara tried to imagine Gretchen driving a U-Haul. “You do know I’m not a lesbian?” she said. She reached for her wineglass and drank fifteen dollars of wine in two gulps.

“I know,” Gretchen said. “It’s what I like about you.” Somehow, this had convinced Tara to stay. She’d slept poorly, then had her attempt at coffee-making foiled by the mice, and now these two stood before her, regarding her warily.

“I’m Tara,” she said. “I’m a friend of your mom’s.”

Tara believed there came a moment in all children’s lives when they understood that their parents were imperfect—foolish or weak or ignorant, human in some complicated way that they were too young to understand but that would disappoint them nonetheless.

The boys nodded. They were young, maybe eight and five, but she was sure they knew that she had had sex with their mother.

"Richard," said the older one.

"Kevin," said the younger.

"Breakfast?" she asked, and both boys nodded again, solemnly.

She beat together a carton of eggs, added un-nibbled cheese from the refrigerator and a clump of wilted herbs. In the midst of this, Gretchen appeared and settled at the table with her sons. She did not offer to help. While Tara scrubbed a baking pan that contained mice droppings, the oven preheated, giving off a stench so pungent it made her head pound. "It's mice feces burning, or maybe urine," Gretchen explained, as though using a word like "feces" changed everything. She opened her computer and chuckled about something as she typed, but she glanced up when Tara began slicing bananas for the boys.

"Use the banana slicer," she said. "It's easier."

Tara kept slicing. Devices that did precisely one thing were never easier.

When the eggs were done, she served Gretchen and the boys, who thanked her shyly.

"Oh my God, did you use the Stilton?" Gretchen asked. Tara shrugged. She did not know whether she had used the Stilton because she did not know what the Stilton was.

There was no U-Haul, just a slow migration of Tara's belongings, a steady weaving together of schedules, though in truth, it was less a weaving than a total subsumption, Tara's days taken over by the needs of the house and the boys, who sat at the kitchen table reading aloud to her from the books on their summer reading lists while she went through the cupboards, cleaning and disinfecting. Gretchen did not work, not really. Mainly, she spent her days examining every little part of herself and trying to make each part perfect, a form of narcissism—Tara believed—engaged in by those who found themselves with plenty of money and time but no way to imbue either with meaning. Gretchen was particularly enamored of therapy, though as far as Tara knew, she had never had anything truly awful happen to her, so Tara thought of Gretchen's twice-weekly sessions as akin to a pedicure or a teeth whitening.

In early October, Gretchen came home from one of these sessions and requested—in words that sounded rehearsed—that Tara quit her waitressing job, framing it as a selfless appeal: there was no need for Tara to spend her nights taking orders from others for a pittance. Tara said something about liking to work, and Gretchen said, "But you do a lot around here," which Tara took to mean that there was still so much more she could do. What Tara did not say was that she needed the income to pay the rent on the caretaker's cottage, where Toots still lived. She had assumed that Toots would move with her, but when she suggested this early on, Gretchen said that it would not work, that a cat on the premises would disturb the mice.

"The mice need to be disturbed," said Tara.

"I couldn't bear to live amidst such savagery," Gretchen said dramatically, and they had not mentioned Toots again, though Tara visited him daily.

That fall, Richard, the older boy, was often in trouble at school. The boys were enrolled in a bilingual school, where they had two teachers, Mrs. Garcia, who spoke to them in English, and the Spanish teacher, Mrs. Ramirez, who was from Mexico and was the one who always called about Richard's behavior. Tara believed that she was right to call, that children needed to learn discipline, how to stand in line and put their own needs behind those of others sometimes. They were not going to learn these things from Gretchen.

When Tara asked him what the trouble was about, he shrugged and said that he did not know how to keep his hands to himself. "What do you mean?" she asked, and he said that he liked to touch his classmates. "Touch how?" she asked. Richard looked perplexed, and then he said, "Like this," and held up his index finger, moving it steadily toward her as though her hair were a flame toward which it was drawn. When it settled on her head, stroking, it was as light as the wings of a moth.

Another day, as they were driving home from school, Richard told her that one of his classmates, Malcolm, had a long needle that he could pound into people's heads until their brains leaked out. "Is he your friend?" she asked, and he said that they were not friends but that he had to pay attention to Malcolm or he would get The Needle.

"Have you actually seen this needle?" she asked, and Richard turned away and stared out the car window.

"I want you to tell Mrs. Ramirez about Malcolm," Tara told Richard that evening as she tucked him into bed, but when he did, the very next day, Mrs. Ramirez said, "You need to watch out for your own body," a cryptic comment that left him more terrified, for it seemed to imply that Mrs. Ramirez was afraid of The Needle also, that it was each person for themselves.

When Tara went in to discuss the situation with Mrs. Ramirez, alone because Gretchen had an appointment with her therapist, Mrs. Ramirez said that she had meant only that Richard should keep away from Malcolm. "He follows Malcolm like a little puppy," she said.

"Richard," she said as they drove home. "Where's your father?"

She knew that Gretchen had been married until she was nearly forty-five but that she had fallen in love with a woman when she was forty. "It was our maid," she told Tara, laughing the way she did when she was pleased with herself.

"My father?" said Richard. "He's with God."

Tara had not been expecting this. "Oh," she said. "I'm sorry, Richard. I didn't know."

"It's okay," said Richard. "We see him sometimes."

That night, as she and Gretchen lay in Gretchen's bed, which was made from some sort of sturdy African wood, Tara said, "Is your ex-husband, um, dead?"

"I wish," said Gretchen.

"Richard said that he was with God," Tara told her.

"Well, that's one way to put it," Gretchen said. "He joined some cult right after I kicked him out. He gave them all his money."

"What sort of cult?" Tara asked.

"One of those cults where grown men and women all live together in very cramped quarters and know way too much about one another's bodily functions. They begin each day with a group orgasm, which they consider a form of prayer, and they spend their afternoons selling candy bars door-to-door like high schoolers raising money for the prom."

"What about the money he gave them?" Tara said.

"It wasn't much. Just the million I gave him to get him to leave."

"Dollars?" said Tara, and Gretchen leaned over and kissed her the way she had when Tara told her that she had never tried persimmons or capers or, most recently, arugula.

Tara had stopped attending the memoir class after she met Gretchen, which was for the best since she had never completed—never even started—the essay about her first sexual experience, but one night she was at the grocery store selecting carrots—organic, which she considered a waste of money since the entire world was filled with toxins, but Gretchen insisted—when she heard Dr. Vance say, "Hello, Tara," and there he was, regarding her with his crossed eyes. She started to apologize for dropping the class, but he held up his hand and said, "Why is it that every time I run into a student, they start apologizing?"

He was with a woman, not elderly but older. His mother, Tara thought. "This is Tara, from the memoir class this summer," he said, and the woman smiled kindly, as though recalling something Dr. Vance had told her. "Tara," he said, "this is my lover, Meryl."

Tara pretended not to be shocked. "Pleased to meet you," she said to the lover, who had nice eyes as well as a slight beard, just a bit of fuzz around her jaw. Tara thought that perhaps the professor, with his crossed eyes, had not noticed the beard.

"I enjoyed the class," Tara said. "I just got busy."

"Oh, come on. I scared you off with the sex assignment." Dr. Vance smiled as if to suggest that he understood her perfectly.

"Not really," Tara said. She made her voice firm.

"It's okay," he said, his expression turning gentle, his crossed eyes looking off in directions that Tara could not determine. "It's hard to write about the first time."

She wondered how it felt to have crossed eyes and why she had not thought to wonder this before. "First times aren't always a big deal," she said. "I hardly remember mine."

"How old were you?" asked the professor. He was examining a stalk of celery.

"Thirteen," she said, anticipating a reaction, but he continued to assess the celery. "It was with my best friend," she added. He brought the celery up to the side of his face, holding it there as though listening to it and not her. "Her name was Sheila."

The last time she hung out with Sheila, they had kissed. She did not know how it happened, just that they were sitting in Sheila's room, as usual, with Sheila reading aloud from dirty magazines, as usual, when Sheila started to cry right in the middle of a story about a woman and a Doberman pinscher. Tara stood up from the bed and crouched over Sheila, who was sitting on the floor with her back against the door. Tara was not comfortable with emotional outbursts, did not know how to touch someone's hand or offer an embrace.

"Sit next to me," Sheila sniffled, and Tara sat.

She asked, "Are you okay?"

Sheila rested the magazine with the story about the dog between her legs and crossed her arms in front of her, pushing her hands up inside the sleeves of her sweater. "Do you remember when I fell off the roof when I was eight?" she asked.

What Tara remembered was the ambulance speeding past their house and then running outside with her parents, listening for how far up their dead-end road it went. Her parents said it must be going to the Ericksons' because Mrs. Erickson's ninety-year-old mother lived with them, but it turned out that it was for Sheila. In discussing the accident, which people did a lot over the next few weeks, they said, "Did you hear about the Andersons' adopted girl? Fell off the roof." Even though Sheila had lived there among them her whole life, she was still "the adopted girl," not really from there, not when she did things like fall off a roof.

"Yes," said Tara. "I remember. You slipped and broke your arm."

"I didn't slip," said Sheila. Tara could see Sheila's hands moving beneath her sleeves, scratching hard. "I jumped." Tara expected to see the usual sly look that Sheila wore when she was testing her, but it wasn't there. "Dad was cleaning the gutters. He came down to use the bathroom, and I climbed up."

"You went up . . . to jump?" Tara asked. She wanted to understand the order of things, which came first: opportunity or desire.

Sheila shrugged. "I got up there, and I could see everything, the whole town, fields and lakes and silos, our school in the distance. It was all so familiar, and I thought about how my real family was out there somewhere, beyond what I could see. I thought about how we would always be looking at different things."

"And then you"—Tara hesitated—"jumped?" Sheila looked at her and nodded.

Tara did not know whether she leaned in first or Sheila did, but one of them had and the other responded. They kissed for a long time, and Tara did not think about whether there was anything wrong with it. Nor did she think about whether it felt right. She thought only about Sheila standing on the edge of the roof and then leaping into the air, about Sheila keeping the secret all these years and then choosing her to tell.

Sheila pulled back and whispered, "Do you know who my real family is?" and Tara shook her head. "The Packers," Sheila said. "You know who the Packers are, right?"

Of course Tara knew who the Packers were. They owned radio stations and convenience stores and had their own grocery chain with the slogan "Pack it on at Packers." Sometimes the Packer men ran for political office, always successfully, and especially then there were stories about them on the news, stories in which they gave money to charities, drove drunk, and cheated on their taxes or their wives.

"They're rich," Sheila breathed into her ear, and she reached under Tara's shirt and squeezed her breast, hard, and when Tara said, "Stop. That hurts," Sheila squeezed even harder.

"I said to stop," Tara said, and she stood up, adjusted her shirt, and left.

She did not go back, not the next afternoon or the one after that, nor did she answer the telephone when it rang, because she knew that it was Sheila calling. When Sheila tried to talk to her at school and on the bus, she stared to the side of Sheila's head, as though she did not exist.

"You were a good friend to that girl. She's just got too many problems," Tara's mother told her a week later, a comment that was uncharacteristic of the relationship she had with her mother, except that that afternoon the Andersons left town after it came out that Sheila had tried to harm herself, so everything that day seemed strange, not just her mother sitting on her bed trying to discuss friendship and feelings.

"I wasn't such a good friend," she said.

"You know who her real family is?" said her mother. She sounded excited. "The Packers."

"How do you know that?" Tara asked. She had thought that Sheila was lying.

"Someone at the agency told the Andersons when they adopted her. Her mother got pregnant in the loony bin, and no one even realized until she was four months along." Tara's mother thought that "in the loony bin" was the normal way to say that someone was crazy. "It was probably one of the other patients," her mother said, "which means poor Sheila got a double dose of all that." By "all that" her mother meant craziness.

"I don't really want to talk about it anymore," Tara said. This *was* characteristic of their relationship, and her mother made a huffy noise as she left.

Later, as Tara got ready for bed, she studied the bruise on her breast. It was in the shape of Sheila's hand. Over the next two weeks, it faded slowly, first the mark left by the heel of her hand, and then the fingers, one by one. The thumb mark, which she had to lift her breast to see, went last.

Gretchen had a plan for the mice, which was to catch them in no-kill traps and drive them far from the house. When Tara asked how far was far—because the driving had quickly become her job—Gretchen said at least five miles. Tara knew that it made no sense to chauffeur mice around like that, not just because of the carbon footprint that Gretchen was always talking about but because she did not have time to drive ten miles round-trip to free one mouse only to find his cousin waiting in another trap when she got home. Still, she did it because she could not bear the sound of the mice screeching inside the traps.

The boys often accompanied her, the three of them making a game of it, speculating about whether the released mouse would forge a new life or spend all his time trying to get home. Richard would watch the mouse hesitate at the edge of the open trap door, its nose quivering, and when it finally scurried off, Richard always turned away. Tara knew that he was crying, but he did not say why and she did not know how to coax it out of him. One afternoon in late November, while Kevin chased after yet another newly freed mouse, Richard sat beside her, crying and trying to keep it from her. Without looking at her, he asked, "Tara, do you feel sad about how big the world must seem to him right now?"

"Yes," she whispered back, because she did.

When they got in the car to go home, she found herself taking them instead to meet Toots. After Toots got over pretending to be uninterested in their affections, they spent an hour lounging together on the bed, where they rubbed Toots's stomach as she told them the story of how he had killed the rabbit. At first, she worried that the story would upset them, especially Richard, but the rabbit was an abstraction while Toots was right there in front of them, purring and showing them his belly, and they refused to regard him as anything but heroic.

"I wish we could live here," said Kevin. "It's like a playhouse."

"Shut up," said Richard because he understood that Tara might be hurt by the implication that her home was too small for anything but playing.

"Toots would like that," she said. "Wouldn't you, Toots?" She made *toot*ing noises and Toots purred, and later when they pulled out of the driveway, the boys waved and yelled, "Toot! Toot!" even though Toots was inside and could not see or hear them.

As they neared their own house, Richard turned to her. "Don't worry," he said. "We won't tell her about Toots."

Tara left Gretchen in December, the morning after the lesbian club came over for drinks. She did not try to explain why she was leaving because she thought that Gretchen would say she was making too big a deal out of things, and maybe she was. Maybe the lesbian club was just the last straw. She had never even heard of the lesbian club until Gretchen announced that they were coming over. "We meet monthly to hike or have drinks and talk," Gretchen said. "We're a group of professional lesbians."

"As opposed to novices like me," Tara replied, though she rarely attempted humor.

Gretchen, who was straddling her hips while pouring maple syrup into her navel, said, "Ha ha. I mean that we're women with professions."

Tara thought two things: that she hated to be sticky and that Gretchen had no profession because she had no job. She said neither.

The lesbian club consisted of six women, all of them coiffed and made-up and looking, Tara thought, like they were trying very hard not to be lesbians. They sat in Gretchen's living room, admiring the Javanese loom table. "What I wouldn't give to be a weaver," said one of them wistfully. "You wouldn't believe the day I had."

The night they leg wrestled, Gretchen had told Tara that she and her ex-husband purchased the weaving platform on a tour of Java. "And I bought this on the same trip," she said, showing her the textile draped over the back of the sofa, "from a woman in a market. I had to bargain hard, but I got her down to thirty bucks. It took her a month to make it." She sounded pleased with herself, and Tara had said nothing.

Gretchen showed the professional lesbians the textile, repeating the story of how she had bargained for it. The women clapped, and one of them said, "I hate the way they treat you in some of those countries, like you're a dumb tourist." They began sharing stories of similar bargaining triumphs, and in the midst of this, Gretchen turned to Tara and said, "Do you suppose you could serve the wine? I'm too comfortable to even think about moving." She did look comfortable, stretched out on the sofa with her shoes off and the Javanese textile that had taken a woman thirty days to make covering her legs.

Tara stood. "Would everyone like wine?" she asked. The professional lesbians all nodded, and one asked whether Tara might bring out some nuts or crackers, just something small to keep her stomach happy. "Of course," said Tara. "Anything else?"

"Water?" said another, and the one who had had such a hard day that she wanted to become a weaver thought she might need a shot of something stronger.

"Coming right up," said Tara, and she went down the hallway to the kitchen. She had put the boys to bed early, so the house was quiet, and she heard one of the women say something, and then Gretchen, who tended toward loudness, replied, "Best customer service in town," and the professional lesbians laughed. Tara filled the wineglasses and carried them on a tray to the living room. She brought out cheese and crackers, mixed nuts, coasters, and water to go around. She placed a shot of Jack Daniel's in front of the weaver wannabe.

"Can I get anything else for anyone?" she asked, but they were too busy talking about the summer opera lineup to answer, so she went upstairs to bed.

The next morning, while Gretchen was still asleep, Tara made the boys breakfast and told them that she was leaving. "Why?" asked Kevin. "Don't you like us?"

"I like both of you. Very much. But you know adults have their own way of doing things, and this is like that. It's stuff between me and your mom." She knew this sounded like bullshit. Richard began to cry, and she went over and hugged both of them. "Come on," she said. "The bus will be here any second." She gathered their things and walked them to the door, where they stood not talking until the bus arrived. Kevin hugged her and ran out, but Richard stayed behind, tapping the toe of his shoe against the doorframe.

"Just ask my mom to pay you more," he said. "I'll ask her. I'll *tell* her." He kicked the door hard to show that he meant business, and she tried to put her arm around him, but he ran out without saying goodbye.

When Gretchen finally came down, looking pale, Tara said that she was leaving.

"I've got a headache," Gretchen said. "Can we please just discuss this later?"

Tara went upstairs and packed her suitcase, an old-fashioned, wheelless thing that her parents had given her when she graduated from high school. When she appeared with it, Gretchen stood up without speaking and went over to the small desk in the foyer and took out her checkbook. She did not find it necessary to use checks in order or keep track of those she had written, so she opened the checkbook up to any old place and began to write. When she was finished, she blew on the check and tore it out. "Here," she said, waving it in the air as she had done with the bill that first night in the restaurant, a woman used to staying seated when it came to money.

Tara set down her suitcase. She walked over and took the check from Gretchen's hand, saw her name after *Pay to the Order of,* the surname misspelled by a letter. She stared at the amount. $500,000.

"I can't take this," she said. She did not say that Gretchen had paid her ex-husband twice as much.

"It's not a gift," Gretchen said. "I want you to hold on to it, until you realize you've made a mistake. Deposit it, and I'll know."

"Know what?" Tara asked.

"That you're ready to come back."

"What if I just cash it and run away?" Tara asked.

"You won't," Gretchen said. "I know you."

Tara wanted to say that Gretchen did not know her, but she just put the check in her wallet and picked up her suitcase. It was heavy, and she had to walk in a lopsided way, as though one leg were shorter than the other. It was not the way that she wanted to look making her exit. She drove directly to the bank, where she sat in her car holding the check for a long time because she knew it was the closest she would ever come to half a million dollars. She pressed it to her cheek, remembering the way Dr. Vance had held the stalk of celery, and she understood then that that was how he saw the world best—peripherally. She tore the check into very small pieces, which she released out the window like confetti as she drove home.

Toots did not greet her when she came in, did not crawl inside her open suitcase or sniff the items she took out of it. He had spent the last four months indoors, with little to keep him company or challenge him. It had left him dazed and slow-witted, and this was her fault. Tara opened the sliding door that led to the backyard and left it open, but for the rest of the day, Toots did not go near it. Tara fell asleep early that night because there were no dishes to do, no boys to tuck in and read to, but she awakened suddenly, hours later she thought, to find Toots standing in the still-open doorway, looking out into the backyard as though recalling something: a scent, the taste of rabbit fur, the memory of a braver self.

That morning, after the boys left for school, she had gone through the house opening every trap, thinking about the mice, about their tiny lives and how Richard used to cry upon their release. She should have taken the trapped creatures home with her. She knew that now. How lovely it would be to lie in bed listening to Toots thrash about in pursuit, engaging in some long-overdue savagery.

Just Another Family: A Novella

My father spent the last year of his life discontinent. He'd always had trouble with prefixes. The day after he died, I entered my parents' house—the house I grew up in—to the smell of piss, the humid night air thick with it. "It's the mattress," my mother explained, and I said, well, then the mattress had to go.

I tried to haul it out right then, just dropped my bag and went down the hallway to their bedroom. I started with the soda bottles. There were five of them, scattered beneath their bed, three with urine still sloshing around inside from when my father had relieved himself during the night. I used a broom to maneuver them out while my mother watched, lying on the floor on the far side of the bed, peering at me across its underbelly and demanding that I call them "pop" bottles. She was sure that I was saying "soda" to bother her because she said there was no way a person could grow up saying "pop" and then find herself one day just thinking "soda."

As I knelt beside their bed, I felt something hard beneath my right knee. "Why are there cough drops all over the carpet?" I asked, using the plural, for I could see then that the floor was dotted with them, half-sucked and smooth like sea glass washed up in the dingy blue shag of my parents' bedroom.

"Your father coughs a lot at night. He sucks on them until he's just about to doze off, and then he'd spit them on the floor," my mother explained, her sentence beginning in the present tense but ending in the past, because that's the way death worked, the fact of it lost for whole seconds, whole sentences. "I used to pick them up in the morning, but he'd get after me for wasting perfectly good cough drops."

"Bettina's not here yet?" I asked. My sister lived just an hour away, so I was annoyed that she had not arrived, but I was also admitting defeat: the mattress was too much for me to handle alone.

"You know she has a family," my mother said, by way of excusing her absence.

Rachel and I had been together eight years. We had a house, jobs, two cats, and a dog, so I thought of myself as having a family, also.

"You know what I mean, Sybil," my mother replied. I did know. She meant that I didn't have children, but mainly she meant that two women together was not a family.

"Well, if she's not here in the morning, I'll call a neighbor to help," I said, but my mother did not like this plan. She felt a mattress soaked with urine was a family affair.

My father was dead, I said, so what did it matter, and she said, "Why can't you say 'passed away' like everyone else?" This was a good question.

From where she lay on the floor on the far side of the bed, she announced that she was putting me in my old bedroom. "So you'll be comfortable," she added, and I did not say that I had never been comfortable in that room and could not imagine I'd start being comfortable in it now, nor did I remind her that Rachel would be arriving the next day, which meant that I would not really be in my old room long enough to get comfortable because

Rachel and I always slept in the basement, in the rec room that my father had built years ago with teenagers in mind. My parents did not approve of our sharing a bed, and the rec room was a compromise: it allowed us to sleep together, a technical win for us, but *together* on separate sofas, unlike my sister and her husband, Carl, who slept upstairs in her old room, in a double bed that my parents had purchased for this very purpose.

"Why are you lying on the floor?" I asked, bending low to peer beneath the bed at her.

"You're getting rid of my bed," she said, and then she pulled herself slowly up, using the mattress as support, and I picked up my bag from where I'd dropped it and went down the hallway to the room my mother somehow imagined I would be comfortable in, this room that I had spent my childhood in—with walls that my father had painted pink as a surprise, the orange shag carpet, the framed print of a child kneeling to pray.

Years ago, soon after I brought Rachel here to my parents' house for the first time, I'd returned for a solo visit having to do with one of many health scares related to my father. Though my parents had just met Rachel, they did not engage in even the basic courtesy of inquiring how she was. Then, on my second night here, my mother came into my room, *this* room, to announce that she—and not just *she* but everyone she knew—was ashamed of it. She was carrying Bibles, a stack of three, as though they did not all say the same thing.

"It?" I said. "What, exactly, is *it*?"

"You know what *it* is." This was what an education had done to me, she said. I couldn't just talk about stuff like normal people.

"Well, then I guess I'm not normal," I said, "because I want you to say what this *it* is that you and every single person you know is so ashamed of." I was speaking to her from the bed I had occupied as a child, before I went away and became the kind of person who thought of her life as something more than *it*.

"If you can't say what you mean," I said, "then we're not going to talk about it."

My mother had left, but not before turning to set the Bibles, stacked atop one another, on my dresser, where they remained these seven years; on the nightstand, a fourth had been added—just in case.

Now, there was something new beneath the praying child, pointing upward: a row of hunting rifles, six in total, butts nestled in the orange shag rug.

I went into the kitchen, where my mother was doing something with cottage cheese. "Why are Dad's guns in my room?" I asked.

"They were in the entryway, but you know how your sister gets about the kids."

"You mean how she gets about not wanting them to blow their heads off?" I said.

Earlier that evening, after a day spent flying backward from Albuquerque to Los Angeles in order to get a flight to Minnesota, I had stopped to pick up my rental car at the airport, and the young man at the counter asked whether I was here on vacation. He was making small talk, but also, he didn't think I was from here, for reasons having to do with the way that I speak, the Minnesota accent that I no longer have. I had not made a point to lose it, not that I could recall, though Rachel says that by the time we met, it was already gone. Sometimes, my mother says she can't understand me anymore. "It's your brogue," she says, as if I have suddenly become Scottish.

"Actually, my father just died," I told the young man, which surely struck him as further proof that I was not from here, because if you were from here, you knew not to say such things to strangers. Quickly, he handed me the keys, and I got into the rental car and drove two hours up the interstate, exiting onto the highway that led through my hometown. All around me was darkness, but I knew what was out there: lakes and fields, cows and barns and silos, the occasional house. Three miles out of town, I turned onto a gravel road and then, half a mile later, into the driveway, at the top of which I shut off the engine and rested my head on the steering wheel, the way one does at the end of a long trip, especially when there's more to come.

I lifted my head, and there was my mother, staring in at me like all the gas station attendants of my youth. I rolled down the window. "Fill 'er up," I said, but she didn't get the joke, or maybe she did get it but didn't get why I was making a joke at a time like this, with my father so recently dead.

Passed away.

"Oh, you're awake," she said. "I thought you were planning to sleep out here."

My mother often said things like this, things along the lines of suggesting that I might be planning to sleep in a rental car in the driveway. My father and I had been alike in the way that such things irritated us. "Why would I sleep in the car?"

"I thought you might be tired from the drive," she said.

"I am tired," I said, and then I tried to play the game where I kept my mouth shut, just once—the game I always lost. "But why would I sleep in the car?"

"Shirley's been at it again," my mother said.

Shirley Koerber lived on the lot behind my parents, her sole companions a band of dogs at which she yelled for various infractions. She was a stout woman with legs that bowed severely, as though she were straddling an invisible barrel as she walked, and she possessed a deep hatred of small animals—squirrels, chipmunks, birds—all of which the dogs chased with limited success and at which she shot with far greater. As a child, I'd awakened often to the sound of her gun, rising to watch from my window as the dogs circled the felled animal, howling, while Shirley rode her imaginary barrel toward them. Once when I was hanging laundry on the backyard line, a bullet whizzed past my head and I ran inside, leaving the basket of wet clothes behind. When my mother came home and asked about the abandoned clothes, I explained that Shirley had been shooting again, and my mother nodded as if I'd said it had started to rain, my options akin to opening an umbrella or going inside, for there was no option that involved making the rain stop.

"This is crazy," Rachel said the first time she visited my parents' house, a visit that I kicked off with a tour of the bullet holes speckling the back wall. "Why didn't your parents do something?"

Rachel grew up in the suburbs of New York, in an intellectual Jewish family with parents who were refugees from war and violence. Until she met me, Rachel had not known people who discussed guns in a personal way, as objects they owned and fired.

"What could they have done?" I asked, trying to see the bullet holes through her eyes. Until I met Rachel, I had not known people who had never held a gun.

"What could they have done?" Rachel repeated, sounding incredulous. "They could have called the police."

"And what could the police have done?" I said, equally incredulous. "Take the gun?"

"Yes," Rachel said. "They could have taken the gun."

I made a list once—pre-Rachel—a list of the things that I considered nonnegotiable in a partner. It was a short list, reasonable in its expectations. I met Rachel just two months later, at a lesbian potluck of all things. Not long after we moved in together, I read an article in the *New York Times*—back when we used to have it delivered instead of reading it on the computer—about professional matchmakers, all of whom said that the key to successful matchmaking was to pair up people with the same pasts, people who recognized themselves in their potential mate's childhood and family and beliefs: Italian Catholic from Long Island with Italian Catholic from Long Island. People want familiarity in a mate, want to recognize themselves, their youth, in the other person. That's what all the matchmakers said. It's not that I didn't believe this. I did—maybe especially of the sorts who would consult a matchmaker—but I also believed that matching a person with someone who resembled a cousin more than a lover suggested a lack of imagination. Until then, I'd assumed, naively I suppose, that most couples were like us, drawn to each other precisely because we were so unfamiliar.

At night, when we lay in bed, Rachel told me stories about her family's arrival in this country, and I listened. Her father and grandparents had fled Russia because they were Mensheviks, one of her stories began; she dropped in "Menshevik" as though the word were common knowledge. This was right after we had sex the first time, so I did not say, "What is a Menshevik?" though later I realized that nobody knew what Mensheviks were, that Mensheviks were *not* common knowledge, except in the very specific world of Russian Jews in exile.

Her grandparents had first gone to France, where they continued to be Mensheviks, and then came to this country, where they kept on gathering with other Mensheviks. Even after her grandparents were dead and her father had his own family—Rachel, her mother, and sister—the tradition continued. One of the other Menshevik offspring had a house on the Hudson River where all of them would meet on weekends in the summer to eat and drink vodka and discuss Russia, its past, its future. Once, Stalin's daughter was there, Rachel told me. This was after a different night of sex. She wasn't Jewish, of course, Stalin's daughter, but she was Russian and in exile. Imagine growing up with parents who knew Stalin's daughter. I couldn't imagine it, not at first, but I wanted to, just as she could not imagine parents who rose at dawn, who did not smoke or drink, who did not speak of ideas or question God, his existence or his decisions.

My great-great-grandparents left Sweden in 1867 after the crops had failed yet again, failed because so much rain fell that year that the potatoes rotted in the ground. They left with eight children and arrived in Minnesota a year and a half later with five, two of whom eventually continued on to Washington, where they became fishermen, while the other three settled in Minnesota and resumed farming, the two factions forming—or so I like to imagine—a poetic yin-yang of land and sea. According to my father, the Minnesota side never forgave the Washington brothers for choosing water, not after all the misery that water had brought to their family: first, the absence of it, droughts that stole the crops year after year, and then the abundance of it taking their crops yet again, and finally the water that surrounded them during those agonizing weeks at sea as they crouched, vomiting, between decks, and watched three children die.

By the time that I was born in this same small town in Minnesota, my father had long ago given up farming to run a hardware store that he purchased in the late forties, soon after he came home from the war. He had enlisted right out of high school, but when the war ended, he had gone no farther away than Florida, where he was being trained as an airplane mechanic. Something about the experience unsettled him greatly, put him off the world. He came home to this town and never left again. He spoke of this as the best decision he ever made. I suppose that there is a sanity in this, in claiming to want exactly what one has; still, perhaps because my father and I were alike in all of the most problematic ways—stubborn yet shy, prone to solitude, sarcastic at moments when it did not behoove us to be so, overly fond of the subterfuge of words—I thought that I understood things about him that others might not: that is, I believed that he was not beyond regret, that he longed for a life that he—to be fair—had not chosen and never alluded to but that I sometimes imagined for him, college in place of family, in place of us.

For starters, he took no pleasure in family time. Every evening of my childhood, he went back to his hardware store, where he watched television and tended to the books, and though I was relieved at his chronic disinterest in us—for the house took on a different shape when he and his anger were part of it—I wondered at his decision to become a father in the first place, especially as he had waited forty years to begin. Occasionally, well-intentioned people—people who are parents—ask why I do not have children, referring to the fact that I am "good" with children, that I like them.

"No," I tell these people. "I like *some* children." You see, I am selfish, but just unselfish enough to accept that I would not be a good parent. I never wanted to be a parent. In this way, I suspect, my father and I were also alike.

Thus, when he ridiculed me for going far away from this town and the world of hardware and childbearing, I could not help but see his ridicule as an expression of his own remorse. I imagined that my father would someday speak to me with an openness that belied the daily narrative of this place. He never did, so what remains is the narrative, a fairly standard one for those who grew up how and where I did, about hard work and toeing the line. Still, I do not think it possible to tell the story of my father's death without first telling the story of how we came to be in this country, this place, the place my father ran back to, the place I ran away from.

Early in our relationship, Rachel and I decided that the best way to keep our relationship sound was to live a plane flight away from our families. This, we believed, would save us from middle-of-the-night phone calls from a parent who needed help relighting the heater or procuring medicine that had "suddenly" run out. Of course, this was a plan built on logic, and middle-of-the-night calls—middle-of-the-night anythings—are not. They are built on the fears that daytime holds at bay, fears that do not keep company with reason. I say this not in a critical way, for I am not impervious to the terror of deepest night, but perhaps I am just hopeful enough, still, to know that morning will come.

The night that my father died, Rachel and I had returned from New Jersey, where we had been visiting her mother, and when we got home, the pet sitter had refused to leave. She just sat there, telling story after story of all the adorable things our pets had done in our absence, and when she was finally gone, Bettina called, but by then, we had vowed not to answer the phone for the rest of the evening. I did not even listen to my sister's message, but Rachel said that there was something odd about her tone and that I needed to call her back at once.

Bettina answered in her usual way, a hello and then right down to business. "So, I just talked to Mom, and she said that Dad might be dead."

"*Might?*" I said, seizing on this as the starting point.

She explained that my mother had called her a few minutes earlier, and when my sister asked, "What's up?"—brusquely because she'd been trying to get my mother to stop calling at the kids' bedtime—my mother had said, "Oh, not much," and then, "Dad's not doing so good." My sister thought this meant that my father's cough had worsened or that he was just being his usual cranky self. "What's wrong with him?" she'd said.

"Well," my mother had said, "he's on the floor, and the paramedics are working on him, but it's been an hour, so I think they think he's dead."

My sister and I were both laughing. Rachel was not.

"Let me know when they're sure," I said.

An hour later, my sister called again. My father was definitely dead.

I would like to say that I did not sleep well that first night back in my old room, but I did. The night before, by way of letting Rachel know that I had arrived, I texted her a photo of the guns lined up beside my bed with the caption *Fresh sheets.* I awakened in the morning to a text from her letting me know that she had finally managed to locate a house sitter—she had given in and called the same loquacious woman we had been unable to get rid of two days earlier—and was on her way to the airport at last. Of the photo and its caption, she said nothing.

Then, I called the neighbor, and he said that he would come right over to help me with the mattress, but by noon the neighbor had still not arrived. My mother set the table with food that people had dropped off: hotdishes and Jell-O salads made with walnuts and sour cream and shredded carrots, the kind of food that I had grown up on, that we ate in the basements of churches and brought to others. Protestant food, I described it to Rachel.

The night before, I'd found a pair of suede mittens in a drawer, and I had them on now, despite the heat. I could not eat with them on, but I liked the way they felt.

"What was his last meal?" I asked.

"He had a frozen pizza around five," my mother said. "Then a couple of potpies at six. There was a TV dinner in the oven when he had the heart attack. One of the paramedics smelled it, or it might have burned down the house."

When I was two months old, my father came home from ice fishing one Sunday to find me in the oven. "She wouldn't stop crying," my mother had explained as my father lifted me—like a Thanksgiving turkey!—from the bottom rack.

That was the way my father told the story, making my presence in the oven sound festive. My mother never told the story.

"Did he always eat four dinners?" I asked.

"He didn't actually eat the TV dinner," she said. "Why are you wearing mittens?"

The neighbor arrived then, bringing a jar of sauerkraut made by his wife. He and I turned the mattress on its side and carried it through the house while my mother stood in the entryway holding the door for us. As we passed through, I saw that she was crying, but I said nothing because what came to mind to say was "It's just a mattress soaked in piss." That is the person I am here. When I'm not here, I tell myself that the person I am here is not who I really am. Rachel is the only person who knows both, and that is no small thing.

"Your father was really proud of you girls," the neighbor said.

"I don't think he was *that* proud," I said. My mother cried harder.

The neighbor was Bettina's age—not some old man is my point—and I wanted to say something about his use of "girls," but he'd come in the middle of a busy workday, so I didn't. This, I thought fleetingly, was how injustice grew.

On three, we heaved the mattress into the bed of my father's truck.

"You're pretty strong," said the neighbor. He meant for a girl. "So, did you ever end up getting married?"

"End up?" I said. I understood the way his mind worked.

"You know what I mean," he said.

"Not really," I said. "Anyway, I'm a lesbian, so I can't get married. It's against the law." I knew that he knew I was a lesbian. Everyone in town knew, despite my parents' best efforts.

"Tell Bettina I said hello," he said.

I had forgotten until then that he and my sister had once dated. Not exactly dated—they snuck out at night sometimes and met in the woods between our houses, his the house he still lived in these twenty-five years later. They met in a fort that we had all built together, and when I asked Bettina what she and the neighbor boy did in that fort on the nights they met, she said that they played house, which I had taken to mean that they sat around eating the cans of baked beans that we stole from our parents' cupboard and stocked the fort with so that it would feel real, like a place we could live if we needed to, if the Rapture happened or we ran away from home.

I slammed the tailgate of the truck. "Thank you for your help, and thank your wife for the sauerkraut. I'd forgotten how neighborly everyone is."

The neighbor looked at me uncertainly, as if he thought I maybe meant something more by this. "I'm sorry about your father," he said at last.

I'd last seen my sister six months earlier, a visit that ended abruptly because of what happened on Christmas Eve. The evening had unfolded as usual—supper, church, the midnight opening-of-gifts, a progression of events throughout which we acted like just another family together for the holidays, ignoring slights and feigning enthusiasm for our gifts, most of them chosen with little regard for the recipient's taste or needs. Only Rachel was safe from having to pretend, for she never received gifts from anyone in my family.

When I'd pointed this out once, early on, my mother said, "But isn't she Jewish?"

Rachel was Jewish. This did not stop us from spending every other Christmas with her mother in New Jersey, alternating under the pretense of fairness, though I suspected that it was Rachel's way of minimizing the time spent with my family, not because she disliked my family but because she disliked who I was when I was with my family. I felt similarly, so I should have been better disposed toward her position, but mainly I brimmed with unjust thoughts: that if Rachel really loved me, she would love me *most* when I was around my family, saying and doing awful things.

On the night that would turn out to be our father's last Christmas Eve, he sat in his recliner opening gifts: a shirt, gloves, another shirt. He studied each, demanded loudly but of no one in particular, "What do I need this for?" and then, with a solid dropkick, sent it ricocheting off the ceiling and tree while we, his family, continued to unwrap our own disappointing gifts.

For several years, our father had been relearning Swedish, which he had spoken as a child, so in the weeks prior to Christmas, I'd gone to every used bookstore in Albuquerque, searching for something, anything, in Swedish. I'd finally found Zola in hardcover for ten dollars, which seemed like both nothing and a lot, nothing when considered against the fact that it was the seventh bookstore I'd tried, a lot when I stopped to think about how few people in Albuquerque would be interested in Zola to begin with, in Swedish to top it off.

My father tore the wrapping from the book with his usual angry haste, and I braced for the sound of his shoe on hardcover. For several long minutes, he stared at the cover, taking in the words in Swedish, and then he began to read. Eventually, he rose from his recliner and went, with Zola, to his room. He had had enough of Christmas, enough of us.

As my mother scurried around retrieving his gifts and sobbing while the rest of us sat watching her, Bettina turned to me from where she sat on the sofa. "The Swedish book was my idea," she said.

"I was the one who said the only thing he cares about anymore is Swedish."

This was true. She had said it during a telephone conversation that summer, not as a gift idea but as a complaint. She had taken the kids to visit my parents, and our father had barely spoken to any of them. He just lay on his bed listening to Swedish on tape, hitting pause to yell for my nephew and niece when he needed something, another cup of coffee or a jar of herring.

"The important thing," I said, looking up at her from where I sat on the floor, "is that he actually got one gift he didn't kick. What does it matter whose idea it was?"

And just like that, she was on me.

To be clear, I don't condone fighting, but neither do I think it's worse for two women to go at it than two men, even if those two women are "sisters who should love each other," as Rachel kept saying afterward, after she and Carl had pulled us apart and the two of us had gone down to our rec room quarters. When we undressed for bed, she pointed at my arm, at the scratches from the tree that Bettina and I had rolled against, nearly toppling it as we each struggled to get on top.

The next morning when I awoke, Rachel's sofa was empty. I went upstairs, and there they were, the two spouses huddled together at the table, between them the leftover potato sausage from supper, which they began—only then—to eat. When I sat down at the table, they pretended that they had not been talking about what happened the night before. Carl took out a shell casing and showed it to Rachel, who touched it the way one would a talisman, as though it contained power that should not be doubted or taken for granted. Did Rachel even understand what a shell casing was, I wondered, that it was what remained behind, empty, after a gun had been fired?

My brother-in-law was once a large man. He woke up on his twenty-fifth birthday and decided that he did not want to be large any longer, so he picked up the first object he laid eyes on—a shell casing from the top of his dresser—and put it in his pocket. Whenever he felt like eating, he had once told me, he reached into his pocket and the casing acted like an electric shock, the memory of his life as a fat teenager and then a fat man jolting his resolve.

My sister had not known her husband then, and when he told us—my mother, my sister, and me—the story of his weight loss, the way that half his body just melted away, he explained it like this: "When I was twenty-five, I lost my twin brother."

We were driving in his van at the time, and my mother, who was in the passenger seat, turned and stared at him with a stricken look. "Carl," she said, "I didn't know you had a twin."

We all laughed, except my mother, who liked things to mean what they meant.

I knew that clarity often arrived unexpectedly, a moment in which one saw one's life plainly—that it was not working, what needed to be done to fix it—but these moments were fleeting. This was what I admired about my brother-in-law, that he could hold on to his moment of clarity all these years, was still holding on to it.

I sat at the kitchen table with him and Rachel in silence, watching them pretend to enjoy the potato sausage until Bettina appeared. She went directly to the toaster, inserted a slice of bread, then stood awaiting its transformation.

"Remember when you tried to smother me?" I said.

She laughed. "Of course."

I laughed also.

The first year of my life, Bettina and I had shared a room, the room that now houses my father's guns, the room that Rachel and I are forbidden to sleep in together. This—the story of what happened in that room, which is the story of why Bettina was moved to her own room, the room with the double bed purchased for her and Carl by my parents—was one of the stories that Rachel did know about my childhood, but Rachel did not think the story was funny.

What happened was this: Our mother found Bettina inside my crib one morning, holding a pillow over my face. "I want to smother the baby," she'd explained. She was not yet three, but she knew not only the word "smother" but apparently how smothering worked, for she'd brought a pillow with her when she crawled up and over the railing and into my crib.

"Maybe she meant 'mother,'" my grandmother said when the adults whispered about it in the years to come. "She heard all this talk of mothering and got the word wrong." Nobody stated the obvious: that "mother" was not a verb, not where we came from.

"She had a pillow over her face," my mother had asserted once. Just once.

As we retold the story that morning, Bettina and I continued to laugh. Our spouses continued not to laugh. They did not approve of the way that our family settled problems: the way that we downplayed one egregious event by invoking a time when our behavior had been even worse. Had the outcome been different, our response might have been different, but you didn't respond to the thing that hadn't happened. You responded to what had, and what had happened was nothing. We were just another family whose members had not killed one another.

We'd never liked each other, my sister and I—who knows why, animosity is nearly always harder to explain than love—and Christmas, with its expectations of good cheer, seemed only to intensify our hostility. Indeed, I could not recall a Christmas when this tradition of ill will had not made itself known. The year that I was ten, Bettina twelve, we were ordered to help with the erecting and trimming of the tree, a task that began with the two of us standing behind our crouching mother, each plotting how to make the endeavor unpleasant for the other, while our mother hacked away at the trunk with a flimsy saw, paring it down to fit into the stand, a tripod with three large screws. Our mother had a vision, I think, of the three of us tightening the screws just so to achieve a perfectly erect tree, of us working together.

As she sawed, I selected a small glass ornament from one of the boxes and put it in my mouth, then smiled at Bettina, my lips pulled back to reveal the smooth green glass.

"Mom, Sybil put a bulb in her mouth," Bettina reported, as I knew she would.

"Sybil, spit out the bulb," our mother said, her weary voice muffled by the tree, and Bettina smiled at me smugly.

I chomped down hard. I had a plan—fuzzy at best—to assert that my sister had smacked the top of my head, causing the bulb to shatter.

My mother stood up. "Spit it out," she said again, cupping her hand beneath my mouth. She did not yet know what I had done.

I opened my mouth wide. I could see the fear in my mother's eyes, feel it in the way that she gripped my head in the viselike bend of her elbow and worked like a dentist on my mouth, all the while pleading in a loud, panicky voice for me not to swallow.

Just over my mother's shoulder, Bettina peered down at me, smiling.

This was not our first glass scare of the year. The first, just months earlier, was on a Sunday, steak day at our house. After church, Bettina and I set the table, which we managed to do quietly—in deference to our father—though we circled each other warily, using our hips and elbows to force the other aside. Bettina, because she was older, carried the steak knives, marching toward me with the blades pointed out in a game of cutlery chicken. Meanwhile, our mother stood before the oven, its door cracked open as the steaks crackled and smoked beneath the broiler. It was then, as she bent to peer inside, that we heard it: a small pop, our mother's "oh no." The bulb in the oven had exploded.

"A little glass isn't going to kill anyone," said our father when he saw the glittering steaks. "We're not wasting perfectly good meat."

Our mother did not argue. She went into the front yard, held the steaks up beneath the brilliant sun, and—in a dress rehearsal for what she would do with my open mouth just months later—extracted shards. Then she came back inside and set the platter of lukewarm meat on the table, crying just a little. We ate tentatively, except for my father, who acted as though there was nothing he welcomed more than the opportunity to eat glass.

I had not told Rachel either story. I knew what she would say. "How is it possible for a family to have two stories about eating glass?"

Six weeks after the ornament incident, on a morning during which we had been tasked with removing the remaining Christmas ornaments, Bettina and I took our Christmas gifts—tennis rackets that we had begged for, separately, after watching Wimbledon on television—and practiced our swings against the tree that our mother had tried, without success, to teach us to erect together. In a rare display of teamwork, we backhanded and lobbed and forehanded until entire boughs of the desiccated tree were bare, their needles embedded so deeply into the shag carpet that the vacuum, which my mother drove frantically around the room, proved useless. Bettina and I spent the afternoon on our knees, extracting needles by hand and dropping them into the large bowl generally reserved for popcorn, but when we went to report that we were finished—arguing about who had done more—we could not find our mother anywhere.

"She's gone," one of us said, and seeing nothing more in our mother's disappearance than possibility, we went into our parents' bedroom to snoop. We tried first to shake quarters out of the large plastic piggy bank in the corner and, after failing, spent several minutes jumping on the bed. Bored, we began opening dresser drawers, looking for something that would shock or appall us, though we did not know what.

"What's that?" Bettina said. We'd both heard it, a sound that seemed to come from beneath the bed.

"Maybe we broke it when we were jumping," I said.

We lay on the mattress and hung our heads over the side. There was our mother, lying perfectly still beneath the bed. She did not turn to look at us, did not acknowledge our presence, and finally Bettina asked, "Are you dead?"

I laughed, not at the thought that she might be dead but at the silliness of the question.

"Go away," said our mother, still not looking at us. "I'm sick of you both."

She began to cry then, and we did not know what to do, so I said to Bettina, "It's your fault," and she replied that it was mine, and we went back and forth like this for several minutes so that we would not have to think about the fact that our mother was lying beneath the bed.

Three hours later, our father's headlights came up the driveway. We always dreaded his arrival because whatever we were doing—watching television, playing games, reading—made him angry. That evening, we were sitting at the table, waiting.

"Just sitting there doing nothing?" he yelled from the entryway as he took off his coat and boots.

We told him that our mother was under the bed.

"Under the bed?" he said, sounding more confused than angry.

"She's hiding," Bettina explained.

"From us," I clarified. "She's tired of us."

"Who isn't?" said our father.

Our father was afraid of nothing. When a noise awakened us in the middle of the night, he got out of bed and went directly toward the source, catching over the years bats and squirrels, a skunk that had worked its way into the dryer, but that night he stood staring down the hallway toward the room in which our mother, his wife, lay under the bed whose urine-soaked mattress I would find myself removing nearly three decades later. Finally, he turned and went into the living room, where he sat in his recliner, the needleless tree nearby, and read the paper. After a while, our mother came out from under the bed and went into the kitchen, and when supper was ready, we all sat down at the table and ate the meal that she had crawled out to prepare, and we asked nothing about why she had been under the bed to begin with.

It was past two when Rachel pulled up in the driveway. She got out of her rental car, and my mother came out of the house, and they stood ten feet apart, greeting each other like two people on opposite banks of a fast-flowing river. Rachel extended a card, which my mother reached toward her to receive, still holding the door ajar behind her; then, without inviting my partner of eight years to follow, my mother turned and went back inside, where she would add the card to the stack that I had pulled out of the mailbox that morning. I rolled my eyes at Rachel, and she did not roll hers back at me.

Inside, my mother stood beside the pile of cards, and when Rachel asked what she could do to help, my mother told her to open each of them and log the donation amount, and Rachel set down her bag and began—using a steak knife supplied by my mother—to do just that. I sat with her, not asking about her flight or making any of the small talk that people make. I did not want my mother to think we had a relationship that in any way resembled what my mother believed of relationships.

Most of the cards contained two one-dollar bills, but when Rachel opened her own card, I saw that inside was a receipt for a $100 donation to Amnesty International in memory of Harold Berglund. I did not know which seemed more absurd—the amount or the organization, which my father would have suspected, as he did most charities, of being communist. She looked at me, then slipped the receipt into her pocket, replacing it with two bills. On the log that she was keeping for my mother, she wrote: *Rachel $2.*

She made a point to read each of the cards, and I made a point not to. I could not help but feel that the task felt to her anthropological, a study of this place that she often described to others, our friends, with succinctness: "It's the most foreign place I've ever been that does not require a passport."

"What do you think this means?" she asked, and she read from a card that said, "Once we visited your family and Harold told us about the Amish."

"How would I know?" I said, meaning that I did not want to be made the expert.

When we finished, my sister was still not there, so Rachel and I got into my father's truck and drove to the town dump, where we paid a small fee to discard my father's urine-soaked mattress amid appliances and furniture and bags of clothing, the detritus of his neighbors' lives.

"I can't believe this place," Rachel said. "It's so strange to think this is where you're from."

"I'm not actually from the dump," I joked. I tended to fill silences with unfunny comments when things between us were tense, which seemed the case now, even if Rachel had reached over and twirled my hair while I drove. "I did learn to shoot here, though."

This was true. When I was twelve, my father had enrolled me in a gun safety course and we'd practiced here, in this place where we could do little harm because everything around us was beyond fixing.

"Have you talked to Bettina?" Rachel asked.

"Why?" I said.

Rachel sighed. "She's your sister, your only sibling, and you just lost your father."

We climbed out of the truck's cab and into the bed, where we strained to expel the mattress.

"I talked to Carl," she said. "On the phone last night."

"Carl?" I said. "Since when do you and Carl talk on the phone?"

"We're worried," she said.

I wanted to ask which of them had placed the call because that would indicate which of them was more worried, but I knew she would say that it didn't matter who had called. It mattered that they were worried.

"Carl told me about the oven," she said quietly. Quiet definitely meant angry.

"What about the oven?" I said, but I knew what Carl had told her. The oven story was the story that always got told in my family when we were worried about my mother.

"The oven wasn't even on," I added, though I imagined she knew that I was lying. I laughed suggestively, but she looked at me as if I were the crazy one.

"It's not funny," she said, and then, "Are you worried?" She meant worried about my mother, now that my father was dead.

"It was a long time ago," I said. "Anyway, that story is none of Carl's business."

"What do you mean?" she said. "He's part of this family."

I thought about the way she said "this family," including herself even though I had done everything I could to make her feel outside my family because I could not imagine her wanting to be inside. I reached into the cab of the truck, behind the seat, where my father kept a rifle and a box of ammunition. "Do you want to try?" I asked, holding out the gun.

Rachel stared—at me, at the gun.

"There's no one around," I said. I pointed at the mattress, which lay where it had landed, propped against a doorless refrigerator. "It's your chance to finally shoot a gun."

I said this as though shooting a gun were something she had aspired to, a bucket list item that I was giving her the chance to tick off.

Rachel looked around the dump rather than at me, this woman with whom she lived who was now offering her a gun, this woman whose mother had tried to bake her. "How is it that we've been together eight years yet you've never told me that story?" she asked softly.

I walked out into the distance with my father's rifle—away from the mattress, away from Rachel—and knelt behind an abandoned bathtub, loaded the gun, and pressed the butt to my shoulder.

"What are you doing?" Rachel yelled, and I pulled the trigger. Even from a distance, I could see the hole that it tore in the stained yellow mattress.

Each year on my mother's birthday, my father and mother would go into the aisles of the hardware store devoted to household goods, and my father would instruct my mother to pick out a gift for herself. One year, she chose a vacuum cleaner, another year a coffeemaker. "This doesn't seem like a birthday present," I said the year of the Crock-Pot. "It's really a present for the whole house. I mean, we all eat. Plus, it comes from our store, so she already owns it."

I would like to revise history, to claim this comment as a reflection of my nascent feminism, but I know better. I was simply stating the obvious, for I was that sort of child, one who embraced logic (though if I were going to belabor the point, I would note that feminism is simply that: a stating of the obvious). I was ten at the time, still of an age when presents meant something. An appliance was not a gift. I suppose all children feel this way about adults. They watch them stare at the news or listen to them speak of what milk cost today and what it cost a year ago, and feel nothing but amazed horror, and soon enough they stop listening because they understand that from adults nothing interesting can be expected.

After just a few meals, my father had unplugged the Crock-Pot from the wall. "Nothing tastes right," he announced. To be clear, the Crock-Pot had produced meals far better than those on which we usually dined, and I could not imagine that my father did not agree. What I have come to suspect is that he took offense at the very thing that attracted my mother to the Crock-Pot in the first place: it made her life easier.

The next morning, he took the stew-encrusted Crock-Pot with him when he left for work, placing it on the seat of the truck that, all these years later, Rachel and I used to drive his mattress to the dump. This is what it means to have a vertical history: your family arrives in a place and stays, and everything gets built on top of itself so that the dump where you take the mattress might also be the dump where your father took the Crock-Pot all those years earlier, which might also be the dump where your partner, watching you with a rifle pressed to your shoulder, thinks that she has had enough.

She did not actually say that she had had enough. What she said was "I don't understand you people." What she meant was that I was one of *them*.

When we got back to the house, Bettina, Carl, and the kids were there, and Bettina greeted us by saying something about how we should not have run off and left my mother all alone, and I said something about how she should not have taken her own sweet time getting there. Then, we sat down to eat dinner, in silence, but after several minutes Petra, my niece, set down her fork and asked, "Were Sybil and Rachel born together in a big bubble?"

She was seven, trying to make sense of our relationship, of the way that we disappeared into the basement while the rest of the family stayed aboveground. I thought of my mother saying, "Everyone's ashamed of it."

"Yes," I told my niece while the others looked down at their plates. "Rachel and I were born in a bubble, and every day we wait for it to burst."

The next morning, my mother came into the dining room, where we all sat eating various versions of breakfast, and stood before us holding one of the Bibles from my childhood room, the room she now occupied because I had taken her mattress to the dump and shot it like an old horse being put out of its misery. I preferred to think of my actions that way, as vaguely beneficent. Of course, Rachel was the only person who knew that I'd shot the mattress, and we had not talked about it since. We had not really talked at all. She was waiting for me to explain not just about the mattress but about the fact that, years earlier, my mother had put me in the oven and turned it on, granted with the door ajar, my father arriving and plucking me out before it had time to get hot. Really, though, she was waiting for me to explain why I had not told her any of this.

My mother did not greet us or ask how everyone slept. She simply cleared her throat and began reading to us from the Bible. We all stared at her, not listening exactly, except when she paused to tell us that at night when she and my father lay in bed together, this is what they did. They read scripture. Once, years earlier, when my sister and Carl were first dating, my mother gathered the two of us—her daughters—and explained that sex was only for *after* marriage, but also that it was very important to marry someone with whom you were sexually compatible. When I pointed out the contradiction her advice involved—for how were you to know that you were marrying a sexually compatible partner if you did not have sex with that person, pre-marriage, to determine it?—my mother became indignant and said that this was why she did not talk to us about such things. We always thought we knew better. Then, with a note of finality, she said, "Your father and I have always been compatible in bed."

All these years later, I no more wanted to know that they read Bible verses in bed than that they had sex. I did not want to hear about the intimacies of their relationship. That is what it came down to.

Rachel is a nurse, which means that she knows how to take charge and provide comfort, so as our mother stood in the middle of the dining room, reading from the Bible and sobbing, and Bettina and I looked away in Protestant embarrassment, Rachel said, "That's lovely. I think it would be nice for the service."

We were leaving soon to meet with the minister, who was not the minister of my youth, that benign figure who had overseen my baptism and confirmation, the singular most interesting thing about him being that he wore platform shoes because there was some notion that he would be better served by height, that parishioners did not want to look down on their pastor. This new minister, my mother had told me repeatedly, led letter-writing campaigns to stop other Lutherans from embracing homosexuality. Who were these

Lutherans that they were writing to, I had wondered. Was there a mailing list of homosexuality-embracing Lutherans?

"What is the purpose of this meeting with the pastor?" I asked warily.

My mother stopped sobbing but continued to stand before us in her frayed robe, the Bible aloft in her hands. "Apostolic" was the word that came to mind, though I knew that this was anachronistic thinking. The Apostles had not had Bibles because the Apostles wrote the Bible.

"We have to talk about our ideas for the service," my mother replied. "You know, your father's favorite hymns and verses. Maybe you girls have some anecdotes for the eulogy."

"What does 'eulogy' mean?" my nephew asked. Lars was nine, the sort of child who liked words purely for the pleasure of knowing them—not as weapons, that is. The adults looked at him the way that adults often look at children who ask perfectly good questions.

I said, "In Greek, *eu* means 'good' or 'true' and *logia* means 'word,' so 'good word.'"

You see, I did regard words as weapons; early on, when I was first figuring out who I was in the world, I decided to make myself unassailable—unassailable in my new life, that is, the world of books and words and people for whom education was generational, a given—and so I became a student of grammar and etymology, both of which had contributed to my "brogue" and my very specific and unlucrative skill set.

My nephew appreciated my response, as I knew he would. Children like to be taken seriously. "Does that mean that they can't lie about Grandpa?" he asked, and I said that, on the contrary, lying was generally required in eulogies, that it is nearly impossible to speak words that are at once good and true about any of us.

Needless to say, I was not keen to meet the new minister. Bettina said that he was fine, but Bettina had a tendency to set the bar low and also to enjoy the low-hanging fruit of normalcy that heterosexuality conferred upon her. The spouses remained behind with strict orders to keep the children out of my room, which was now my mother's room and—more to the point—the room that housed my father's hunting rifles, so it was just the three of us knocking at the pastor's office door. He immediately called out for us to enter, not pausing the way that people usually do as they shift from their private to their public selves.

As we pushed open the door, an overwhelming stench greeted us, leapt at us like a badly trained dog meeting guests. Perhaps the minister had been snacking on cheese, I thought, the stinky kind, but the minister explained, without being asked and with disturbing unselfconsciousness, that it was his feet we smelled. My mother responded to this news as though it were not news at all—as though her pastor's foot odor was common knowledge. She shook her head sympathetically and told him that the whole prayer chain had been working on it.

"You've been praying about his feet?" I said.

When I was young, the phone rang frequently with such requests, mainly involving illnesses and accidents. Even then, I was an inveterate eavesdropper, so I knew the drill. Before sitting down to pray, my mother dialed the next three members of the chain and described the nature of the request—a church member with a weak heart or Melvin Bergstrom's brother, who had run over his bare foot with the lawn mower. Regarding the chain, two things struck me: that a prayer chain seemed nothing more than God-sanctioned gossip, and that the most interesting subjects of it lived elsewhere—a nephew in Fargo who had begun tattooing his body with strange symbols, a brother-in-law who had been arrested in a park in Saint Paul. I had tried to imagine what could be done in a park that required the police or prayer or the hushed tones with which my mother spoke of it to others, but I could not, nor could I ask my mother, who had already explained that some requests were almost beyond prayer. Once, my mother caught me listening and suggested that I join in. "The more prayers the better," she said. I asked whether God had a number in mind, but she said that praying did not work that way—did not require a consensus of opinion—which I imagined was part of its attraction.

"It means a lot to me that your mother and the other ladies pray for my feet like this," the pastor said solely to me, and then he turned to my mother. "The doctor says it's probably some sort of fungus, and the hot weather's sure not helping."

The three of us were still standing, but instead of inviting us to sit down, the pastor rose and came out from behind his desk. He was barefoot.

"Maybe we can get down to business," I said, because I feared where this was headed: the four of us, heads bowed, hands joined as we prayed together for what? Less humidity?

"Business?" said the pastor.

"I mean my father's funeral."

"Oh, yes. There's plenty of time for that," he said, "but I hope you won't mind if I offer my condolences first?" He opened his arms wide and asked whether he might hug me specifically, as though I were the only one with someone dead.

I had not come from a world of huggers but of people who greeted one another from a duelers' distance, twenty paces, so I suspected that his plan was to draw me in by invoking the world of my present and, in this way, to hoodwink me into letting down my guard, at which point he would turn the conversation to that whole trite dichotomy of sin versus sinners—of hating one and loving the other—which would end with me saying that, first of all, sin was a construct and that moreover the two were inextricable: how could a sin even exist if there was not a body to accommodate it? It was like the fungus on his feet, in need of a host.

This was a conversation that would not end well. I knew that. So as he lunged confidently forward, I stepped swiftly aside, directly onto his foot, his funky, fungus-ridden foot. He yelped, and Bettina laughed, and my mother looked at once horrified and ashamed, as though she could not believe the hand God had dealt her—burdened with a clumsy, solicitude-adverse lesbian of a daughter.

"My mother has ideas for Bible verses," I offered instructively, and the pastor limped back behind his desk. The three of us, taking this as a cue to be seated finally, settled on the folding chairs arranged before it. "And I've got an anecdote," I added, looking at neither my mother nor my sister before I plunged ahead:

"We used to have steak every Sunday after church, and one Sunday the bulb in the oven blew. The steak was covered with glass, but my father made us eat it anyway. He said he wasn't going to sit by and watch us waste good food."

The pastor studied me for a very long time. It was a sympathetic look—I could see that, could see that my anecdote or possibly the fact that I felt driven to offer it stirred in him feelings of pity, but just as I understood the absurdity in speaking of "sin" as separate from "sinner," it struck me as impossible to accept this sympathy as sincere, proffered as it was by someone whose life's work was to make my life more difficult.

"Can I pray for you?" he said.

"I'd prefer that you didn't," I said.

"I will anyway," he said.

Rachel and Carl were at the dining room table with the kids, all four of them drawing. I sat down and took a sip from Rachel's coffee, and Petra said, "Look, Aunt Sybil. I drew you and Rachel in the bubble." She held up a piece of paper on which she had sketched two stick figures with breasts holding hands inside a clumsily drawn circle.

"I love it," I said. I did love it.

"Rachel said she's going to frame it and hang it in your bedroom so it's the first thing you guys see every morning when you wake up."

"Well, if Rachel said it, then it must be true. Rachel does not lie."

Rachel gave me a sharp look, as though she thought I meant something more by this, but I didn't. Rachel does not lie.

"Care to descend with me into the Infernal Region?" I said to Rachel, which was how we referred to the basement—Hell, Hades, the Infernal Region—and she rose from the table, promised Petra that she would be back up to claim her drawing, and together we descended.

"How were things while we were gone?" I asked. Really I wanted her to ask me how things had gone with the pastor, but Rachel instead chose to answer my question.

"Carl is a mensch," she said.

"A mensch?" I said.

She started to explain what a mensch was, and I said that I knew what a mensch was, that my consternation had to do with the fact that I had never once in all of the years we were together heard her use "mensch," or really anything Yiddish for that matter.

"I use 'schlepp' all the time," she said.

"You do," I agreed, "and your response has confirmed my point."

"How does proving to you that you have heard me use Yiddish somehow prove that you have not?" she asked.

"Because you know I'm right, so you reverted to the exception."

"Okay," she said. "I get it. You're mad that Carl and I are friends."

"I'm not mad," I said. "I'm not."

"Okay."

"Anyway, you're not friends. You're in-laws."

"The two outsiders, you mean. Is that your point?"

"I don't really have a point," I said. As far as I knew, I didn't.

"You don't have a point, and yet here we are, talking about why I don't have the right to call Carl a mensch or a friend."

"I'd hardly call that a point," I said.

"I give up," she said. "I hate coming here. It's like you disappear right in front of me."

"You mean that I become one of 'you people'?" The sentence was a syntactical mess. I knew that.

"So that's what you're mad about? That I said I don't understand 'you people'?"

I had hoped that she would not understand my reference, which would mean that her comment at the dump the day before was nothing more than a fleeting moment of frustration, but she did remember, and this gave it import. "I told you I'm not mad," I said again.

"That doesn't mean you aren't. It means you don't want to accept that you're mad. What I don't understand, I guess, is who you're mad at. Me or them?"

"The meeting was all a setup," I said, and when she looked confused, I clarified, "Just now. With the pastor."

"What do you mean a setup?" she asked.

"To get me in the anti-homosexual letter-writing pastor's office so that he could exorcize my sapphic demons."

Rachel laughed, and though I had meant for her to laugh, her laughter galled me.

"It's not funny," I said.

"So what are you saying? That your father's death was purely strategic, a tactical move designed to get you back here and into that man's office?" Her tone was at once incredulous and amused.

"It's possible," I said.

"Yes," she said, "I guess anything is possible."

I hated when she said stuff like this, placating clichés that meant I was being ridiculous, and hated it even more when I knew I *was* being ridiculous.

"Do you remember the shell casing that Carl showed you?" I said.

"What are you talking about?"

"The shell casing that your mensch friend Carl showed you at Christmas? Remember when I came upstairs and the two of you were talking about how crazy your spouses were, and then he showed you the shell casing that he carries to remind him not to give into temptation?"

"The talisman?" she said.

"Yes, the talisman. It's from a gun, you know."

I could see from her face that she did not know.

"How would I know that?" she said. "I know nothing about guns. You know that."

"So Carl didn't tell you where that shell casing came from?" And then I proceeded to tell her the story of Carl's uncle, how Carl had gotten off the school bus one afternoon and come home to find his mother and sister in the kitchen drinking coffee. "You'll need to clean up the mess," his mother had said, nodding toward the living room. The mess was his uncle. While Carl was at school that day, his uncle had shot himself in the head.

I looked over at Rachel, who was lying on her sofa, perfectly still, breathing in and out, in and out.

"So, you see, Carl is just as crazy as the rest of us. He's one of us."

"Okay," she said.

I looked away. "Okay," I replied.

Fathers die first. Rachel and I both knew this to be true. Her father had died four years earlier, after several months of rapid decline. Just before he died, he announced that he and Rachel's mother would be moving out of the family home, the house in which Rachel and her sister had grown up, and into one of those upscale retirement residences in a neighboring suburb. We could not imagine him in such a place, so we knew what this meant: that he was ready to die and that even now, at the end of his life, he was doing what he had done throughout it, taking care of Rachel's mother, who lacked skills of the sort that would have allowed her to continue on in that house alone. She did not drive, never had, mainly because she lacked any spatial sense whatsoever, including the ability to find her way home amid the familiar topography of a place where she had spent most of her adult life, nor did she know how to shop for groceries or how to combine the discrete elements of the refrigerator and cupboard into the simplest of meals. Within weeks of completing the move, Rachel's father got pneumonia and rode it down.

Now, when we visited Rachel's mother, we stayed in one of the guest suites at the retirement residence, a place that was like a cruise ship—people eating and playing bridge, socializing and hooking up on the sly—except on this cruise ship everyone was old and Jewish, and they never set sail. Rachel, her mother, and I ate breakfast each morning with her mother's three usual breakfast companions, all six of us wedged in around a table meant for four, while her mother's friends tried to remember whether Rachel was Rachel or her sister.

"And who are you?" they asked me each time.

"Rachel's friend," her mother replied each time, in a way that made clear that she had not told them about Rachel.

Once, I suggested to Rachel, unhelpfully perhaps, that maybe this wasn't proof of her mother's disapproval so much as her mother's general lack of interest in her life. "They probably don't know you're a nurse either," I'd added.

On our last visit, the one we returned from the day that my father died, one of the servers came over and scolded us for having too many people at our table. Even one extra chair at the table was not safe, she said, and we had two. I stood up to move, but one of the women ordered me to sit down. She said this loudly. These women said everything loudly. Just a few minutes earlier, they had pointed to a woman at the table next to ours who was missing an arm. "Look," they screamed. "She's missing an arm but you'd never know it, the way she eats." Everyone turned to look at the amazing one-armed woman who was eating her eggs like someone with two arms.

One of the breakfast companions, Helga, was reading a book as thick as an encyclopedia, which turned out to be one of those large-print tomes. In addition to her eyesight, Helga's memory was going, just the short-term, which meant that she could talk as though it had happened yesterday about walking, orphaned, back to Berlin after the camps were liberated; about arriving in England and going to live with a family that refused to let her speak, ever, of her life before she came to them. She did not hold it against them, she said, because that was the way people thought then, that life was best treated as a series of doors slamming shut behind you. She could remember that her sons were both dead and that she had wanted girls, that her husband, who was also dead, once baked a birthday cake for her out of potatoes.

A man pulled up a chair—a seventh chair!—and sat down. "You've been reading that book forever," he said to Helga. Rachel's mother had told us about this man. His name was Saul, and he was courting someone at the table, though they did not know which of them it was.

"Yes," Helga said. "That's the good thing about not being able to remember what I read yesterday. I just start over on page one every morning, and it feels like a new book." We all laughed, and Helga looked pleased. I thought about this, about how her brain did not forget that she was funny, did not forget the subtleties of delivery or perspective that contributed to humor.

Saul read the title of Helga's book aloud. "*The Good German*? Does such a thing exist?" he asked, and the women laughed. I laughed.

Rachel gave me a look. "What?" I said. "I'm not German."

"I'll have orange juice," Helga told the server who had scolded us, and Rachel's mother reminded her that she had given up orange juice because it was hard on her stomach.

"Is that right?" she said thoughtfully, as though being introduced to some delightful fact about someone who was not her. "Grapefruit juice?" she said then, uncertainly, and Rachel's mother gave a small shake of her head.

"You hate grapefruit," she said. "You better stick with the cranberry."

Helga turned to the server and said brightly, "I will stick with the cranberry."

How did it feel, I had wondered, to exist, increasingly, from outside oneself, to rely on others to tell you who you were, to lose the secrets that you had told no one, the secrets that defined who you were, for better or worse, because they belonged only to you?

The morning of my father's funeral, I woke up on my sofa and turned to Rachel on hers. "Did you bring the purse?" I asked.

Normally, we had pockets, which was another lesbian thing about us, not that straight women don't have pockets, but lesbians seem more likely to prioritize practicality over fashion. Every once in a while, though, we went somewhere in clothes without pockets—the opera, for example—and for those occasions, we had the purse. We called it "the purse" because it did not belong to either of us, which meant that often we would arrive back at our car and realize that everything we needed, beginning with our car keys, was in the purse and the purse was somewhere else, usually under the seats that we had just occupied. We would argue about whose fault it was, but it was both of our faults and neither. That is the reassuring part of having a collective purse, a collective anything, I suppose.

Rachel sat up on her sofa and said that she had not brought the purse. What she actually said was "You didn't tell me to bring the purse." She still felt some sort of way about the events of the last few days.

It was true that I had not asked her to bring the purse. I had not thought about the purse until that very moment, when I woke up the day of my father's funeral and saw dangling haphazardly from an unused nail the skirt that I had emergency-purchased the evening before. It was long and drab and pocketless, and I had already determined that I had no need of it in my regular life. I would leave it here, hanging in the closet of my childhood room for when I needed it the next time: when I returned to bury my mother.

Already, the day was humid, and what came to mind was the pastor's feet. I did not want to be thinking about his feet, certainly not now, hours before my father's funeral, but once I started, I could not stop. Everything reminded me of them—the constant patter and thump of my family above us, the rancid moisturizer that Rachel found in the bathroom, shoes, oatmeal, the buttermilky tang of the kitchen sponge.

Around ten, we loaded everyone into Bettina and Carl's van and Rachel's rental car, because they were parked last in the driveway, and we drove the three miles into town. My mother insisted on riding in the van, and I did not argue with her, even though I knew it was because she did not want to arrive at the church in a car driven by lesbians. The businesses in town—there were only six or seven of them—were all closed for two hours to give the 418 people enumerated on the population sign the opportunity to attend my father's funeral; my parents had owned their store for fifty-five years, so they were known.

My parents' store—Berglund Hardware—was permanently closed. The sign on the door read *Closed Until Further Notice*, but everyone knew what that meant. My father had planned to keep it going until he died, but a few years earlier, he had begun sleeping much of the day, not out of laziness but because his body's needs had shifted—he was like a cat, napping for hours and then awakening to a terrible desire for protein. The preceding winter, just two days before we wrestled beneath the Christmas tree, Bettina and I had staged an intervention. We told our father that our mother was too old to keep the store going, biting our tongues to keep from adding "by herself," though that was what it had come down to. Our father was not ready to let go of it, for reasons that were probably symbolic but felt to us like hubris. He accused us of meddling in their marriage. While we pleaded with him to consider the burden that it placed on our mother, she sat in the other room. She knew what we were up to, but she did not know how to say these things herself. "Lunchtime," she called out instead, working against herself. Bettina and I had given up, accepted failure, gone into the kitchen to eat. We did not speak of it again. Then, months later, it became clear to us that the store was closed. There had been no formal announcement by either of them, just the use of past tense instead of present when they referred to it.

Halfway through the service, I feared that I had not silenced my ringer. I took out my phone, the eyes of the congregation on me. I believed that they thought of me—on the rare occasion that they did think of me—as someone who had left a place she considered herself too good for, which is to say that that morning they looked at me, phone in hand, and surely saw a woman bored by her own father's funeral.

I began to laugh. Beside me, Rachel turned, which only made me laugh harder.

The minister, busy eulogizing, announced that he had a story about my father, a memory that the deceased's younger daughter had shared with him the day before, a memory that said a lot about who Harold Berglund was. I stopped laughing.

"Every Sunday after church, the Berglunds had steak." From his pulpit, the minister looked around the church. "Every Sunday," he repeated. He nodded deeply, at once sanctioning the story and letting us know that it was over.

I began to laugh again, and soon my sister joined in. Rachel once more turned to regard me, to regard us both.

Those were the good words about my father. And why not? Every Sunday we had eaten steak. Only once had there been glass.

When Rachel told me that I needed to talk to my sister, truly talk to her, I was not troubled. That is, I did not read into her suggestion anything that seemed to imperil the agreement to keep our families at bay that we had made all those years earlier. It was the day after my father's funeral, and we were standing out in the driveway, wedged between her rental car and my father's truck. She was going home to our dog and cats, leaving me behind with my mother who did not think that I had a family to go home to. Bettina, Carl, and the kids were leaving also, and when I pointed out to Rachel the unfairness of this, that my sister had come late and was leaving early, Rachel said that I needed to consider that children, even those as delightful as my niece and nephew, were not always what one—by which she meant my mother—wanted to deal with in the midst of grief.

"I mean it," she said. "Talk to Bettina. Soon it will be just the two of you."

I was staying, simply put, because my mother did not seem capable of being alone. I watched her banging through her new life, lost amid the detritus of the past; it was a lostness that I at least recognized, an unmoored look in her eyes that she used to get on the rare occasion that my father had to be away. My parents did not take vacations, but each fall my father drove off with a group of other men from town to hunt. They would be gone for two or three nights, and each time my grandfather came to stay. Later, I would realize that my grandfather came because it was understood—by everyone but Bettina and me—that my mother could not be left alone with us, could not be left alone with herself.

But Bettina and I did not sit down to talk, at least not then, because even as Rachel and I were saying goodbye, Bettina and Carl and the kids came out and said that they were also hitting the road. The kids laughed because they thought that "hitting the road" was funny, and then they both flopped down on the driveway and proceeded to pummel it with their fists and scream, "I'm hitting the road. Look! I'm hitting the road!"

Rachel glanced over at me as if to say, *You see?*

I had been waiting to see how Rachel would say goodbye, whether she would tell me she loved me or skip that part, and whether I would believe it to still be true either way, but then the kids got up from the driveway—well, were yanked up—and before I knew it, everyone was driving away except me.

That night we sat alone together—my mother and I—she at the table eating microwave popcorn and reading her Bible. One of her Bibles.

"I'm going to call Rachel," I announced and stood up, and she looked at me as though she had no idea what I was talking about. "Rachel," I said again. "My partner. The woman I have been with for eight years." I huffed off, down to the basement.

I did not call, of course, even though I wanted to know that Rachel had arrived home safely, wanted to know how Gertrude and Alice and Frederick the dog were doing, whether they missed me. But I was waiting for *her* to call, and I fell asleep waiting—fell asleep on Rachel's sofa, which was where I had decided to sleep because the basement frightened me in ways that it did not when Rachel was there with me.

Deep in the night, my cell phone rang and I sat up, thinking it was her, but it was my mother's voice whispering into my ear: "Someone's here. There's a car in the driveway. I'm scared, and your father's gone."

It was not clear which meaning of "gone" she had in mind—whether she thought that my father was off hunting or whether she knew that he was dead.

"I need you to come home," she said. "Right now."

I started to say, "I am home," but caught myself. "I am here," I said instead, worrying about semantics even as my mother was going crazy above me.

"I've got the gun," she said.

"Which gun?" I asked softly.

"The pistol," she said, referring to the gun that my father had always kept, loaded, above the stove, believing that his children would never be stupid enough to touch it. It turned out I was stupid enough. The Sunday we ate glass, after our parents disappeared into the bedroom to rest, I climbed up on the stove and stood with my feet on the burners that were still warm from string beans and potatoes and took down the loaded pistol, two stupidities rolled into one. I pointed this gun at any number of things—the toaster, the relentlessly dripping faucet, a loaf of whole wheat bread—and when my sister came in from outside and saw me there, standing atop the stove with the gun that we were forbidden to touch, she said, "I'm telling," and I turned the pistol on her.

"That gun is loaded," I said, speaking loudly this time, fearfully.

"They're in the basement!" my mother cried out, both into my ear and through the floorboards. "I hear them talking."

"There is no one down there," I said, whispering again.

And she said, "I'm going down."

"Do not go down there," I said. "Do not."

We were both silent for a moment. Above me, she paced.

"I'll call the police," I told her at last and hung up, and then I called Rachel, who answered on the fifth ring, sounding not at all groggy, though it was after midnight back home. I described the situation—that my mother had become confused and mistaken my rental car for the car of a stranger, an intruder whom she believed to be in her house at this very moment.

"She's got the pistol," I said, but the pistol was one more story I had not told Rachel, one more story at which she would not have laughed. I wanted her to laugh, even though I could see what laughing meant, how it allowed us to live with everything that was wrong. I backtracked to explain only that such a pistol existed, that my mother was holding that pistol now.

"Do not go up there," Rachel said. "Whatever you do, do not go up there." On the other end of the line, in our home miles and miles away, Rachel began to cry.

"I won't go up there," I said, but she did not stop crying. "Hey, I'm sleeping on your sofa," I said.

"Are you all crazy?" she said. She wanted an answer.

"Yes," I said. "We are all crazy." But she only cried harder.

We will steal the gun together, Bettina and I. That is what we decide when I call her at dawn after a sleepless night spent listening to my mother above me. My task will be to get the gun, to physically remove it from my mother's room, my old room, and then baton it off to my sister, who will take it away with her, though not home to the house where she lives with children whose heads none of us want blown off. My sister says she cannot be the one to remove the gun for reasons having to do with the Ten Commandments—the one about stealing, I wonder, or about obeying your mother and father?—and I cannot be the one to dispose of it, for reasons having to do with the fact that neither I nor anyone I know possesses knowledge of this sort. And so, my sister and I will work together.

My mother does not seem surprised to see me when I come up for breakfast, nor does she mention her middle-of-the-night call. She is in her robe, the one that had seemed apostolic just days earlier, but now seems simply ratty. She is not carrying the pistol. I do not mention that Bettina is coming, but when she pulls into the driveway at lunchtime, my mother says, "You see? Your sister is here." Perhaps she has been expecting her all along. Perhaps in some tucked-away corner of her brain, you call one daughter and both appear.

Then, while Bettina distracts our mother, I go into her bedroom, my old bedroom, and rummage around. The six rifles still stand at attention; the kneeling child still prays over them. If my mother discovers me, my plan is to pick up one of the Bibles and pretend to be reading it. She will believe it because she will want to believe it. But my mother does not come in and I do not find the gun. When I'm about to give up, I kneel beside the bed, like the girl in the picture, like the girl I used to be. In this way, my trip has symmetry: it begins and ends with me kneeling.

I lean sideways. Beneath the bed are old newspapers and shoes, broken toasters and irons, boxes of ammunition, presumably for the six guns leaning against the wall, but it's hard to know whether the ammunition was placed there with proximity in mind, or simply abandoned there years ago for no other reason than that there was space.

What there is *not* is the pistol.

As I rise, my arm rests briefly atop the bed, atop something hard. I pull back the blanket: nestled like a kitten or a hot water bottle is the loaded gun.

"Have you heard of the Mandela effect?" I ask Bettina.

Four hours have passed since she arrived, four hours during which we ate lunch and stole a gun, and now Bettina and I are standing in the driveway, pretending to say goodbye but really trying to hand off the pistol. If there is anything that should make my mother suspicious, it is this, her two daughters making a point to bid each other farewell.

As I waited for my sister to arrive this morning, I graded papers, for though a substitute was covering my four freshman composition classes, the grading was all mine. The assignment was to write about something they knew nothing about, something they had never even heard of before, an assignment that angered them greatly, for how—they had wondered aloud at the beginning and middle and end of each class for two solid weeks—were they supposed to arrive at a topic they did not even know existed. In response, I said all of the annoying things that they expected me to say: that instead of asking this same question over and over, they should simply get started, that this was meant to be an exercise in exploration or learning or curiosity, that they had come into this world knowing nothing and look at them now. Of the one hundred and three papers submitted, only one introduced *me* to something new: the Mandela effect.

Bettina says that she has not heard of it, glancing past my shoulder at the doorway, and I say, "It's when a whole group of people remembers something that never actually happened, a collective false memory, like Mandela dying in prison."

"He did die in prison," my sister says.

"No, he didn't," I say. "That's the point. He got out and became the president of South Africa."

She is quiet for a moment, not thinking about Mandela specifically, I suspect, because my sister is not the sort to know much about Mandela, but wondering why I have brought this up now, as we stand here attempting to pass off my mother's loaded gun. My sister likes to figure out what people are thinking and why, without having to ask, though eventually she will ask.

"Why are you telling me about this right now?" she says.

"I don't know." This is true. Partly true. "I guess I'm just trying to imagine what it's like to have a memory that you're so sure of, and that all these other people have also, but the memory's wrong. I mean, how is it possible that all over the world people share the memory of Mandela dying in prison?"

"And?" she says.

"Sometimes, I think we're like that."

"We?" she says. She knows that I am referring to our family, though not whether I mean all four of us, or just me and her. "What memories do we have that aren't true?"

She is right. We are the opposite: a family with memories so true, so vivid, we rarely dare to recall them.

I say, "Remember when Mom put me in the oven, and Dad came home and took me out?"

"Like a Thanksgiving turkey," Bettina says.

Rachel believes that I did not tell her this story because of her, but the truth, I realize only now, is this: the child's mind cannot live in a constant state of contradiction. I could not sit down at the table each day of my childhood to eat the food that had come from that oven—food that had been prepared and placed inside it by my mother—unless I chose not to think about the fact that, once, my mother had placed me in that same oven and turned it on. In this way, perhaps childhood always involves a degree of Stockholm syndrome.

"I like Rachel," Bettina says then, as if she is reading my mind.

"I like Carl," I reply, even though I know that compliments given in response to compliments always sound insincere. But it's true. I do like Carl. Carl is a mensch. He grew up with his own crazy family, but he is still willing to deal with ours. This is probably how it will always be with my sister: we will always like each other's spouses better than we like each other. We will always exist at this one degree of separation.

I look back over my shoulder at the house to make sure that my mother is not watching, and then I slip the gun out of my hoodie pocket and hold it out to my sister, and we stand like that for a moment—me holding the gun, her on the other end of it—and I know that we are reliving the same moment.

Then, she takes the gun, opens the large tote bag that she brought with her for this very purpose, drops the gun inside, and extracts a cardboard tube, which she holds out to me.

"I promised Petra that I wouldn't forget, and then I nearly did," she says. "Petra was very upset that she forgot to give this to Rachel."

Later, I will take the drawing out of the tube and unfurl it, and I will see that Petra has made some changes. Rachel and I are still there, of course, two stick figures with breasts, but Petra has added two cats and a dog, and has fortified the circle around us with a series of thick crayon lines. Across the top she has written

The Bubble Family. This is how Petra sees us, I think. We are just another family.

I take the tube with my niece's drawing from my sister. "Well," I say. "A gun for a drawing."

Bettina laughs, and I laugh. It's a good trade.

Tomorrow, I will leave behind my mother and her failing mind and go home to the bubble that has still not burst and tell the woman I love the story of this place, which is the story of who I am:

The father who plucked me from the oven fed us steak peppered with glass, and the mother who placed me in that oven removed that glass, shard by shard, in the bright light of a Sunday afternoon.

Above that oven was a loaded gun, and it was meant to keep us safe.

Once, I pointed that gun at my sister, but did not pull the trigger.

Once, my sister tried to smother me.

Once, together, my sister and I stole a gun. We left six more behind.

Acknowledgments

I am deeply grateful to my agent, Henry Dunow, who loved these stories from the start and took me and my collection on at a time when story collections are regarded by some as a fool's mission, and who was wise enough to point me toward the title that this collection needed, and my extraordinary editor, Emily Bell, who is a whirlwind of energy, enthusiasm, and insight. I am thankful to be working with her and with the whole Astra House team, including Ben Schrank, Rachael Small, Alexis Nowicki, Tiffany Gonzalez, Olivia Dontsov, Frankie DiGiovanni, Maya Raiford Cohen, and anyone else who helped bring this book out into the world. I am fortunate to have found a home at Astra House.

Short story writers owe so much to the journals and editors who keep putting our stories out in the world. I am indebted to the journals and editors who first published these stories: Carolyn Kuebler, who has supported my work from the very beginning, and Ernest McLeod at *New England Review*, in the pages of which "Just Another Family" appeared; Laura Cogan and Oscar Villalon at *ZYZZYVA*, which published two of these stories ("Clear as Cake" and "A Little Customer Service," republished in Literary Hub); Steven Schwartz and Stephanie G'Schwind at *Colorado Review* ("Are You Happy?");

Michael Nye at *Story* magazine ("The Bus Driver"; republished in *We Can See into Another Place: Mile-High Writers on Social Justice*); Cara Blue Adams and Emily Nemens, former editors at *The Southern Review* ("The Gap Year," republished in *New Stories from the Midwest*); various editors at *The Kenyon Review* ("The Peeping Toms"); Matthew Baker, former editor at *Nashville Review* ("Aaron Englund and the Great Great," originally published as "Aaron Englund, July 1970"). My deepest thanks also goes to Heidi Pitlor, who served as series editor of Best American Short Stories for many years and who was an early supporter of my stories, including "Just Another Family," which appeared in *The Best American Short Stories 2024*, and to Lauren Groff for choosing the story for inclusion. Thank you to Edward P. Jones, guest editor, and Jenny Minton Quigley, series editor, for awarding "Just Another Family" an O. Henry Prize and including it in *The Best Short Stories 2025: The O. Henry Prize Winners*. Over the years, Roxane Gay and Richard Russo have provided enthusiasm for my work in ways and at times that made a difference. I feel fortunate to have had so many people in the world of publishing keeping me steady and buoyed.

Young writers have occasionally asked my advice on the best way to become a better writer, and I generally answer in terms of what I know to be true for myself: what makes you a better person will also make you a better writer. For me, this has meant building and sustaining meaningful relationships and work, traveling, and walking a lot, but also engaging in the world beyond writing. At times, especially during the pandemic years, these various goals found themselves at odds, and there were years when I wrote very little. Ultimately, in order to write, I need to feel hopeful, and so this page would not be complete without an acknowledgment of the various ways that I have found meaning and hope.

Though I write best and most often in solitude, I have benefitted deeply from my friendships with both writers and non-writers. Albeit an incomplete list, I am grateful to the following people who have brought so much to my life: Debbie Weissman, Molly Luethi, Nancy (D.D.) Gaustad, Blaine Gaustad, Annette Dozier, Clavere Brown, Sue Guynn, Rosana Vantuyl, Matthew Lansburgh, Pam Durban, Katherine Proctor, Nick Pauley, Aiko Tani, Krista Bremer, Carolina Franquiz, Ann Cummins, Steve Willis, Minrose Gwin, Ruth Salvaggio, Sylvia Brownrigg, Jessica Treadway, Catherine Raeff, the Ladies Who Lunch (Lucy Jane Bledsoe, Pat Mullan, Genanne Walsh, Lauren Whittemore, Barb Johnson, Lucie Faulknor, Dawn Logsdon), Seth Borgen, Ann Gately, Hema Padhu, Cynthia Wooley, May Lee Watase, Sachi Watase, Will Tyner, Clara Speer, Renee Perry, Laine Snowman, Maryanne Berry, Mary Taugher, Laurie Doyle, Alice Templeton, Joan Pfeiffer, Carmen Croonquist, Jill Kuntz Aguayo, Hassan Khoudri and the whole Khoudri family (a second family for the last thirty years), Mark Vinz (who told me forty years ago that I could write), my siblings, who knew me from the beginning, when stories were first taking shape in my head (Julie Ostlund, Wayne Ostlund, ViAnn Ostlund, Mark Ostlund), Cabrel Ngounou, Liese Mayer, Joe Di Prisco, Alec Scott, Barbara Ridley, Judy Kerr, and Mira T. Lee, website creator extraordinaire.

My life has also been made more complete by the years that I have spent teaching and by the many lifelong friendships that have developed with both students and colleagues. This book began to take shape during my two years as the Kenan Visiting Writer at the University of North Carolina at Chapel Hill, and more recently has benefitted from several years at Golden Gate University, the eight years that I taught for the Mile-High MFA, and my ongoing gigs at the San Francisco Writing Salon.

I also feel fortunate to have served as the series editor of the Flannery O'Connor Award for Short Fiction since 2022. My own big break as a writer happened when my first collection won this award in 2008, chosen by the late Nancy Zafris, to whose memory this book is dedicated. Nancy was an amazing writer, teacher, editor, and supporter of writers. In a world—publishing—where many focus on currying favor with those more established, above them on the publishing pecking order, Nancy was an exception, always most interested in reaching downward to pull new writers up beside her. I know this well, for I was one of many she yanked upward. She had a sharp tongue and a gentle spirit. Nancy Zafris died in 2021. She is deeply missed by me and numerous others. I am grateful to the University of Georgia Press for continuing to celebrate the short story and for offering me the opportunity to share that mission with them.

Ultimately, to write I need to feel hopeful, and to feel hopeful I need to feel useful. Perhaps this is my residual Midwesterness at play or simply the state of being human. Most recently, two organizations have given me a sense of purpose and thus a sense of hope: the Barbara Deming Foundation, whose board I have served on since 2022 beside a group of wonderful women, with a mission of providing financial support to feminist writers and artists; and Rainbow Railroad, an organization that my wife and I began volunteering with in 2023 and that brings LGBTQ+ refugees fleeing discrimination, imprisonment, and violence to safety.

I remain indebted to The Rona Jaffe Foundation, which provided me with early financial support as well as a boost of confidence. I am indebted also to Tony Huang and Nancy He, who contacted me and my wife out of the blue in 2017 and invited us to spend several weeks as visiting writers in Tianjin, China, and who have remained dear friends.

I reserve this final paragraph for Juztice Solána Yarborough, who came into our lives in 2019 and changed them. Of course, my biggest thank-you goes to my wife, the writer Anne Raeff, with whom I have spent the last thirty-three years of my life. Once upon a time, she was the only other writer I knew, and she continues to be my first reader, the one who allows me to mine small moments of our daily lives together and who always laughs in the right place.

Photo by Dennis Hearne

About the Author

Lori Ostlund is the author of the story collection *The Bigness of the World*, which won the Flannery O'Connor Award for Short Fiction, the California Book Award for First Fiction, the Edmund White Debut Fiction Award, and was a Lambda Finalist. Her second book, the novel *After the Parade*, was a Barnes & Noble Discover pick and a finalist for the Center for Fiction First Novel Prize, the Ferro-Grumley Award, and the Joyce Carol Oates Prize, and was a New York Times Editor's Choice. Her stories have appeared in *The Best American Short Stories*, *The PEN/O. Henry Prize Stories*, and literary journals such as *New England Review*, *The Kenyon Review*, and *ZYZZYVA*. Lori is the series editor of the Flannery O'Connor Award for Short Fiction. She lives in San Francisco, California.